Just a Simple Love Affair

by

Maeve Kim

Love Stories of the Burlington Bird Club

Cover Art by *Teddi Black*

The Wild Rose Press, Inc.
PO Box 708
Adams Basin, NY 14410-0708
Visit us at www.thewildrosepress.com

Publishing History
First Edition, 2025
Trade Paperback Print ISBN 978-1-5092-6378-3
Digital ISBN 978-1-5092-6379-0

Love Stories of the Burlington Bird Club
Published in the United States of America

Chapter One

The Meeting

Jack didn't feel the July sun beating down on his head and shoulders. He was lost in a world of numbers. He had spent hours studying the two possible sites for the solar array, taking photographs, making sketches, noting trees and hills that would affect the amount and angle of sunlight, calculating how much sun would be available for each daylight hour. He had studied possible access routes for the trucks that would carry in the components of the array, and he'd taken deep soil samples that would dictate the kind of footing needed for the massive collectors. Just a few more calculations and he'd be ready to sit down with Hunt and finalize the contract.

The landowner, a no-nonsense farmer with the unlikely name of Huntley Huntington, wanted enough electric energy for two huge barns, six greenhouses, the main house, and the four trailers used by migrant workers during spring, summer, and fall. The project would be a coup for Jack's little company. It would be a demonstration that solar energy was a natural fit for agriculture even in Vermont, one of the cloudiest states in the nation. And Hunt was the perfect partner: a go-getter who had already secured two grants and was determined to be a trail-breaker.

"Read somewhere about growing crops right under the collectors. Some do better there than in the fields. Winter wheat. Potatoes. Celery. Especially in hot dry years." The creases on Hunt's forehead deepened even more. "Guess that's what's in store for us. Summers so hot and dry every single thing you plant struggles to get started, and then summers so wet you can't even get seeds in the ground. Nothing in between."

"We'll make this work," Jack muttered to himself as he neared the edge of the field. "We can't make Hunt immune to climate change but we are sure gonna help… Oh, hello."

He took a few steps closer to the hedgerow between the field and the farm road.

"You've probably been chipping at me for the last half hour, and I never even noticed."

The small brown bird tipped its head to one side.

"You and your mate have a nest close by, don't you? C'mon, sing for me. Let me hear why you're called a Song Sparrow… Not going to, huh? Just going to keep chipping, warning me to keep my distance… All right. I'm moving away."

There were workers visible in the distance, bent over in the strawberry fields, but near the big house everything was still. The outlines of the hoop houses were blurred by shimmery heat waves. A black and white dog dozed under a giant maple.

Jack opened both front doors of his car to catch the breeze, got in and flipped open his project notebook. When he finally looked up, closing the notebook with a snap, someone was coming around the corner of one of the barns and heading toward the house. The man was small and wiry, with a weathered face that looked, in a phrase loved by one of Jack's high school teachers, like a streak of hard times. Jack stretched his back against the seat and rolled his shoulders, grinning a little when he noticed that the man was wearing two baseball caps, one frontward and one backward.

"Haven't seen that before," Jack muttered. "Fashion statement."

The small man walked to a black pick-up truck, lowered the tail gate, lifted out a huge bag and effortlessly flopped it over his shoulder. After carrying the bag to a pile near the barn, he returned for another, and then another, and then a fourth, before dusting off his hands and his sun-darkened arms and heading toward a distant field.

"Let that be a lesson," Jack muttered. "Back to the gym, this week. That little guy could pick me up with one hand and heave me twenty feet without breaking a sweat." He looked again at the distant field. "After I consume a pint of fresh strawberries with vanilla ice cream."

He flipped the pages of his notebook again, muttering and frowning and occasionally nodding. "Check just one more time. These figures…"

The front door of the farm house slammed and Hunt came out, taking the steps two at a time. He strode to the pick-up truck, bent and peered in the passenger side window, stalked around to the other side and opened that door, and then brought one huge fist down on the top of the truck. He dug in his pocket for his phone, punched in a number and barked a few words. Immediately, a man came out of the largest barn, looked toward the field and shouted. Three farm workers started toward the house, one of them the wiry man Jack had seen a few minutes before.

Hunt stood like a scowling statue. When the men were close enough, he growled, "I am missing a blue canvas bag. From the truck." He slammed his open palm on the truck's door. "Blue. Azul. Um. Bag." He made a rectangle in the air with one finger. "With a zipper." He mimed holding the rectangle from the bottom and zipping it open. "Zipper. Zip."

"Ah. Sí. Zip, zip."

"Yes! Zip. Blue canvas bag with a zipper. Azul. It's not there now. Perdida. No. *Perdido*. Lost." He tilted his head back and bellowed, "Rose!"

A woman appeared at the front of the nearest greenhouse. Her face was shadowed by a wide-brimmed white hat, but Jack watched her quick, fluid walk across the yard and thought she must be quite young. As she got closer, he could see a wide smile below the shadow of her hat.

"Rose. Thank goodness you're here today." Hunt pushed his hair off his forehead. "Tell them there was a bank deposit bag in the truck. A blue canvas thing. I put it on the front seat with some stuff for the Post Office. That stuff is still here but the deposit's gone." He looked at the workers. "All the other men are working in the far field. These three were the only ones close by."

The smile was gone as she turned to the farm workers and began translating. At one point, she lifted one hand and made a series of tight, rapid hand movements that were watched intently by one of the men. All three looked alarmed, shaking their heads vehemently and answering her in machine-gun rapid Spanish.

The woman turned back to Hunt. "These two men

say they haven't been anywhere near the truck. They've been working in the strawberries all morning. Anyelo here unloaded four bags of fertilizer from the back of your truck but he didn't see any blue bag."

Hunt took a deep breath. "I am sorry, Rose. But if Anyelo was near the truck, he *had* to have seen it. It was right on the front seat."

More conversation, more head shakes, more frowning and animated hand gestures. The morning's intermittent breeze caught the rim of her hat and she reached up and yanked it off.

Jack caught his breath. She was lovely. The shape of her face, the mass of red-gold curls, the wide curving lips. He wanted to get closer to her, talk with her, watch that mouth smiling at him.

"He says he took the fertilizer out of your truck, four bags, but he didn't take anything else. He says he didn't see any envelope."

"It didn't just fly out the window!"

Jack got out of his car. "Excuse me." The whole group turned and gaped as if he had materialized from the hot air. "I've been over there, in my car, for the last hour or more. This gentleman did indeed get four bags out of the truck, as he said. He put them over there and walked off in that direction. I didn't see him open either of the truck's doors. I don't think he had anything in his hands when he walked away."

The wiry man was staring intently at Jack, clearly catching some of the English words. "*Sí. Sí. No tomé ninguna sobre. No el tomé.*"

"You watched him the whole time?"

"I did." Jack made a fist and touched his own bicep. "I was impressed by his muscles."

Hunt looked around the yard as if the envelope thief might be hiding behind a shrub. "Doesn't make sense. Oreo would've barked at a stranger."

Jack kept his "yeah, right" to himself. That dog hadn't even lifted her head all the way off the ground when he drove in, parked the car, and walked right by her.

"Dad!" A teenage girl jumped down the front stairs of the house, all flying hair and coltish legs in ragged cutoffs. "Getting a tad senile, are we?" She held out something blue. "I found this in the egg cooler. Trying for cold hard cash?"

For several seconds, the scene was frozen, every single person staring at the canvas pouch in the teenager's hand.

"You're joking. Right? Teasing me?"

"Would I tease my very most favorite father?" The girl pointed to a big red cooler on the porch. Even from a distance, Jack could read the words "EGGS—SELF SERVICE" on the side. "I opened it to check the dates on the eggs, and there it was."

Hunt's big ears and tanned face went several shades darker.

"I checked dates, too. My hands were full. I must have—I must have put the deposit down to look at the bottom row of cartons." He turned toward the three farm workers. "Anyelo. I owe you an apology." He glanced at the other two. "All of you. I'm sorry. Uh… Lo siento. Siento, mucho. I, uh, salto? Salto, jump? I jumped to conclusions. Rose, tell them."

In later years, Jack would tell friends that he knew right then he would share the rest of his life with the lovely interpreter but, truthfully, he was too stunned to think. Rose was a perfect name for her. She was standing in the sun, surrounded by sun-darkened men in denim and mud-smeared khaki, and she was wearing a bright apricot-colored tee-shirt and loose flowered pants tucked into high muck boots, and she looked like a rose in a patch of dying weeds.

"*Gracias, señor.*" The small man's handshake almost crushed Jack's fingers. "*Muchas gracias. Muchas, muchas.*"

"*De nada.*" Jack glanced at Rose to see if she noticed his use of Spanish, but she had turned away and was chatting with Hunt's daughter. From the back, he saw that her hair was caught up in a large plastic clip printed with tiny red-breasted robins.

Birds for the bird lover. It was a sign. He was going to wait around, and he was going to talk with her, and he was going to ask her to have a milkshake with him.

****

"We'll break ground next week. I'll be on site for the first few days anyway, possibly more. Then at least once a week until you're up and running." Jack held out his hand. "I'm excited about this project, Hunt."

"I'll be more excited when I see what kind of difference it makes in my bottom line."

"Understood." Jack looked around. "I'd like a word with that interpreter. Do you know where she might be?"

She was in a big hoop house, with one of the farm workers, both heads bent over a sheet of paper that she was translating.

"Rose?"

"Ah! The hero of the morning!" Her smile was almost blinding. "The man who was in exactly the right place at the right time."

"Not true. Hunt's daughter came out with the bank deposit only a minute after I interrupted you all." He held out his hand. "I'm Jack."

"I'm Rose. This is Eduardo. Eduardo, *aquí es* Jack. Jack *está trabajando con* Hunt. *Con la energía solar.*"

"*O. Sí. Me gusto.*"

"*Yo también*, Eduardo."

"*¿Necesita alguna mas?*"

"No. No." The man touched his hat brim and walked toward the back of the hoop house.

"*¿Usted habla español?*"

"*Un poco. Un poco.* Rose, I'm thinking about going to Goodrich's for a milkshake. Would you be interested… Uh. Would you join me?"

She hesitated, frowning slightly, and Jack rushed in with a spate of words.

"My car's right over there. But you know that. Of course. That's where I was watching Angelo or something. From my car. We can have a shake and then I'll drop you back here. Oh. Of course not. You wouldn't go off in a car with a complete stranger. I'm not dangerous, I promise you, but unknown men in general—But you could tell Hunt you're leaving with me and will be back in a little while and he'll know where you are. No! You can take your car and meet me there. It's just a mile or so—But of course you know where Goodrich's is. Better yet, carpooling. Better for the environment. I could ride along with you." He knew he was babbling but he wanted to overwhelm her with words so she wouldn't say no.

"Jack." She laid a soft hand on his arm. "Your car or mine will be fine. But not a shake. My trusty alarm clock died sometime during the night and I didn't have time for breakfast before class."

"Class?"

"Several local farmers free up the migrant workers for English classes. I see three of Hunt's laborers for an hour every morning and six more in late afternoon."

"A long day for you."

"Long indeed. That's why I need food. Real food. Would you be willing to go to the diner? You can get a milkshake there if that's what you're hungry for, and I can gorge myself on their Starving Farmer's Platter." Rose pursed her mouth and tilted her head. "I'll buy, of course. Your offer was for just a shake."

"Breakfast sounds good to me too. I ate at four." Smiling all over his face, Jack touched her elbow and turned her toward his car.

"Why so early?"

"I wanted to be in the fields when the sun came up."

Oh, yes. She looked perfect in his car. Jack started the engine, feeling that he was starting the best part of his whole life.

****

Jack never thought of himself as macho. But when two men leaving the diner glanced at Rose and then looked again, Jack straightened his shoulders and wanted to crow.

Yeah! Worth looking at, huh? And she's having breakfast with ME!

The place was full of quiet chatter, the clinking of forks against plates, the breakfast smells of coffee and bacon. Rose tipped her head back and inhaled. "Heaven has two main areas. One smells like the outdoors, and the other smells like a diner at breakfast." She headed for the only empty booth. "And this booth has been waiting for the two of us."

He wanted to sit a while and enjoy the top of her head, the piled-up curls, the smooth forehead, the eyelashes against the rounded cheeks, but the waitress was heading their way carrying two mugs and a pot of coffee.

Jack sighed and looked down at the menu.

The Starving Farmer's Platter was described in a large square in the middle of the page. Three eggs any style, two strips of bacon, ham, home fries with onions, cheesy grits, biscuits, coffee, and a large orange juice. Jack couldn't believe the slender woman sitting across from him would be able to finish it all. He thought about the six pounds he'd gained over the last year and settled for a short stack of blueberry pancakes, ham, and orange juice.

As soon as the waitress left, Rose leaned forward with her arms on the table between them. "Tell me more about Hunt's solar array. He's excited about it."

"How can you tell?"

Rose gave a little spurt of laughter, and all the other sounds in the diner faded to nothing. Jack sat frozen, reeling under the realization that he wanted to hear that exact laugh every hour on the hour for the next forty or fifty years. He wanted to watch sunshine on that exact curl of her hair, changing the brown to copper and gold.

"Haven't you ever heard Becca call him gee?"

"Bec…? Oh. Hunt's daughter. Yes. Gee?"

"G for Great. As in Great Stone Face."

"Oh. Yes. Good name for him. And he is excited, yes. He said so anyhow. I am too. Excited." Jack took a deep breath. "Hunt's project is going to be the biggest privately owned solar array in the state. And the biggest agricultural one. It's significant for us, for the company I work for, because we're trying to build a name for ourselves. We're a small company. The president, me, and two field engineers."

"The four of you do everything? The whole kit and caboodle?"

"Yes, ma'am. We specialize in caboodles. Kits too. Says so right on our website."

"Right. So who does what?"

"Planning and meeting, that could be any of us. Derek does the legal work. I'm the geotechnical engineer, so I do the site studies. The other engineers and I work on size of the arrays, and energy output. They do maintenance and keep up with new technology which, believe me, is changing every day. We use subcontractors when we reach the stage where Hunt's project is now. Starting next week, one company will bulldoze a few temporary roads for the trucks, and another will start putting in the ground-mounting system."

"Ground-mounting?" She was still leaning forward, still looking interested, but now there was a sparkle in her eyes. "As opposed to, say, sky hooks? Giant bungees fastened onto nearby trees?"

Jack tilted to one side, dug a notebook out of his pants pocket, clicked his pen, and pretended to take notes. "Those are two interesting ideas, ma'am. With your permission, I'd like to pass them on to the team."

They laughed together, meeting each other's eyes.

Oh, yes. This was for real. It just had to be.

"So, seriously, tell me about ground-mounting."

"Well. Seriously. We know what's under the surface in Hunt's field, so we know where to drive steel support beams into the ground. We don't have to lay a cement foundation for each collector, and that's a whole lot better for the environment. And the pocketbook." Jack leaned forward, warming to the subject. "Big solar collectors can be ground-mounted, or they can rest on cement slabs, or we can use ballast systems or anchor systems or several varieties of hybrid systems. There's one array in the southern part of the state…"

Rose sat and listened with only half a mind. She never missed breakfast, ever. She wondered if he could hear her stomach growling.

Peter was never that excitable in the morning. In the three plus years they'd been dating, he'd stayed overnight four times and he was always the same the morning after. He'd shuffle out to the kitchen in the old man slippers he always packed in a small duffle bag, and he'd take the mug of coffee she held out to him, and he'd open the bakery box he brought with him and take out a bran muffin and sit and eat with his eyes fixed on the wall or out the window. He wasn't much more scintillating when they went out to supper, but at least then he talked. In their three plus years, Rose had heard more than she ever wanted to know about running a successful hardware store.

Now she watched Jack Carmichael's expressive face and thought that he was a pleasing person to see across the breakfast table. His brown eyes glowed, he had a nice speaking voice, he smiled often, and he seemed to have boundless enthusiasm.

Come on, waitress. What's going on with our food?

She studied the man across from her. The broad tanned face and strong cheekbones, and the sturdy build, reminded her of photos of Inuits from her World

Languages text. Or Mongolian horsemen. But his mop of hair was several shades redder than her own, perfect for someone with his Irish last name.

She smiled as he finished telling her about a woman in the southern part of the state who was worried that her neighbor's solar collectors might be stealing so much sunlight that her rose garden would suffer. She made sympathetic noises when he described the federal regulations, state restrictions, and local zoning restrictions that added months and dollars to every single project.

Maybe the cook's out back taking a cigarette break. Maybe they had to send someone to the farm for eggs.

Jack was still talking when their food arrived. "Sorry. Get me started and it isn't easy to turn me off."

"Oh, yum. Oh, seriously yum." She picked up her fork. "We can talk some more in a while, Jack. But right now, food."

****

She leaned back in her seat, touched her mouth with a napkin, and heaved a satisfied sigh. Nothing was left on the Starving Farmer's Platter but half a biscuit.

"That was exactly what I needed." She grinned, and he found himself staring at a dimple in her right cheek and thinking how perfectly perfect it was. "Or exactly what I *wanted*. One of my dad's pet peeves is when people use the word *need* when, of course, there's no real need involved."

"Wise man."

"He is. Moderation in all things, he always says." She looked down at the empty platter and grimaced. "This was not moderate. Why am I feeling so happy about it?"

"It's the American way."

"Too true."

"Your turn. Tell me what you do at Hunt's place."

"Well…" She morphed before his eyes from a happy glutton to a professional with an interesting and demanding job. "My main purpose is to interpret for the workers and the farmers who hire them. And sometimes I interpret in other settings, like going along if one of the workers needs a doctor. Plus I do some teaching, which is my favorite part."

Jack watched, fascinated, as the sparkle in her eyes ramped up a notch and she began using her hands to help her talk.

"This year, nobody on Hunt's crew has kids but there are some on two other farms, so another woman and I meet with ten children for a few hours every afternoon. English language lessons, games in English for the little kids, help with academic work for the older kids. Thanks." She smiled up at the waitress who was refilling their mugs. "And every month I go around and give farm safety lessons in Spanish. State mandated."

"Who's your employer? The farm owners?"

"I work for vee-mep." She grinned at his baffled expression. "Vermont Migrant Education Program."

"And what kind of background does one need to work for vee-mep?"

"Facility with Spanish in this case. And I have a teachers' license."

"Is working for vee-mep what you dreamed of? When you were a little girl?"

"Not exactly. I always thought I'd be an elementary school teacher. Or maybe middle school. But then I took a class in English as a second language, and I was hooked."

"You were using some sort of hand signals with one of the laborers. American Sign Language?"

"Oh. No. Felipe lost a lot of his hearing working with heavy equipment down in Texas. He doesn't know ASL but he's a whiz at finger-spelling Spanish words."

"And you're a whiz also?"

"I'm getting there. It's a relatively new skill for me. I've got a lot of time in the winter so I'll practice up. And I usually take some classes." Her eyes lit up again. "This winter, it's sign language and Bosnian. Vermont is getting more and more immigrants from Bosnia and Herzegovina, so there's a need for interpreters to go with them to doctor's appointments, the DMV, etc."

"Another language. Smart woman."

"I spent two years on Mandarin lessons that turned out fairly useless here in Vermont." The dimple came and went. "Still, I get a kick out of hearing what the staff in the Chinese restaurant is saying about the customers."

"Not always flattering?"

"Hardly!"

"Well, I think the laborers and farmers are lucky to have you."

"Thanks."

"Are you a Vermonter? By birth, I mean?"

She shook her head. "I grew up on a farm in central New York State. My parents started out producing beef and pork but then they discovered a growing market for fresh fruit and vegetables. They have hoop houses, like Hunt's, and an orchard, and several fields of veggies. They sell to local restaurants, and my brother Finn and I used to run a farmstand out by the road."

"Child labor."

"You better believe it. Takes a whole family to run a farm." She sat back, both hands around her coffee mug. "Several years ago they started a CSA, like Hunt's, and it's been great. Their customers come to them, like a roadside farmstand on a larger scale. My cousin does five or six farmers markets all summer long, and he's the liaison between my parents and the state's Farm to School program. He and my brother and sister are full partners now."

"You're proud of them."

"Very. How about you? Have you always lived in Vermont?"

"I have, but I'm first-generation—" His wide grin was partly about what he wanted to say next, but mostly because he was suddenly washed with pure delight about being there, talking so comfortably, seeing this beautiful woman only a few feet away from him and hearing her voice and getting to know her laugh. "So I don't count as a *real* Vermonter. My parents were city folk. Baltimore and Boston. They moved to Vermont as starry-eyed newlyweds with the dream of doing something that fit their mental picture of real Vermont. Community. Social activism. Old-fashioned values. One of their ideas was managing a good-sized food co-op somewhere. No brick-and-mortar store front, just members meeting over hummus and pita bread to decide what to order each month and then meeting again to divide up the order."

"I think that model pretty much died out."

"Yeah. Everyone's too busy. Anyway, my parents took one look at the Tyne Country Store in the Northeast Kingdom and that was it. They had found their calling."

Rose glanced up over his head. "We should probably get going, Jack. There's quite a line waiting to be seated."

"Oh. Right." He signaled the waitress for the check. "The store had been closed and empty for going on five years but it wasn't in bad shape. It's got living quarters upstairs so my mom and dad bought it, moved in, and got to work. I came along a few years later and they put me to work as soon as I could walk." He handed the waitress a twenty and a ten. "No need to bring change."

"Thank you, sir. Thank you both. Have a great north country day."

"You too."

"So…" Rose tipped her face into the sunshine. "Did your parents dream of handing the store to you someday?"

"Hell, no! My parents love me! They don't want their only child spending the best years of his life working ten, twelve hours a day, seven days a week. They always encouraged me to find something else, *any*thing else!"

****

Jack stopped the car in the shade outside Hunt's house and turned toward Rose.

"I enjoyed this."

"Me too, Jack."

"I'll be back here on Monday, when we break ground at Hunt's. Will you have lunch with me? Or breakfast again?"

"Yes—Oh, no. I can't. I'll be up in Newport for the whole week." She frowned. "I'm not looking forward to it."

"Why not? That's a nice little town."

"It is. But I'll be indoors a lot of the time, in a courtroom."

"The fuzz finally caught up with you, huh? Found out about that time you went eight miles over the speed limit on the interstate."

She looked so somber that Jack immediately felt foolish.

"I'm trading locations with a vee-mep woman who has no experience with legal terms. I've interpreted at two trials so far, so I'll be translating in the courtroom at least part of every day. The rest of the time I'll do what she normally does on the two farms she covers."

"What's the trial about? If you can tell me."

"I can't. Not yet." She smiled. "Maybe next time. What about the week after that?"

"Damn. I'm going to be in the Bennington area then. And the week after that. At least."

"After the court thing I'll be down in Addison."

"Addison. Great! I'll be doing site studies in Bristol. Let's make a date for one month from today, at that restaurant on the main drag in Vergennes. Will that work?"

"Lunch?"

"Noon?"

"Noon for lunch in Vergennes. Good."

****

Jack couldn't remember the last time he felt like this. He'd been pretty much solitary and celibate since the divorce. And before that his luck with dates was so abysmal that he'd been forced to invent the Third Girl Project. But today he met a girl, he liked the girl, he asked the girl out, she said yes, they were comfortable with each other, and they had a second date planned. Way better than the Project!

Chapter Two

Jack's Third Girl Project

"Bro. Guess who just came into the library?"

Jack looked up, his eyes glassy from two hours with an Applied Linear Algebra text that must have been written by someone new to the English language.

"Who?"

"Who. He asks who. The object of all your dreams, that's who." His roommate slammed his books down. "Who!"

"Oh."

"So go ask her."

"Don't think so."

"That girl is probably just waiting for you to ask her."

"I strongly doubt that."

"C'mon, man. She knows you. She likes you. She always laughs when you're clowning around. Besides, you've already kissed her!"

"That wasn't a real kiss, dimwit. It was a stage kiss."

"Did not your lips meet her lips? Did not that conjunction of lips last for, oh, five seconds or more? Was not that kiss repeated during rehearsals and then for three nights in a row in front of a vast audience of your peers?"

"Yeeeeesss. But—"

"C'mon, man. You're a popular dude. Everyone on campus likes you. You're funny." He leaned back and regarded Jack solemnly. "And you're not completely hideous to look at."

"Gee. Thanks. So where is she?"

"She's sitting with three other girls at that long table two stacks from here."

"Okay." Jack stood up, squared his shoulders, took a deep breath, and pushed back his chair. "Here goes. The Big Ask. For the Big Date."

Katrina. Exotic. Foreign. Gorgeous beyond words. Katrina, with her dark curls and olive skin and intriguing accent and her red, red lips. When they started practicing that kiss, he expected to end up with red smeared all over his face. But no. The beautiful lips were all natural. If Katrina would go with him to the Drama Club's annual spring dinner dance, his year as a college freshman would be complete.

He could hear light laughter, and then Katrina's best friend, whose voice was louder and less melodious than Katrina's.

"Well, sure. Jack Carmichael is funny. And kinda cute. But he's, you know, like a cartoon character. A peanut."

Jack stopped moving. Peanut? No way! He wasn't built like a basketball star but five-nine-and-a-half hardly qualified as a peanut!

"Peee nut?"

"In the comics. You know. That little round-headed guy."

"Oh, yes. That iss very cute drawing." Jack thought Katrina's laugh was like a distant wind chime. Sweet, musical, tinkling, achingly beautiful. "But that peeenut has a ceer-cle face. Round. And no hair. Jack Carmichael has very good hairs. When we were in play together, I wanted to roo-ful up his hairs."

"Then he's a puppy." Jack recognized the voice of Kristina's second-best friend. "He's like our little labradoodle. You want to pet his hair or rub his belly. And make him groan."

They all laughed this time, and Jack thought the combined sound was more like hyenas than wind chimes. He took a few silent steps backward. Rub his belly! If any of those girls tried rubbing anywhere near his belly, they might get quite a surprise.

"No! I've got it! You were right about a cartoon character, but it's not a person. It's the dog! The beagle! Jack Carmichael is a beagle. Sweet and cute, with beagle eyes! Katrina, when you kissed him in the play, did he feel sorta squishy? Like a cute little stuffed beagle dog?"

"No. Not at all."

You go, Kristina, you tell 'em.

"He is quite moos-cular. He looks, how you say, *pudgy* because he is, what is the right term? Bushel chested. No! Barrel chested." Even her sigh was music. "But I agree with you. He eees not my ideal fabric for dating. Fabric? Cloth?"

"Date material."

"Ah. Yes. He is not date material. He is cute, and he is nice. But he is too short." And then she twisted the knife. "He is not sex-eee. I theeenk."

Jack turned and leaned his forehead against the cool side of the bookstack. Kristina was right. He *was* barrel-chested. And he looked shorter than he was. Back in high school he'd found a chart showing average body dimensions. He was two inches longer than average from the top of his head to his crotch, and his legs were almost an inch shorter than average. The PE teacher said that his broad shoulders, long arms, and barrel chest gave him a perfect wrestling build, but Jack hated wrestling. Rolling around on the floor, grappling with other guys. No way.

He looked chubby, it was true. No wonder he could write his whole dating history on a half sheet of paper. Baggy jeans probably didn't help. Maybe he should start wearing that tight pair his mother gave him for Christmas. There had to be some style that would make him look as *mooscular* as he really was.

Nope. He would still look too short for exotic, dark-haired, gorgeous, unattainable Katrina. She would still want to ruffle his hair, smile her achingly beautiful smile with those achingly gorgeous lips, and then skip off with a taller guy.

****

"So? How'd it go?"

"Look into my face, bro. Are you seeing the face of a man who will be escorting the most beautiful woman on campus to the spring dinner dance?" Jack plopped down into the chair. "I'm too short."

"She said that?"

"Not to me. She said it to her friends. I was hiding in the stacks." He opened his textbook and stared down at it. "I'm too short and I have beagle eyes."

"Ouch."

"True that."

"So what are you gonna do about the dance?"

"I am going to finish this chapter."

"You gotta get out there, bro. You never do anything involving girls. That's why you're so bowled over by that Katrina bitch." Ben leaned across the table. "Be honest. Do you ever meet up with girls when you're doing your bird-watching thing?"

Jack lifted his head. "Yes I do. So there."

"*So there*? What are you, five years old?"

"All right, forget the *so there*. But yes, I do interact with females."

"Yeah? Who?"

"Lucy comes to mind immediately." Jack forced a starry-eyed grin. "Green eyes, lots of smiles, nice tight little bod." He looked back down at his textbook. "Silver hair."

"Your sexy Lucy has gray hair??"

"Yeah, well, *I'm* not ageist. Unlike some people I know."

Ben was looking sadly at his friend, slowly shaking his head from side to side. "You are fast approaching pitiful."

"Probably true. But right now, I'm going to understand just enough Applied Linear Algebra for tomorrow's test." He looked up, his usually smiling face glum and determined. "And then I am going to walk out of here and I am going to ask the very first girl who meets my eyes." He shook his head. "No. Not the first one. When I was a kid, three was my lucky number. I am going to walk out of here and ask the third girl who meets my eyes if she will be my date for the Drama Club's spring dinner dance."

"No matter who she is? Even if she's that scary mean-looking girl from bio?"

"No matter anything. I have struck out with the girl I wanted. It'll be the third girl. Random. No matter what."

****

23

Jack sagged against the door frame. His eyes were wide. His mouth gaped open. He clutched the front of his jacket in one clenched fist.

"Wore you out, huh? Doing the dirty?"

Jack took two staggering steps and fell into his desk chair.

"Bro, the only dirty in the last four hours of my life, which I might add were the *long*est four hours of my life, was the food being masticated and swirled around in her open mouth as she talked."

"Barf."

"I almost did."

"So the date was not a success."

"The date was a disaster. She never stopped talking. Never. Not for a second. She started talking before we were out of her dorm and she was still talking when I dropped her off." He fixed his roommate with an agonized look. "Did you know that some guy wrote a piece of so-called music that's twenty-nine minutes of silence?"

"I did not know that."

"Maybe it's twenty-five minutes. I forget." He clutched his forehead hard enough to leave imprints of his fingertips. "Must forget. *Must* forget. Forget the whole evening. Forget what her parents do for work. What her grandparents did. The name of her second-grade teacher. Where she buried her pet turtle. Must forget that she has a slight scoliosis of the spine and some kid made fun of her when she took Red Cross swimming lessons at age eleven."

"You gonna give up on the Third Girl Project?"

Jack sighed. "Not sure. Ask me tomorrow. Right now I am going to take an exceedingly long shower and wash away the entire evening."

****

Back in high school, Jack's mother teased him about his mad social whirl. It was true that he went to a lot of sporting events and school dances and parties, but he was almost always part of a group. And in the last two years of school, he was always the designated driver. The one who was too sober to laugh at the hysterically funny jokes, stumbles, and witticisms. The one out in the cold at two in the morning cleaning the vomit from the back floor of his car. He had exactly three dates in all four years of high school, and one was when his parents asked him to take a visiting cousin to the movies.

Now, at the beginning of his sophomore year of college, Jack faced the fact that he had no dating skills. He didn't know how to choose a girl. He didn't know how to ask one out. He didn't know what to talk about on a date. He was a virgin and would probably be a virgin forever. He would have to resurrect the Third Girl Project.

He never would have approached Vera if it weren't for the Project. She was a few inches taller than he was, with snapping black eyes and a wild mane of black curls that looked like steel wool. He'd seen her striding along the walkways and through the halls with her long legs in tight jeans and her feet in black boots, always with a leather backpack slung over one shoulder. Jack assumed she was a lesbian. Or maybe a vampire, with that white, white skin and black, black hair. But she was the third girl.

Third *woman*. Calling Vera a girl was like calling Mt. Everest a hill. Vera was the third woman who met his eyes on his way back to the dorm after breakfast on the second morning of his sophomore year, so he walked right up to her and grinned.

"Vera? I'm Jack."

"I know."

He raised his eyebrows, and she said they'd been in the same freshman American Lit class.

"Oh. Yes."

"What do you want, Jack?"

"I want to ask you to get coffee with me sometime."

"How about now?"

"Oh. Yes. That's good."

As they walked back across campus, Jack felt his usual fluttery stomach, the one that always accompanied being one-to-one with a girl. A *woman*. But then Vera started grilling him on his plans for the future and, after a few stammering starts, he found himself explaining his dream of working in some field related to environmental protection. Solar energy or wind power or maybe geothermal.

"You read about that proposed geothermal project near Bend, Oregon?"

"Super-hot rock? Steam at supercritical temperatures?"

"You'll do, Jack."

He knew he had just passed a test, but he didn't want her to see him gloating so he stifled his grin, put his hand on the small of her back, and guided her to an isolated table.

"What do you take in your coffee?"

"Cream. Lots."

"Pastry?"

"Lots."

He came back with a tray of two mugs, two

chocolate hazelnut croissants, a muffin, and a giant peanut butter cookie.

"What do you want to do, Vera? After college?"

She took a sip of coffee, nodded her approval, and gave a gusty sigh.

"Not graduate school, I don't think. I think I was born to be an activist. Greenpeace, maybe? Signing up new voters in red states? Chaining myself to trees in old growth forests?" She fixed him with a fierce stare. "I have GOT to find something like that. Something worthwhile. I *have* to make a difference, now, when I'm young and healthy." She shrugged. "I can go to grad school once I start slowing down."

"In what?"

"Eh?"

"What would you study? If you went?"

"Oh, I don't know. A decade or so of activism should make it clear what field of study will do the most good." She split the cookie and gave him half. "Tell me what you know about Iceland and geothermal energy."

They were still talking when students started coming in for lunch.

"Share a 'za?"

"Sure."

They were still talking when the cafeteria had almost emptied again.

Vera looked at him, considering.

"Lunch is over."

"I noticed."

"You got any place we can go and fuck?"

One of Jack's teachers used him as an example of the word *glib*. Now he wasted several stunned seconds stammering and trying to catch his breath.

"Oh. I… My… Yes. My roommate is visiting his parents. So, yes. Yes. My room. A suite. Two bedrooms, bathroom, study area."

She gave him another sideways look.

"Study area, huh?" She hefted her backpack and started walking.

****

"Huh. It *is* a study area." Vera stood in the doorway, looking at the two big bookcases, two desks and two chairs, separated by the moveable divider. "I expected a giant flatscreen TV. Couches. Gigantoid music center. Stacks of empty beer cans." She turned and looked directly at him. "I'm liking you, Jack Whatever-your-last-name-is."

"Carmichael."

"Doesn't matter." She dropped her backpack to the floor. "You got condoms?"

"Yes."

"So here's what we're going to do. You're on top first. The second time we do it, I'm on top. Then you, then me. Just fucking. No oral sex. No anal sex. No declarations of undying love."

"That's—All right."

****

If he hadn't bought a box of twenty-four condoms as part of this-year-I'm-going-to-get-lucky preparations, Jack would have had no idea how many times they had sex over the next two days and two nights. But by Sunday evening there were nine condoms left. The room reeked of sex, pizza, and left-over Chinese food, and he was sure he didn't have a functional muscle left in his entire body.

"Got an eight a.m. class tomorrow." Vera stood up,

majestically naked, the bush between her legs as wild and dark as the one on her head. "That was good, Jack. Great way to spend a weekend."

"When's the next time?"

"Never. Probably." She picked up her t-shirt off the floor. "We've done it with each other. Time to move on."

****

There were a few other Third Girls.

There was the moody Poli. Sci. major who wanted Jack to help her go canvassing door-to-door in the scariest part of the city, campaigning for someone no one would vote for but her. There were several girls in the first half of his junior year, each for one date only and no regrets after. And then there was Jazmine, a lovely and lively dance major with skin the color of café au lait and eyes that were truly black. They were together the rest of that academic year and all summer, when they both had work internships on campus, and they were together for the first half of Jack's senior year. But Jazmine quit school after New Year's to join a professional dance troupe in New York City. Jack promised to follow her career online and said he would surprise her by showing up at one of her performances and sitting in the very middle of the very front row and being the first person in the audience to jump to his feet and start a standing ovation. But he never did.

And then came the Third Girl he ended up marrying. And divorcing. That was, if not a total unmitigated disaster, such a colossal failure that he gave up on the Project. If love came to him, great. If not, well, he didn't hate being alone. He liked himself. He was starting a career that fascinated him. He knew that he was doing something fine with his life. He would be all right.

Chapter Three

Second Date

"This is idiotic."

Rose pulled into an empty slot in front of the restaurant.

"It is moronic. Half-witted." She unfastened her seat belt. "This feels like a blind date and I have always hated blind dates." She looked up and down the street. "I can't remember what his car looks like, so I can't even tell if he's here already. I should leave. I have plenty to do without starting the afternoon with a blind date." She eyeballed the picture window to the right of the restaurant's main door. "He's probably sitting in there right now, watching me sitting out here." She listened to the little pings as the engine cooled. "I met the man exactly once. A month ago. For an hour. Plus, we've exchanged two single-sentence texts confirming this idiotic almost-blind date."

She pushed open the truck door.

The diner near Hunt's had shiny surfaces, with hard red plastic booths and silver chrome edges around the tables. This place was all wood, with old narrow boards on the floor and wooden tables and chairs of various styles and generations. Even the walls were narrow wooden boards, whitewashed and covered with old or made-to-look-old advertising posters. Aside from the straight aisle directly in front of her, the place was full of people. Two waitresses carrying coffee pots and plates of food wove their way between tables, expertly bending now toward the right and now toward the left, lifting their burdens over the heads of oblivious customers. The noise and bustle were daunting, and Rose couldn't see Jack anywhere. For several long moments, she stood by the door trying to convince herself to turn around and leave. But then she caught sight of tousled red-brown hair at a small table way in the back, up against the half-wall separating the dining area from the cooking area.

Well, she'd recognized him at least. She wasn't meeting a complete stranger.

When she touched Jack's shoulder, he stood up so abruptly that his elbow knocked the passing waitress and there was a breath-held moment as Rose gasped, Jack reached out both hands, and the waitress juggled two sandwich plates.

"Great save."

"Thank you." The waitress looked from Jack to Rose and back again. "If it was just you, I might do some scolding. But you're too pretty a couple for that."

"Thank you." He held out the chair for Rose. "She just earned herself a mega tip."

"Yes indeed." She picked up a menu. "Have you eaten here before?"

"Nope."

"So no recommendations, huh?"

"Breakfasts and lunches are always good in diners and small restaurants."

"True."

This *was* a blind date. Uncomfortable, silly, and awkward.

"So." She flopped the menu down on the table and looked directly at him. "How have you been?"

"Busy. Very."

"Happy, though?"

"Mostly."

"You sounded like you enjoyed your job. Before."

"I do. This last couple of weeks, though—" He leaned forward. "I have been dealing with three landowners who are driving me bonkers. I've been looking forward to this meal like a drowning sailor grabbing for a life preserver."

"My gracious. That bad, huh?"

"Worse." He glanced up. "Let's order."

As soon as the waitress left, he leaned forward again.

"First there's the guy whose whole property sits on ledge. I call him Papa Bear, because his bed is too hard."

She started to smile.

"Then there's Mama Bear, who wants a solar array in nothing but swamp. I keep having to explain about wetland rules and she keeps smiling and feeding me raisin cookies and saying that we—she always says *we*—should have no trouble convincing the state that the ecological benefits of solar outweigh any possible damage to a few measly wetlands."

"Oh dear."

"And then…" He heaved a huge sigh. "Then there's Goldilocks. Not a single thing is right. This site plan is too *jarring*. Quote. This one's downright *ugly*. This one blocks the view from her guest room window. This one might require cutting down her favorite tree. On and on and on."

"You think you'll ever come up with something that

works for her?"

"I don't know. All four of us have visited the site. All four of us have met with her, talked with her, listened to hours and hours of stuff we don't need to know. Like where she found Jack-in-the-Pulpits last spring, in a spot that's not anywhere near any of the proposed sites so it's completely irrelevant."

The waitress brought coffee for Rose and a mason jar of root beer for him.

"Anyway, that's enough. What happened with your court case?"

"It was nasty." She wrapped her hands around her coffee mug and leaned back in her chair. "Three immigrant farm workers saw their boss knock his wife against a wall and then backhand his eleven-year-old son when the boy intervened. It wasn't the first time he hit her, but he never hit one of the kids before so she called the state police." Rose shook her head. "The guy went ballistic. He couldn't believe his wife reported him and he couldn't believe his son would back her up. And he was *livid* that his farm workers were willing to testify." Her whole face tightened, her blue eyes snapping and furious. "*Ignorant immigrants. Don't even know how to speak English. He could get them deported. Only a numskull would take their word against his.*"

She made a motion with her head and shoulders as if shaking off the memories. "The guy's well-known in town. He ran for Selectboard. He's a Rotarian, for Pete's sake. Which he told the officers. And when they weren't impressed, he took a swing at one of them."

"Whoops."

"Huge whoops. Assaulting an officer, abuse of both a spouse and a minor, and then resisting arrest."

"And what happened?"

"Significant fine. Stern warning. Public embarrassment. And the wife moved into town, with the boy."

"Are the workers still on his farm?"

"Gosh, no. They're working for one of his neighbors now. Which adds insult to injury, because now he's short-staffed for harvest season."

"Sweet. The bully got what was coming to him."

"I am sincerely glad my part of the whole thing is over." She sighed. "And I hope I won't be assigned to that area next year. It'll be hard for him to hire workers unless he goes with a different labor exchange. He'll be furious all over again and he's the kind who holds a grudge." She did the odd shrugging motion again. "Here comes our food. Just in time."

"Are you always hungry?"

"Pretty much." Her eyes were on the heaping plate the waitress set in front of her. "Rapid metabolism or something. I'm always ravenous, I always eat humongous meals, and I always burn it off."

"Lucky you."

There was quiet for several minutes as they dealt with huge messy sandwiches and piles of slaw and fries. Rose finished half her food before she started talking again.

"I know you're passionate about your work. What do you do when you're not passionately working?"

"Birding."

"What?"

"Bird-watching. I'm a birding geek. Big time."

Her expression was a mixture of disbelief and amusement.

"Tell me, birding geek. What exactly does that involve?"

"I spend hours and hours a week tramping through woods and around ponds and along the lake shore, binoculars slung around my neck and notepad in my pocket, looking for birds."

"What's the notepad for?"

"To write down everything I see. Of course! You can't be a birder without making lists. It just isn't done."

"Oh." She was almost grinning. "And what do birding geeks do with their lists?"

"If they're socially responsible, they enter their sightings on e-bird."

"Never heard of it." She picked up the other half of her sandwich.

"It's a gigantic database run by the Cornell Lab of Ornithology. Birders all over the world report what they're seeing, and where and when, and scientists use the information to keep track of population declines, migration trends, and so forth."

She nodded, chewing.

"The e-bird site keeps track of my personal lists too. Life list. Vermont life list. Current year list. Other years' lists." He almost laughed at her expression. "Lists of what birders have submitted the most lists and who has seen the most species."

"So it's competitive."

"It is for a lot of birders. Definitely for me." His brown eyes lit up. "For five glorious days in mid-June, I was number fourteen in the state for species seen. Since then I've been straight out with work so I'm way down the Top 100 list, but it was good while it lasted."

"So sorry." She picked up a fry. "Bird-watchers on

TV or in movies always wear tan. And high boots. And pith helmets. Do you?"

"Not a pith helmet to my name. But I do have lots of tan."

The waitress refilled Rose's coffee and she murmured her thanks.

"What's more fun? The birds, or the lists?"

"Hmmmm. I like watching birds, a lot, but the lists add excitement. Some birders even keep county lists. And lists of species they've seen nesting. Or mating. Or pooping."

"Not true."

"Swear to god."

"My mom always shakes her head when she hears about some hobby or interest that's new to her. Worlds within worlds, she says. You just gave me a glimpse into a world within the world."

"Birding is a very big world, Rose. I forget the exact numbers but millions and millions of people watch birds and feed birds and buy bird-related things like nest boxes and spotting scopes. And take pricy birding tours."

"Have you ever? Taken a tour, I mean?"

"Not yet. But I hope to, someday." He looked to his left, where a glass case held rows of pies, brownies, cookies, and cakes.

"Dessert?"

"For sure!" She looked embarrassed and amused at herself. "There's this restaurant in the Adirondacks that's famous for pies. On one trip home to see my parents, I stopped there and had nothing but pie for lunch. I'm all grown up! I don't have to eat proper food first! So I had a piece of apple pie, then a piece of strawberry-rhubarb with ice cream, and I finished up with warm pecan pie for dessert."

"That sounds like a thoroughly wonderful meal."

"It was. It was." She unexpectedly frowned. "I shouldn't have snickered at your birding, Jack. You're a bird geek, and I'm a plant dweeb. Both my parents know a lot about wild plants, and soon after I moved to Vermont I took a weekend course in ferns, mosses, and lichen. One thing I love about my job is that I get to see plants in so many parts of the state."

Jack looked up from under his brows. "And make a list?"

For the first time, Rose laughed out loud. "I do! I bought a gorgeous leather-bound notebook a few years ago and I write down every new plant I see. Plant that's new to me, I mean. Plus the date and location. Realizing how many different plants are right around here, where we all walk and drive every single day without even noticing them—It has—It has made my world three-dimensional. It's as if before I started noticing plants, I was seeing woods and fields as flat. Like a painting or a drawing or a photograph. But then I started seeing INTO the woods and fields. Like an x-ray but better because of all the colors and variety and beauty."

Jack started nodding about halfway through. "That's exactly it, Rose. That's what birding does for me. I feel like I'm *in* the world when I'm walking outdoors and watching birds. I'm not just walking *by* the world."

Their attentive waitress was at their table, notepad in hand. Jack knew he'd regret it the next time he stepped on his bathroom scale, but he and Rose ordered a brownie sundae and a piece of pecan pie and agreed to share. The waitress left, and Jack found himself looking past her to an elderly couple who were sitting with all four hands joined across their table.

"Call me sentimental, but I like seeing that."

Rose was about to say "I thought your name was Jack" but she looked over and had to agree. She liked seeing it too.

"Have you ever been there, Jack, where they are? Married?"

"Maybe they're not married. Maybe they're having an illicit tryst." He met her eyes again. "But to answer your question, yes. Briefly. Not even three years."

"Oh, dear. I want to ask what happened but if it's too personal, just ignore me."

"You know, in a way, it was too *im*personal. Samantha was the last of my Third Girl Project."

"Third Girl."

"Gonna need coffee for this story." He caught the waitress's eye and pointed to Rose's coffee cup and then to his own chest. "Okay. I was not a roaring success at dating in high school. So in my freshman year at college, I decided to opt out of decision-making entirely. I would let fate and random selection find me a mate. I would choose a day and I would ask out the third girl who met my eyes on that day."

She sat back, her face amused and intrigued. "How did that work out?"

"Not all that badly, actually. There were a few disasters, but it was way better than my high school social life."

The waitress topped off Rose's coffee and plunked down a mug for him.

"You are possibly the best restaurant server in the entire universe."

"I try."

Jack stirred in a container of half-and-half and sighed. "So a few months before college graduation, my sweetheart at the time quit school and ran off to New York City to become a professional dancer."

"Oh dear."

"It wasn't too awful. We both knew what she wanted, if she ever got the chance. I was happy for her and only mildly sad for me. I spent a few weeks at loose ends and then decided to resurrect the Third Girl Project. Samantha was the third girl who met my eyes so I asked her out for pizza and mini-golf."

"And it was love at first date."

"No. But it was affection, at least on my part. And the always perilous URL."

"I'll bite. What is that?"

"Unthinking Raging Lust."

They both laughed.

"I'd been accepted to grad school. I had an apartment lined up. I had a part-time job. I knew where I was going next and what I was doing." He sighed. "Sam, on the other hand, was a very unenthusiastic sophomore. She was a lousy student, and she didn't seem curious about any particular subject."

"Why on earth was she in college?"

"Her parents were not what you might call flexible individuals. Their little Samantha was going to college and that was the end of the discussion."

"What did she *want* to do, instead of college?"

"That's a good question. I don't know." He flushed, staring down into his coffee. "Quite an admission from a man who was married to her for almost three years. I don't know what she wanted in life. I think she expected college to be an extension of high school. She'd be with her high school friends, or new friends just like them, and they'd go on talking about boys and waxing their legs and getting their nails done." He grimaced. "That sounds phenomenally sexist, but Sam *liked* those things. And going to the movies and texting and trying out different mixed drinks whenever they could raid their fathers' alcohol cabinets or find a bartender who was lax about IDs." He shook his head. "Sadly, and it *was* sad for her, her high school friends got better grades and better test scores than she did. They had the chance to go to big universities out of state while Sam ended up at a rinky-dink college where she didn't know a single soul."

He looked up, his eyes puzzled and pained. "She was lonely and bored and angry. Angry at her parents for making her go to college. Angry at her high school teachers for not helping her get better grades." He gave a little laugh. "For not *giving* her better grades. Angry at the rinky-dink college and just about every person there. And she was furious about the triples."

"Triples?"

"State colleges are infamous for accepting more students than they have room for, so lots of dorm rooms designed for two get turned into triples. Samantha had been in a triple as a freshman, she was in a triple as a sophomore, and she had just been told she'd probably be in a triple as a junior. Unless she moved off-campus."

"She did *not* get married just to avoid living in a triple room."

"I think she did. Oh, wow. Look at these desserts."

Jack waited until the waitress left and then dug his spoon into the brownie, ice cream, and chocolate sauce. "Oh my god. This is paradise. Nirvana. Close to ecstasy."

There was silence for several minutes. Then Rose pushed her pie plate across the little table, reached out, and pulled the brownie concoction closer. Jack watched her lick her spoon and stopped breathing.

"I wouldn't have thought anything could equal that pie, but I think what you ordered just might measure up. So. There's, um, Samantha hating school. What next?"

"Sam. Right. Well, she grew up in the Bronx. In a high-rise. She said she could listen in on every conversation from the apartments on both sides plus most of what went on across the hall. She was supposed to think her family was lucky because they had three bedrooms, but there was mom, dad, Samantha, a brother, and a grandmother. Her brother slept on a folding cot in the living room. He studied in a tiny closet. Sam said she felt crowded her whole life. Anyway, to cut a long story short—" He gave Rose a lopsided grin. "Cutting a long story short isn't exactly one of my talents. Anyway, one night we were in the rec room of her dorm. We'd been on five dates. Five, that's all. We were on the couch, necking. I was—Well, I was a guy in my early twenties. A guy who'd had the same girlfriend for almost a year and then hadn't had sex for months." He glanced up under his brows and met Rose's eyes. "I was close to exploding when she moved her fingers toward the only part of me capable of volition at that moment. And then she said we should get married." His eyes widened as if he was as surprised now as he'd been then.

"A bit sudden."

"Yup."

"What did you say?"

"You know, I'm not sure. I've never been able to remember. It was probably something flippant. *Why not?*

Or *Sure thing.* But by noon the next day, she had contacted the school to tell them she wouldn't be back the following year. She'd called her parents. She'd even started looking into retail jobs where I'd be going to grad school."

"Yipes."

"Double yipes."

"And you just went along?"

"I did. I felt like, I felt like I was caught in a tornado or something. And she was glowing, Rose. Samantha was happy for the first time since I'd met her. I liked being able to make someone that happy. Heady stuff for a guy who could count every girl he'd ever dated on the fingers of two hands, and have a few fingers left over." He shrugged. "We were married the day after I graduated, before a Justice of the Peace, with nobody there but my parents and hers." He half-laughed. "Her mother kept glaring at me, sure that I'd knocked her daughter up." The humor faded from his mobile face. "That was what my parents thought too. I'd never mentioned Sam to them, not once. And there I was, out of the blue, marrying her." He took a deep breath. "The next day we moved to Dartmouth and set up housekeeping."

"And…" Rose was reluctant to ask but she really wanted to know. "How was it?"

"It didn't seem real. It felt like we were playing house. Pretending. Hubby going off to earn his degree, wifey working at the neighborhood grocery store." He frowned. "We tried. I think. For a while. But I always knew that her main reasons for getting married were to get away from college and get out from under her parents." His snort was so loud the couple at the next table looked over, startled. "One day I came right out and asked her. Did you propose to me just to avoid living in a triple?"

"And what did she say?"

"She said she wanted to get off campus. And I was sort of cute."

"Ouch."

"Yup. That was as lovey-dovey as she ever got. As *we* ever got. She thought I was cute and she was grateful to me for getting her out of a life she hated. I liked her and sometimes I felt sorry for her, and I was getting regular sex. But I started resenting her after only a few months. She was always there when I was trying to study. She never wanted to hear about what I was learning. I can get very enthusiastic, as you probably can guess. I'd start blathering about some amazing fact or some article, or I'd want her to look at my computer screen and see some amazing photos, and she'd sit down next to me and ask me when I was going to invite friends over. People we could hang out with. Have what she called fun."

"How long did you say you were married?" Rose jerked her head back, her eyes widening. "You're not still married, are you?"

"God, no. Would I be sitting here with you, sharing a booth and a—" He looked at the remains of their desserts. "About two trillion calories, on what counts as a second date, if I were still married?"

"I don't think you would, no. But this is, as you said, a second date. There must be a great deal about you that I don't know."

"Nope. With me, what you see is pretty much what you get."

What you get, Rose. I would like very much for you to get me.

The silence lengthened until Jack finally started talking again, quickly. "But to answer your question, we divorced just short of our third anniversary."

"Any children?"

"God, no! Luckily! I was immersed in graduate studies and she—Sam had felt hemmed in, limited, her whole life. A baby would limit her even more. We were very, very careful."

"So how did it end? Your marriage?"

"It ended, my marriage of not very much convenience, when my unemotional, shallow, unromantic wife sat down beside me on the couch, took my hand, patted it, and told me she had met someone and they were deeply in love."

"Oh. Dear. Well, good for her, I suppose."

"I think so. I lost track of her, so I have no way of knowing if it worked out." He shrugged. "That's my sad marriage story. What about you? Have you ever tied and then untied the knot?"

"Sort of." Her forehead wrinkled and she looked down and watched her hands rearrange the catsup and mustard and the salt and pepper shakers. "I stood up with my fiancé in a church full of friends and relatives, after walking up the aisle to the strains of the wedding march, and then I didn't get married."

"That poor guy! You left him at the altar."

"No."

"Do not tell me he left you. Because I won't believe you."

"I—Thank you." Rose sighed. "No. He didn't leave. I didn't leave. We stood there together, hand in hand, facing everybody, and we told them we had decided not to get married. We loved each other since we were toddlers but it wasn't the kind of loving people should feel if they're going to be married. Not the kind my folks have. Or my sister and her husband."

"What happened then?"

"Then we had the reception, at my parents' farm. Food, music, dancing, just like a regular wedding reception. He and I danced together. We laughed. We had a great time." A shadow passed over her face. "And later that night, I found out something that made me incredibly glad I hadn't married him."

Jack waited for what felt like several minutes. When he couldn't stand it…

"And? What was it?"

She looked up, her blue eyes narrowed and stormy. "I found out that my best friend in the world, the friend of my entire childhood, had proposed marriage because his parents threatened to disown him if he didn't settle down. He wanted their lovely moolah, so he was *willing* to marry me."

"Ouch. Big huge ouch. What happened then?"

"He went on being a boy for several more years. Riding his horses, sailing his boat, driving too fast, partying with his buds. Offending the old fuddy-duddies at the country club. And then one day." She adjusted the napkins. "Whit was driving too fast, as usual, and he almost hit a little boy. He threw himself out of the car just as an Amazon with the lungs of a drill sergeant raced down the driveway yelling at him."

She grinned, and Jack almost missed her next words because he was watching her dimple.

"That's Whit's description. Amazon and drill

sergeant. She picked up the child, grabbed Whit by the arm, and took them both up to the house where there was a frazzled foster mother and a half dozen other kids. The feisty Amazon assigned Whit the job of turning the crank on an old-fashioned ice cream maker. They all ate strawberry ice cream, Whit fell for the social worker, she fell for him, he turned into a grown-up, and they've been married for something like eight years." The dimple reappeared in her left cheek and her eyes sparkled again. "And they adopted the boy. That boy Whit almost hit."

"Are you still friends with him? With Whit?"

"Oh, yes. I even went to his wedding. We're still friends and I think Cynthia is amazing. And they have two more adopted kids now."

Loyalty to her childhood friend kept her from mentioning Whit's pregnancy scare, the alarm that pushed his mother into delivering the marriage ultimatum, and the irony that he was infertile so the whole brouhaha was for nothing.

After a moment, Jack broke the silence. "Rose? Would you like to do something next weekend? Something outdoors this time?"

"Instead of another episode of sinful gorging?"

"It's not the greatest time of year for birding, with the excitement of courting and nesting and raising young pretty much winding down. But my partner Derek and his wife have gotten into geocaching and I've been wanting to try it."

"That's where you follow clues and a compass to find prizes or something?"

"Or something. Yes."

"I would like to try that. Where were you thinking of going?"

"Supposedly there's a good course, or whatever it's called, not far from you, right outside Stowe. Want to go Saturday?"

"Is there anything I should bring? Do we have to dress like mighty hunters or anything?"

"I don't think so. But if you have a huntress costume you're dying to wear, Rose, I'm dying to see it." He waggled his eyebrows like a younger, cuter Groucho, and she laughed. "Just bring yourself, Rose, and some water. And good shoes. And bug spray. I've got compasses and GPS units and I'll get specific instructions from Derek. What say I e-mail you with a start time and place?"

"Jack, I will look forward to it all week." Rose reached out and curled her fingers around his lower arm. "I have thoroughly enjoyed today. I wasn't sure I wanted to come in, but I'm glad I did."

"Me too. Very."

He leaned forward at the same time she did, and what might have been a real kiss ended up two air kisses beside two cheeks.

Chapter Four

The Almost Wedding

Every time Rose turned in the driveway at 112 Spring Street in Morrisville, Vermont, she whispered a thanks into the sky for Stuart Farmer-Abernathy and his hair.

No. That wasn't true. Sometimes she silently thanked the gorgeous young man with the gorgeous hair, but other times she grinned a wicked grin and sent a "nyah nyah nyah" winging through the air toward Manhattan.

Rose wanted to live in the little building hidden behind the main house at 112 Spring Street the minute she saw it, seven years ago, ready to start her new life. She was finally done with school. She had a brand-new degree in English as a Second Language with a Minor in Spanish, and a brand-new job translating for migrant farm workers. Her worldly possessions were in her little truck and she was in Vermont and she had just signed a six-month lease with option to renew. A new job, a new home, and a landlady named Max.

"Poopie."

Both women turned and stared at the young man standing stock still a few yards away, a look of exaggerated dismay on his handsome face.

"You just rented the place, didn't you?"

"I did indeed."

He grabbed the front of his scarf in one fist. "Alas!" He stepped forward and held out two business cards. "Stuart Farmer-Abernathy. I'm in search of a little *pied-à-terre* so I can come up to visit Mummy—" He shuddered. "Without having to stay in her condo. But I made a disastrous miscalculation. I stopped in Montpelier to have Gianpietro cut my hair."

"Your hair looks very nice," Rose said politely, and Max nodded.

"It always does, with Gianpietro. Gianpietro does a better job than anyone I've found in Manhattan." The young man heaved a dramatic sigh. "But I have paid dearly for my vanity if I have lost the chance to stay in this delectable little retreat." He widened his eyes, tilted his head, and gave Rose a toothy and winsome smile. "Would you accept a roomie for a three-day weekend every now and then? I'm quiet and clean, and I'd pay of course."

"I don't think so. No."

"Plus a few days between Christmas and New Year's. And for her birthday."

"Your mother is fortunate to have such an attentive son."

"My mother is charming and witty and I love her dearly. But after a few hours in her over-crowded, over-heated, and over-perfumed dwelling I am ready to pull out my newly feathered and washed and cosseted hair." Another huge sigh, and he turned his golden eyes on the other woman. "Do you know of any other places I might investigate, now that I'm here in Morrisville?"

Max flipped the first several pages on her clipboard, ripped out a blank sheet of paper, and scrawled a short list. "The first name is a realtor who works only with rental property. The next three are friends of mine who have either rooms or apartments to let."

Stuart Farmer-Abernathy reached out in slow motion and took the note as if it were a sacred screed.

"Thank you. Thank you. I am forever in your debt. What is your name, may I ask?"

"Max."

Both perfectly shaped eyebrows rose.

"Maxine. And you're not in my debt yet, Stu. Not until you actually find something."

He winced at the nickname but his winning smile didn't dim.

"I will. I know it. I feel the strong vibe." He turned the smile on Rose. "And you. If you change your mind about a now-and-then roomie, call me. Or text. Or e-mail. Or send a pigeon. Do anything to get in contact. Please."

"Nice meeting you, Stuart."

He hesitated a moment and then turned on his heel and walked away.

"Well," Max huffed. "He's just too pretty for words. What do you think? Rich college kid?"

"Hairdresser, like the marvelous Gianpietro?"

"Nah. He's too young to have a career yet."

"Whatever he is, I am very grateful to that young man and his vanity. If he hadn't stopped in Montpelier, he would have been here first and I would have been too late."

"I have to say, Rose. I'm glad it's going to be you."

"Me too, Max. Me too."

Moving into Max's little red barn was the absolutely perfect thing to do.

And right now, it was absolutely perfect to sit in her truck and gaze at her little home and relive her date with Jack Carmichael, solar engineering wizard.

But then she remembered telling him about her almost-marriage. And it all came back. The anxiety. The increasing uncertainty. The faces of everyone in the church when they made their announcement. The giddy fun of the reception. And then the staggering sense of loss.

****

Everything was going wrong.

Every single thing.

Whit might not even be able to get a flight home. He joked about his best man standing in as a proxy groom. About doing the whole wedding by videoconference. It was dark when he finally called, tired and strung out, to tell her he was renting a car and driving the last three hundred miles.

And Rose's truck wouldn't start the next morning and when she finally got it going, the darn thing lurched and bucked down the whole driveway and her beautiful wedding dress slid off the seat and probably got covered with god-knows-what from the icky floor. And then she had to make a left turn and she was in the right lane and there was morning commuter traffic stretching in back of her as far as she could see.

She thought about honking her horn, flooring it, and cutting across all three lanes.

Bride-to-be Commits Vehicular Suicide on Her Wedding Day.

She would have to take the next right and find a driveway or a parking lot where she could turn around and go back to the intersection and sit there staring at the longest red light in the county. And she would be late. All six bridesmaids would think she changed her mind and was about to break Whit's heart.

Rose's big blue eyes opened even wider. That was impossible! She had known Whit since they were toddlers. She knew him better than she knew her own brother. Suddenly, absolutely, she knew Whit's heart would not be broken if their wedding didn't happen. He might even be relieved. He would be afraid of what his mother might do, that went without saying. But sitting there in traffic, Rose knew without a doubt that Carleton "Whit" Whittaker IV, her best friend in the world, was really, truly, absolutely not ready to be a married man. He wanted to go on being a carefree, rich, gorgeous, unattached *boy*. He wanted to go on taking his sailboat out on the lake in the middle of the night if he felt like it. He wanted to go on riding his horses. He wanted to think up more of his intricate practical jokes, jokes he never played on Rose because she would clobber him, and he didn't play on his mother because she was one scary woman, but jokes he played on everyone else he knew. Whit wanted many more afternoons at the golf course with his friends, all of them dressed in outfits chosen to shock and offend the older club members. And he wanted many more "manventures", with not a care in the world for a little wifey sitting alone at home.

He wanted to keep flirting, too, supremely confident that any woman or any girl he flashed that smile at would respond the way every woman and every girl always did. Always, his whole life. They all melted, no matter what their age or marital status, no matter if they'd been tired or angry or upset just seconds earlier. Their shoulders relaxed, their faces softened, their eyes began to sparkle, and they smiled right back at him.

No. Whit would not be heartbroken.

A parking lot. Rose pulled in, stopped the truck, and got out her cell phone.

"Whit. It's me. Pick up." Big gasp for breath. "Whit. Oh, I really want to talk to you. Whit?"

"It's me."

"Oh thank goodness!" Another gasp. "I'm sitting in a parking lot, on my way to church, and I just realized something. Whit, I can't get married today. Even more important, *you* can't get married today. It just can't happen."

"What?"

"We've been best friends forever and a day. We've always told each other everything. I have to tell you this and I hope, hope, hope you understand. We can't get married, Whit. It wasn't our idea anyway, and I don't think either of us wants it, at least not now. At least I hope, hope, *hope* you don't because if you do, I'm going to really hurt your feelings and I hate the idea but—"

"You don't want to go through with it?"

"Not really. No."

"Oh."

His long, long sigh sounded like that of a broken man.

Oh no oh no no.

But his next sound was a chuckle.

"Rose, I love you better than life itself." And then a deep belly laugh. "My mother is going to hit the proverbial roof. She might even follow through on her threat to disown me. But Rose, I love you and love you and love you some more."

"You..." She started laughing too. "You aren't

upset? Oh my goodness, Whit, you're just as relieved as I am!"

"I am probably *more* relieved than you are. You, at least, are almost grown up. I am not, and I don't want to be." His voice sobered. "I would never have left you at the altar, you know that. But I hugely DO NOT want to be a married man."

"How on earth did we let it get this far? There's a very expensive gown here next to me. There are six, count them, *six* bridesmaids waiting at the church. That whole building is going to be full, every single person waiting to see the county's most eligible bachelor tie the knot." She laughed again, a bubbly sound of pure delight. "But he wants to go right on being the most eligible bachelor in the county."

"Correction." His chuckle came over the line again. "The most eligible bachelor in central New York State."

"Confidence has never been a problem for you."

"Nope. So—What are we going to do?"

"Are you in your tux?"

"Tux. Cummerbund. Silly little tie. The whole bit."

"I'm still in jeans. Do you have anything in your car? One of those hideous outfits you guys wear when you play golf? Anything that screams WE ARE SO NOT GETTING MARRIED TODAY?"

"That's a brilliant idea, Rose! We will stand up, together, boldly—"

"Bravely. Resolutely."

"In grungy old clothes and we will declare, before the assembled friends and family—"

"And Reverend Cummings. Mustn't forget the esteemed Reverend."

"And Reverend Cummings. That we are not getting

married today."

"Maybe never."

"Maybe never." He gave a laughing, shaky whoop. "You'll go on being my best friend?"

"Forever and ever."

"Then let's do this thing."

By the time Rose got to the church, her hands hurt from clutching the steering wheel, the hair near her forehead was damp, and her armpits were pouring sweat. She glanced over at the wedding gown and then leapt out of the truck and raced into the church. Breathless, she threw open the door on the left of the foyer, and six women in gowns of various shades of teal and dyed-to-match shoes gaped, gasped, and stared at her decrepit jeans and faded t-shirt and the sneakers that probably had manure on them. The four bridesmaids chosen by Whit's mother looked meaningfully at each other and elevated their artfully plucked eyebrows. But Rose's sister Lily and her neighbor Sally looked at her and then at each other and grinned. They knew she wasn't going through with the wedding, and they were happy for her.

"We're not getting married," Rose blurted. "Whit and I. We agree."

There was a tap on the door and Sally dashed over and opened the door only a few inches. "Just one more minute." Then she closed the door and leaned against it. "So what are you going to do?"

"Whit is already here. I think he might be changing his clothes. And then…" Rose took a deep breath and squared her shoulders. "Then we are going to stand up before everyone and tell them. Together."

"This is waaaaaay past absurd. A total farrrrce. I for one am leaving." The blonde with the horsey face plucked a tiny beaded purse off a bookshelf. "I won't be part of this churrrrr-ahhhhd." She turned and shot evil looks at the other three.

"I wish you'd stay," Rose said earnestly. "I wish you would all walk up the aisle with me, the way we practiced."

"Like that would ever happen."

The four women glared at Sally, still barring the door with her body.

"Let them go, Sal. Whit and I didn't want them anyway."

As they swept through the door, the brunette said loudly, "We'll never find anybody to take these ghastly dresses off our hands. What was Mrs. Whittaker thinking?"

The door closed.

"Well. Ladies. Friends. Here we are. Not what we planned, but it should be interesting."

Lily hugged her, ignoring the sweat and possible manure. "I am so happy for you, Rose."

"I am too. Hugely. Can you peek out and see if he's here?"

"He's waiting, and he has definitely changed his clothes." Sally grinned mischievously. "And there's a whole lot more muttering and craning of necks than usual right before a wedding."

"Let them start the music. We are doing this non-wedding right."

The music started, that overused march his mother insisted on. As the two remaining bridesmaids started up the aisle, the gasps and mutters and murmurs became louder.

"Okay, Mother Whittaker," Rose muttered from her

post in the foyer. "As if I could ever have called you that! I bet your scary frown lines are deeper than canyons right now. And your mean little eyes are pure ice. And you know what? *I. Don't. Care.*"

The whole congregation turned as she started up the aisle. They all saw her dirty clothes and the messed-up hair that had looked so elegant at the salon that morning. But she saw only one person. Whit. Waiting for her, in the gag tee-shirt with a tux front and the old geezer ice-cream plaid shorts and his favorite once-red but now faded-to-pink high-tops with neon green laces. She met his eyes from the whole length of the church away, and they both smiled. Glorious smiles. Radiant smiles. She loved him since they were four years old, but she never loved him more than at that moment. She took a deep breath, lifted her chin, and strode purposefully to the front of the church. He took her hand in his, and they both faced the congregation.

"You first?"

She nodded. "Friends, relatives." A little spurt of happy laughter escaped. "The whole county. Whit and I love each other. You all know that. We have loved each other our whole lives. But we—" She looked up at him and he nodded. "We don't love each other like people should if they're going to be husband and wife." She smiled down at her parents, thinking for the thousandth time how much like siblings they looked, both of them lean and weathered, both with warm blue eyes, wearing identical smiles and nodding in unison. "Not like the love my mother and father feel for each other." She turned to her maid-of-honor. "Not like my sister Lily and her Geoff. They love each other so much they held the whole church hostage last year."

People on the Whittaker side of the aisle looked baffled. Everyone on the Gilhooly side grinned and nodded and murmured to each other, recalling how Reverend Cummings had been delayed by a freak May snowstorm and how Geoff had barricaded the church door so no one could leave until the preacher arrived and he and Lily were wed.

Rose stopped talking when Whit's fingers clenched around hers. He looked down at the tight-lipped woman sitting so stiffly in the front pew. "Mother. Father. I know you want me to settle down. To start being a responsible adult. But I'm not ready." He looked around at the congregation and slowly smiled *that* smile, the smile that made females melt and guys want to be his best friend. "We're going ahead with the reception at the Gilhooly farm." He glanced over at Rose and she nodded, her eyes starry. "It's gonna be the biggest shindig this town has ever seen. We're gonna eat 'til we can't waddle, and then we're gonna dance. We are gonna celebrate, goddamnit, this non-wedding like no non-wedding in all of history has ever been celebrated before. And now, the non-groom may kiss the non-bride."

****

Rose always fell asleep immediately and slept like a log. But not that night. She sat up and stared out the window. She heard a barred owl. She listened to the faint sounds of the animals in the barn, shifting their positions, nosing around to see if there was any grain left in the feed trough.

She wondered how it would have been if she and Whit had gone through with it, if they were together now in the heart-shaped mega-bed in the bridal suite chosen for them by Mrs. Whittaker.

She liked kissing Whit. She had liked it for years. But she had never wanted more. She never once felt what Lily must have been feeling that time Rose walked into the barn and found her sister and Geoff, tightly pressed together, their hands kneading and clutching and caressing, their mouths seeking cheeks, necks, shoulders, lips. Lily's eyes were closed. Her hips were pushing against his, and she was making a low throaty moan.

Rose had never moaned. Not even once. She had never pulled Whit closer. The two times when he clearly wanted more than kissing, they both stopped, appalled, and pulled apart. And he apologized. Apologized for wanting something that should have been a natural thing for both of them to want. Nope. She couldn't imagine them in bed together. And she was happy the suite and the heart-shaped bed weren't being wasted, that Lily and her husband were undoubtedly making very good use of it.

She wanted to talk with Whit. She had to. As soon as she heard his voice, thick and groggy with sleep, Rose asked the question she always asked when she called him in the middle of the night.

"Whit? Are you awake?"

And Whit gave the answer he always gave, every single time.

"Now I am."

She smiled in the darkness. They had done the right thing. He was still Whit, her best friend, the person she knew better than anyone in the whole world.

"But were you truly? Did I wake you up?"

His laugh, so familiar, so warm, made her hug herself and grin.

"You didn't wake me up. I'm sleepy and tired and I've been playing video games for almost three hours but I just can't sleep."

"Are you still okay with what we did this morning?"

"Definitely! You too?"

"I'm very pleased with it, Whit. With us." Rose laughed. "My mother said if I had married you, when you want a few more years to play, you would have been quite a handful."

"A handful, huh? You don't have any regrets that I'm not *your* handful right this very minute?"

"I would be the envy of almost every woman for miles around if I, if I had a couple of hands full of you this night. But no. I'm not having any regrets."

"Me neither. Of course, I don't know yet if I've been disinherited. Once that shoe drops, I might be feeling a tad regretful."

"Did anything happen between you and your parents, after the party?"

"Nope. That ax has yet to fall."

"Your mother looked okay at the party."

"Of course she did. She was the star." Whit's voice became high and saccharine. "That poor brave woman. She always gives her all for that son of hers and now he goes and humiliates her in front of all her friends. I can't *imagine* how she keeps on smiling."

Rose gave a little snorting laugh. "I guess she *would* love that kind of attention. But once she's alone…"

"Dunt-da-Dunt-dun."

"What?"

"That noise. You know. That noise that signals impending doom."

"Oh. Yes."

"Rose?"

"Yes?"

"I… I should have… I didn't tell you the whole story."

"Not possible, Whit. You *always* tell me the whole story, even when I have absolutely no interest in the disgusting details."

"Yeah. Well. This time I didn't. And there are definitely a few disgusting details."

Rose sat up straighter against the headboard of her bed. "Tell me now."

"Well. Where to start? You know that Mother said it was time for me to settle down."

"Yes."

"And I guess my father agreed. He nodded a lot anyway." Whit snorted. "My father is not exactly famous for what might be called cajónes. But…" There was a silence and then a sigh. "There's more, Rose. Why I asked you to marry me. Why I pressured you."

"You said your father's health wasn't good and he wanted us to present him with some grandchildren before he died."

"Oh. Yes. I did say that." There was a silence and then a sigh. "That's not—I made that up, Rose. Because you wanted to wait 'til we finished college and I didn't want to wait."

"In other words, you lied."

"I—Yes. I lied. Because I didn't want to tell you the real reason."

"The real reason you wanted to marry me."

"The real reason I wanted to marry you *now*, not next year."

Rose picked up the extra pillow and held it tight

against her with her free arm. "Go on."

"All right. Just out with it. Remember when I went away to deer camp?"

"Beer camp."

"Yeah. None of us have hunting licenses. Or guns. We just thought it would be a blast to rent a cabin off in the woods and hang out with no parents around and eat crud food and drink more than we ever drunk before. And cuss and swear and tell dirty jokes."

"And spit on the floor. And write your names in the snow with your pee."

"Not enough snow for that. But, yeah, that was the general idea. But—Will, my cousin Will, remember him?"

"Of course."

"Well, Will decided that, uh, that there should also be, uh, women." He was quiet, and Rose waited. "On the fourth night, Will went on a food-and-beer run and came back with four women. Four hookers, for our fourth night for the four of us."

Rose knew Whit had had sex before. But she didn't want to hear about it.

"We all did it. Each of us with one of the women and then another one of the women and then, for those of us who were still, uh, up to the task, with the third woman and then the fourth. It wasn't…" There was a long pause. "It wasn't all that wonderful, Rose. Coming was good, the first time. Of course. Coming is always good. But then it was work. Sort of grim. We had to keep doing it because the other guys expected it." He gave a harsh laugh. "I thought, I guess we all thought, it would be a story for us to tell whenever we got together, for the rest of our lives. A manventure we shared back when we were young and wild." There was another pause. "Rose? Are you still there?"

"I'm here."

"Anyway. It was weird. I think we were all embarrassed, to varying degrees." He inhaled noisily. "I figured it was over and done with."

Rose waited.

"Until one of the women showed up at the house."

This time the silence went on until Rose made an impatient noise.

"She—God. This is hard. She said she was pregnant, Rose. And she said it was mine. She—"

Rose interrupted. "You didn't use condoms?"

"Of course we used condoms. We're not total assholes! But she, the woman, Amy, her name is Amy, she said I looked away when I was, when I was pulling out of her, I looked away because somebody made an ungodly noise and I jerked around and she said I, my, I came out of the condom, partly, and she thought some of my, my—You know. She thought some of it ended up inside her." Whit started talking faster. "She was the first for me and I was the first for her so when the other guys got to her, they had already come at least once. She said that meant I was the only one with lots of, lots of—"

"Jizzum?"

"Christ, Rose. You don't use words like that! *Sperm*. She said the other guys got rid of most of their viable *sperm* the first time. Her exact words. She sounded like a frigging doctor or something. I told her I would need a paternity test, of course, and I'd pay for it. Of course. And that's when Mother opened the door."

Rose didn't know if he heard her gasp. He was talking even faster, eager to be done.

"Maybe she was listening at the keyhole the whole time. She took one look at Amy and shrieked 'Carleton' and he popped his head out of his study and she told him to escort the young lady out. She ordered me to stay put until he got back and she stood in the doorway with both arms out like some sort of crossing guard." He gave a little snort. "I turned around and went out the French doors and ran to catch up with the woman's car. Amy's car. So I could give her my cell phone number. Then I went and stayed with Stuart for a whole week."

"Whit. Wait." Rose frowned into her dark bedroom. "Beer camp was months ago. You've known about the baby—You've known you're going to be a father all those months."

"I'm not. There isn't a baby. She called, Amy called, and asked me to meet her at Gracey's. She'd been to the doctor. She wasn't pregnant. We both—" He made a sound that was part gasp, part laugh and maybe part sob. "Rose, we sat there in that back booth, and we both got teary and we both laughed and we talked. She's not a hooker. Three of them weren't, that night. They'd been in school with the other woman and she was, pretty much. A hooker. Not on street corners, but she did parties and made a few porn films and she kept talking about all the big money she was making so the others agreed to do one party with her. That night was the first for three of them. She, Amy, said she wasn't going to do it ever again even though the money was, in her words, friggin' amazin' great."

Rose was staring fixedly at the blur on her bedroom wall from the neighbor's porch light, her back straight, her voice even. "How much did you guys fork over?"

"Don't know. Will paid them. He said it was his gift.

We're…" His voice faded. "We're not so much friends now. Not like we used to be." He exhaled gustily. "Anyway. No baby. I gave Amy a check for $500 and said I'd send another in a couple of months so she wouldn't have to do any more parties. She kissed me on the cheek, and I went home." Another huge sigh. "I sat down with my parents and I told them the woman wasn't pregnant. And Mother freaked out."

"She freaked out because you *weren't* going to be a father? That doesn't make sense."

"It does, in a way. She said the three of us had been given a wake-up call. She and my father were not going to wait until I got some other bimbo knocked up for real. They wanted to see the Whittaker name on a grandchild, but only if that baby had what she called proper parentage. If not, she would make sure not one single penny of the Whittaker family money went to the child. Or to me. I would get my inheritance from my grandfather but nothing from my parents. Not one cent, not ever."

Rose kept her voice even, quiet. "And there goes the law degree. And the fancy office."

"She said I was to get married immediately and I was to limit what she called my sexual shenanigans to the marriage bed. And, oh by the way, I had to choose someone in Our Set."

"Your father agreed?"

"Hah. I never know what he's thinking." Whit's voice was lighter now, less tense. "Anyway, I got pissed. I said there was only one person I could see myself marrying and that was you. My best friend ever. Mother looked at Dad and he looked at her and they both nodded and then she said 'All right'. I could marry you. She said you—You wouldn't be their first choice but it was clear that I cared for you so maybe I would keep my pants zipped around other women."

There was no way Rose could make her voice sound normal anymore. "And you hightailed it over here and bugged me until I agreed to marry you. Because you didn't want to lose a shitload of money."

"I—Yes."

"And you lied to me."

"I'm sorry, Rose."

"You said, that day—" She took a deep breath and started again. "You said you had just realized I was the only woman you could ever marry." Abruptly, blessedly, Rose was furious. "I believed you, Whit! And I believed that stupid sob story about your father! I loved that you were so worried about him. And I thought—" She pulled a tissue out of the box on her bedstand and blew her nose. "I thought you were so eager to get married because you loved me."

"I do love you! You know that, Rose!"

"Right. You love me. But not nearly as much as you love the Whittaker gidzillions."

"Rose! I said I'm sorry. I said I should have told you." He shifted to defensive. "But think about it, Rose. Would you have agreed to get married if you'd known it was for, it was *partly* for, the money?"

"Good night, Whit."

"Rose! Don't—"

She sat, the phone still cuddled against her face, listening to silence. After a long minute, she slid down under the covers, curled up on her side, and sobbed.

Chapter Five

The Geocaching

In later years Jack described their third date as hours and hours of death-defying peril. White-knuckle adventure in the deep woods, far from civilization. Just the two of them, with their wits and a GPS.

In reality, there was an hour or so of mild excitement followed by two hours slogging through mud and wet ferns while battling giant mosquitos, followed by a little pain and a lot of embarrassment.

And then... Heaven. Euphoria. The beginning of the most glorious thing that ever happened to him.

****

The previous day's thunderstorms had finally ended a long hot spell, and the air was crisp, dry, cool, scented with pine and ferns.

"Trails are going to be muddy. And slippery."

Rose looked up from spraying something on her hiking boots.

"Forewarned is forearmed. Want some tick repellant?"

"Oh. Yes. Good idea."

She looked different than she had the day they met at Hunt's farm, or when they'd met for lunch in Vergennes. Before, she looked soft and feminine, with pastel colors and flowers on her clothes. Today she was monochromatic: brown long-sleeved shirt, tan baseball cap, khaki pants tucked into wool socks rolled down over well-worn hiking boots. The robin-decorated hairclip was replaced by a no-nonsense rubber band. This Rose looked hardy and competent, like a pioneering woodswoman. Well, Jack thought, if my backcountry skills aren't good enough, she'll rescue us both. He dug a piece of paper out of his shirt pocket.

"I got the first clue by e-mail. *Geocacher, here's what you should do. Walk not a mile but an eighth of two. And in a lovely little glade—Find something of purest jade*. There's only one trail out of the parking lot, so I guess that's the way we go."

"An eighth of two. One quarter. So in a quarter mile, we should hit, what did it say, a pretty glade?"

"A lovely little glade. It should be obvious, but I'll keep track of distance with the GPS anyway."

"Good idea." She gave him an incandescent smile, as if he had just come up with an idea so brilliant that no other man in the whole world could have dreamed of it.

The well-worn trail zigzagged, giving them a quick view down onto the parking lot and the dirt road beyond before heading into deeper woods. There was no bird song, and Jack thanked whatever intuition had decided him against birdwatching.

Neither of them had any doubts when they reached the glade. The trail widened and then entered a clearing with giant oaks and maples making an almost perfect circle.

"Something jade." Rose turned in a full circle. "Every single thing is green, except for brown tree trunks."

"I bet it'll be man-made."

"That makes sense. Jade… jade… Oh!" Rose darted to a large beech and pointed to a small green metal circle nailed into the bark above her head.

"We're not supposed to take it off the tree, are we?"

"Nope." Jack had his head down, looking at the base of the tree. "Anything like that gets left for the next geocacher. But there should be something… Ah." He reached between two huge roots and pulled out a little metal box.

"Outstanding!"

Jack sat back on his heels, opened the box, and showed Rose a notebook and three pens.

"We're supposed to sign—" He opened the notebook. "Here's the clue, on the inside cover. *Not gonna tell you the distance—Just that you'll need some persistence—Keep on walkin' and walkin' some more— till you're looking right at a door. The Vermont stone wall will tell you all.*"

"Sounds like it's quite a ways."

He looked up at her, squinting into a ray of sunlight. "You feel like you've got persistence, to go the distance?"

"Lead on."

Water was using the trail as the fastest way down the mountain, and the footing was getting wetter and more slippery.

"We should have brought hiking poles."

"They definitely would help. Do you want to turn back?"

"Absolutely not!" Rose smacked her hand against her forehead. "But it's unfortunate that the rain hatched out all these mosquitos. I'm going to stop for a minute and bathe in bug stuff."

"Do you have extra?"

She held out a small spray bottle. "Go for it. I don't like the smell but it's better than being carried off by insects the size of rescue helicopters."

They'd been hiking for almost forty minutes when Jack skidded to a stop. "Look."

Twenty yards or so into the woods was a small outbuilding.

"A door. Facing right at us. And there's a stone wall."

"You go that way. I'll check it out in this direction."

"Ah! Got it!" Jack held up a metal box, a twin to the first one. "Wedged between two stones in the wall."

She crouched next to him as they both read the clue.

This one ain't gonna rhyme 'cause I ain't got the time. Horace was wrong. Try two two point five.

"You know any Horaces?"

"The only one I can think of is that *go west, young man* guy. Greeley. Horace Greeley."

"If it's him, maybe the clue means we shouldn't go west. Because he was wrong."

"Which narrows it down to north, east, south and every point in between."

"We're not supposed to bushwhack, so that limits us to wherever there's a trail." He looked ahead. "Unfortunately, we appear to be at something akin to Essex Junction's Five Corners."

"Maybe two two point five means twenty-two and a half degrees. A quarter of the way between two of the cardinal points." She pulled a small bright yellow compass from one of her pants pockets.

"Crafty thinking, Rose. That's probably it."

"Drat." She was staring down at the compass. "Two

of these trails could be right."

They stood side by side and stared at the intersecting trails.

"You think we should assume it's the one that looks more used?"

"I have no idea." He watched with fascination as a smile started in her cheeks, spread to her lips, and then to her whole face.

"You're saying we have to just guess?"

"Looks like it."

"All right then. I guess—" She hesitated, one finger pointing to one of the possibilities and then the other and then back again. "This one!"

****

"What on earth was that?" Rose stopped dead and turned, wide-eyed.

"I think we just spooked a Wild Turkey. Probably a flock of Wild Turkeys."

"Yipes. It sounded as big as a moose."

"Well, Rose."

It struck her that she didn't mind at all that he was laughing at her.

"Turkeys are good flyers, but not when they're hemmed in. That noise was a dozen or so big strong wings hitting a couple hundred branches."

"Yipes. You're the birder. You take the lead. It'll be you who encounters the next avian explosion."

****

"Hey, Rose!" Jack turned around and called back to her. "We have come to a veritable Grand Canyon."

She looked up. "You think we're on the wrong trail?"

"Well, I would have thought the GPS would have

warned us about it. Or maybe the last clue would have—
Shit!" Jack's eyes widened, his mouth opened, his feet
slipped out from under him, and he disappeared.

"Jack!" Rose scrambled up the little hill and looked
down to see Jack sitting twenty feet below, in a little
stream. His legs were straight out in front of him, and he
was bent forward and clutching his left arm with his right
hand.

"Damn, that hurts!"

"Hold on. Don't move." She looked frantically up
and down the crumbling bank and then grabbed a tree
root and started sliding down. "Did you hit your head?
Don't move! You might have hurt your back."

"Head's fine. Back's fine."

Jack was rocking back and forth, his face contorted
in pain, still clutching his arm. Rose knelt beside him,
running her hands around his neck, up the back of his
head, across his shoulders, across his chest.

"I don't think you're bleeding anywhere. Look at
me."

He looked up.

"Your eyes look fine. Do you think you could have
broken your arm?"

"I'm fine." His grin was more of a grimace but it
was at least an attempt. "I like what you're doing with
your hands though."

She smacked her hand lightly against his shoulder.
"I thought you were really injured. You scared me to
death. I thought I'd have to haul you out of here."

This time Jack's smile came a little more easily.
"Find some sticks and make a travois?"

"No way. Grab your feet and drag."

He pushed himself up onto his knees. "You're a hard

woman, Rose Gilhooly. Damn, that hurts."

"You said you weren't hurt."

"I said nothing's broken." He sucked in his breath. "I smacked my funny bone against a rock." He wiggled his fingers. "Excruciating pain and then the whole arm goes numb. What's funny about that?" He put both hands in the water at his sides and levered himself up. "Do you see the GPS?"

"I... No."

"Wonder if I threw it as I was falling. Shit."

Fifteen minutes later they were both soaked, muddy, and still GPS-less.

"You need that for your work, don't you?"

Jack was making a last-ditch effort, lifting branches, feeling among rocks and fallen branches, patting mud. "I've got a back-up. But that was my good one. For the twentieth time—SHIT!" He straightened up. "If it's up to me, geocaching is done for the day."

"Me too."

Rose headed several yards downstream to a spot with more dirt and rocks than mud. When she got to the top, she turned, held out a hand, and hauled Jack up the last few feet.

"Do you know the way back?"

"I think so. I'm pretty sure." He patted his shirt pocket. "But if all else fails, we still have two prehistoric GPSes. Our trusty compasses."

He moved past Rose and headed down the trail.

Great adventure, he thought. We're both wet and muddy, my arm is still numb, my back and butt hurt, the sun's gone behind the clouds and it's getting chilly, and we never found what we were looking for. If I ever ask her out again, it's gonna be something safe. Like the movies. And I do not want to lose that GPS. The older one's all right but it takes forever to find the satellites. Maybe tomorrow—Yes. Tomorrow I'll go to the office and borrow Derek's metal detector and come back. It's not supposed to rain tonight so it should be all right. Unless I threw the thing with enough force to break it.

Behind him, Rose was focused on thin wet pants clinging to a tight behind and sturdy legs. She didn't know why she was surprised that his thighs and calves looked so muscular. Maybe because he had sort of a baby face. A nice face, but it didn't seem to go with those legs. She was suddenly aware that Jack wasn't quite limping, but he was walking awkwardly.

"Did you hurt either of your legs when you fell?"

"Legs, no. But I landed hard on my tailbone." He held up his hands almost three feet apart. "By tomorrow morning, my butt will have a bruise this big."

"It can't have a bruise that big. You've got a tiny butt."

She had no reason to feel embarrassed about noticing his ass. It was right there in front of her, in sopping wet pants. And it was a nice tight not-big ass.

Jack's face was even redder than hers but he kept walking, staring straight ahead. She was noticing his body. That had to count for something.

Getting back to the car took a lot less time than following the morning's clues up the trail. Rose was fastening her seat belt when her stomach growled loudly, and he gave her a lopsided grin.

"Me too. But we can't go in a restaurant looking like this."

"We could throw open a door, lurch inside gasping, and make out that we're fearless adventurers in desperate need of, of pulled pork sandwiches."

"What about a drive-through? We could get something and take it to… I don't know where we could take it. Your place?"

"My stomach says yes. But my cold wet feet and cold wet legs say that you should drop me at the park-and-ride and we should each head home and get out of wet clothes and into hot showers. And find something to eat in our own homes."

"All right. Yes." He started the car.

****

Neither of them said anything until Jack pulled his car beside her pickup and she started unbuckling her seat belt.

"Rose? I'm sorry about today. It was supposed to be a fun adventure."

She looked at his somber brown eyes, and she reached up to touch his cheek.

"Jack. It *was* an adventure. Bona fide. Once you're warm, dry and fed, you'll realize it'll make a great story. You'll laugh when you tell your coworkers on Monday."

"Maybe."

He had just enough time to feel startled before she pulled him closer and kissed him.

Rose meant to give him a peck. A way of showing this friendly man that she hadn't hated their date. But he put a hand behind her head and moved his mouth against hers and touched her with his tongue. She heard a little noise and realized she made it. Realized that she was pressing closer. That their tongues were touching, stroking, that her hand had moved from his cheek to his neck and then his shoulder and then his chest. That the kiss was going on and on.

She pulled back, appalled. She never responded like that. Never.

Did she start it? She barely touched him, at first. She hadn't expected him to respond the way he did. And she certainly hadn't expected her own response!

"I'm sorry, Jack. No. I'm not. That's a ridiculous thing to say. I mean that I…" She bent to get her fanny pack from the floor. "Thank you, Jack. I very much enjoyed today. And I'm glad you weren't hurt." She met his eyes with an unexpectedly mischievous expression. "And I very much enjoyed this last bit. And now I'm heading home."

Jack sat without moving as she got out of the car, shut the door, headed to her truck, unlocked it, got in, fastened her seatbelt, and drove away. Then a slow, slow grin started, widening and growing until he felt like hugging himself with both arms. Felt like yelling and hooting and cheering and laughing. Felt like getting out of the car and doing a wild dance in the parking lot, sore butt and tingling arm and all.

****

Hours later, after a long shower and two peanut butter, cucumber, and mayonnaise sandwiches, Rose still felt astonished. She had never reacted like that to a kiss. Not with Whit, all those years ago. Not with Peter, her occasional lover for a few years now.

Peter was, as she reminded herself often, a very nice man. Everyone liked and respected him. He ran what had been his father's hardware store, he was a member of the Kiwanis Club, he mentored a preteen from the middle school, he remembered people's birthdays, he had a smile for everyone. But if Peter had any sense of humor, any playfulness, any whimsy, any hint of a wild streak,

Rose hadn't found it yet. They'd had sex only four times and each time it was the same. They got undressed, lay down, shared a few kisses, then he got on top and it was over in ten minutes. Sometimes less. Then he said thank you and fell into a deep sleep. And it was always in her apartment. Peter's mother lived in one wing of his house, and he didn't want to get her hopes up about grandchildren.

Rose always got out of bed after he was asleep and went into the living room and either read for a while or did crossword puzzles on her computer. She knew he'd wake up in an hour or so and get dressed and go home.

She had orgasms all the time when she had solo sex, orgasms that left her limp and gasping and grinning from ear to ear. She never had an orgasm with Peter. She didn't hate sex with him. She looked forward to the sensation of his swollen cock pushing into her, moving inside her. But it never lasted long enough, and the whole thing was so formulaic. She sometimes wondered if it was foolish to wish for excitement, for variety, once you were nearing thirty. But she had seen her parents' faces when they headed up to bed, and she was willing to bet they had excitement and variety aplenty.

Now she had her reaction to Jack to think about, a reaction that told her, loud and clear, that her lack of excitement with Peter was because he was, truly, a very boring man, in bed as well as out. And if she was going to continue seeing Jack, she had better have an uncomfortable talk with Peter, soon.

****

Dumb. Dumb. Dumb.

He should have asked Rose to go geocaching today instead of yesterday. He should have looked at the two-day forecast. He should have realized the trails would be in better shape after an extra day without rain. Maybe then he wouldn't have disgraced himself by landing on his rear in mud, water, and hard pointy rocks. Maybe they wouldn't have ended up wet and filthy and cold.

Then again, if she hadn't felt sorry for him, she might not have kissed him. And there was no question in his mind. That kiss was worth a sore elbow, a bruised rear-end, soggy hiking boots, and a missing GPS.

The GPS was not going to stay missing, though. He was going to find it, and it was going to be in working order, and he'd have it in his pack before he headed home even if he had to stay there in that damned ditch until night fell.

The weather was perfect, with bluer skies, puffier clouds, and a gentler breeze than the day before. Jack powered up the trail, the metal detector over one shoulder. Less than an hour later he was heading back down the trail with the undamaged GPS stowed safely in a zippered pocket. He was within sight of the little outbuilding they'd seen the day before when he noticed someone toiling up the hill, someone wearing a brown long-sleeved shirt, a tan baseball cap, and khaki pants tucked into woolen socks that were rolled down over what looked like new running shoes.

"Rose?"

She looked up, startled.

"Jack! Oh! I was—" She eyeballed what he had in his hand. "A metal detector. What an outstanding idea! Did you find your thingy?"

"I did. It's muddied but unbowed. Or something. What are you doing here?"

She reached around, unzipped her fanny pack, and

pulled out a LED flashlight. "I figured this would light up all those hidey-holes under branches."

"You were going to look for my GPS unit?"

She stuffed the flashlight back in her pack. "It was *our* adventure, Jack. We chose the wrong trail together." She shrugged. "It was our loss, not just yours."

"Rose." Jack could feel another smile starting down near his knees and working its way up until it filled his whole body. "That is one of the nicest things ever. I'm— I'm flabbergasted."

"So. Since we're both here, do you want to find the trail we should have been on?"

"Not a whole lot. How about you?"

"I'd like to spend some time along that little stream, about a quarter of a mile down the trail. I think there might be a patch of *Oxypolis rigidior*."

He looked blank.

"Common Water-Dropwort."

"Dropwort. Of course. Everyone knows that."

"Sometimes called Stiff Cowbane. Even though one of the names has 'common' in it, it's not common in Vermont. I'd love to get a few photos and post them on iNaturalist. That's a citizen science thing like your, um, e-birdy."

"E-bird. Well then. May I join you on the dropwort hunt?"

"Of course. But first, since we're here, let's investigate the shed." She moved off the trail. "The sneaky little shed with the sneaky little clue that led us onto the wrong trail."

"Careful, Rose. The whole thing might be getting ready to collapse."

The door opened with a squeak and Rose peered

inside.

"It looks like it's in good shape."

The building was maybe ten by eight feet, with a plank floor and walls and one window. A wide shelf ran along one long wall, with a narrower shelf on the other wall.

Jack peered over her shoulder. "Way too small for a dwelling."

"A monk."

"What?"

"Like in Ireland. Monks would spend years and years in tiny little huts, all alone and meditating. People thought they were very holy and would leave food for them." She took a step inside and ran her hand along the wide shelf. "This was his bed. He stored all his worldly possessions on the other shelf."

"A meditating monk. Here in Vermont."

"That's not impossible. There's an abbey somewhere south of here. With lots of monks. Weston, I think."

"Oh. True. A monk's hideout then." He backed out of the doorway.

"Jack?"

"Yeah?" His voice came from outside.

"Is that plexiglass covering the window?"

"Yes." His face suddenly appeared only a few inches away. "The screws holding it on look new. Somebody's keeping this little place weatherproof."

His head disappeared and she could hear him rustling around outside. Her eye was caught by a series of marks on the wall to her right, marks that showed up as four lines of words and numbers when she turned on her flashlight.

"Jack!"

"What?"

"Oh! I didn't hear you come back inside. Look at this. The top word looks like s-p-i-l-e. A name, maybe?"

"Spile? Yes! That makes perfect sense."

"It does, huh?"

"Yuppee." He put one hand on her shoulder and leaned over to get a closer look. "Spiles are those things that get tapped into maple trees. To get the sap. The outside of that wall—" He gestured with a lift of his chin. "—is scorched. I bet this part of the woods was a sugar bush, with the sugar house next to the shed. And I bet the sugar house burned down. We could probably find the old stone foundation if we looked hard enough."

"And the shed was for storage! This list was a way to kept track of how many, um, spiles and such." She bent closer. "The second word might be pail, which makes sense. And then there's something that starts with a J."

"Jar? Or maybe jug."

"Jugs for the syrup! Of course." Rose turned off her flashlight and straightened up. "We may have failed at geocaching, Jack, but we solved a mystery anyway!"

He was very close to her, his hand still on her shoulder, still staring at the wall, his eyes oddly unfocused. He straightened up slowly and looked into her face.

"Yesterday, Rose," he said. "Did you kiss me because you felt sorry for me?"

"Oh." She backed up half a step. "I did feel bad for you, Jack. You were sopping wet, and bruised and, and disappointed. And you'd lost your GPS. But that's not why I kissed you. That was because I wanted to."

"Good."

When he pushed his hands into her hair, the rubber band around her ponytail pulled but she was breathless and she didn't want him to stop. She was held in his warm firm hands, held by the intent look on his face, by the closeness of his body, by his breath.

Lips against lips. Gentle pressure. Heads tilting to get a different angle.

Smile against smile.

Jack lifted his head just a little and looked down at her face, her smile, her almost closed eyes. He touched his tongue to one corner of her mouth and then the other and her smile widened and he traced the smile with the tip of his tongue.

"Mmm," she murmured. "*Mentha canadensis*."

"Huh?"

"*Mentha ca*—A kind of mint." She slid her arms around him. "Doesn't matter."

His roving hands were stopped by her fanny pack, and he reached over it to spread his palms over her bottom. She felt him swelling against her. Her breasts were aching, reaching out to fill every bit of space between them. Her hands explored bone and muscle and fabric. She slid both palms down to his high, tight butt and tightened her fingers.

Jack flinched.

"Oh my gosh! I'm so sorry! Your—It hurts! I am so sorry. I forgot!"

He grabbed her hands and put them back at his waist. "Keep touching me. But it'll be like high school. Sort of. The girl's gotta keep her hands above the guy's waist."

His mouth was on her cheek, her jaw, her neck. She

grabbed the back of his shirt in both fists and it came free of his pants and she could slide her hands up to his back. She could feel all the ins and outs of spine and ribs and shoulder blades, warm and smooth and firm. She had the hazy thought that the skin on his face, his throat, his arms and hands and back was all stretched, tight, taut, holding exactly as much as it was made for.

Peter's skin always felt cool. A bit damp. And loose. The first time they made love, she wondered if he had lost a lot of weight.

Peter.

"Oh. Oh Jack. Oh dear. We should stop."

"I would much rather we didn't." He pushed her hair back, his face a study in humor and interrupted passion. "But I suppose this isn't the greatest place to keep going." He loosened his hold on her and gave a lopsided little grin. "Dust. Dirt. Spiders. Probably splinters. But I have a bed. I bet you have a bed." His fingers were gentle as he caressed her cheek and touched her mouth. "I would love to make love with you, Rose."

Her breath was still uneven but her eyes were troubled as she put her hands on his chest and pushed him away, just a little. "I forgot. I almost forgot. I shouldn't have forgotten. I've been—Jack, I've been seeing someone. On and off for a few years now. I can't—We shouldn't go any further until I talk with him."

He took a step back and she immediately missed his body against hers, wanted his hard heat against her. "Are you in love with him?"

He watched the warmth in her eyes cool. "I would not have been kissing you, Jack, if I were. I wouldn't have just forgotten him." She shook her head. "We're not in love. Neither one of us. But we like each other. Respect each other. And it's been—It's been convenient, I guess. There aren't a whole lot of unattached people in Morrisville. Peter and I have become accustomed to being available, for movies or eating out. Or the annual Kiwanis Club Benefit Dinner and Silent Auction. A big event in town." She took a deep breath. "He's a nice man, Jack."

She couldn't tell what he was thinking. He was still flushed and his breathing was still uneven, but he was standing completely still. She reached out a hand and touched his wrist.

"Jack, I'm sure you could tell how much I enjoyed what we were just doing. But I have to tell Peter before we—Before we touch each other again. Kiss each other."

He bobbed his head once in a little nod. "Yes. That's the right thing to do. But I want—I would like—I want to make sure I understand. You're going to tell him what, exactly?"

"That I won't be going out with him anymore."

"I am very glad, Rose."

They didn't talk on the walk back down the trail. She let him lead and again she watched his shoulders and his back and his butt and his strong thighs. She felt stunned. That hadn't been her, back in that shed. She had never felt like that. Never acted like that. She remembered her sister Lily, grasping Geoff's bottom and pulling him closer and trying to crawl inside his very bones. She remembered thinking that would never be her. She just didn't have that kind of passion.

Chapter Six

The Waiting

Home.

A sanctuary after the startling kisses in the shed. A refuge. A retreat. Even after seven years, the little red barn still welcomed and delighted her whenever she turned in the driveway and parked in the third bay of the gigantic garage. Home.

Back when Max and her husband bought the property, they studied the little red building tucked way back in the yard and Xavier climbed a ladder and investigated the roof and they decided the shed could help them pay their new mortgage. They insulated the floor, walls, and ceiling, replaced the old double doors with siding and a front door, added six windows, and went to work on the interior. Now there was a kitchen area to the right and a living area on the left, with a couch, bookcase, and overstuffed easy chair. A miniscule bathroom behind the kitchen. Two tan fabric-covered room dividers, like those used to separate office cubicles, screened off space for a double bed, the dresser Rose got at a used furniture place, and the oak rocker that Lily helped her find. Her parents brought throw pillows and a rug the first time they came to visit and they'd all agreed that the blue chair and couch were Rose's colors. And a few months later, the Vermont Botanical Club took a field trip to Montreal's Botanical Garden and Rose bought two big posters, one with a montage of the native orchids of northeastern America and the other with just one blossom of Narrowleaf Blue-eyed Grass against a dark background. She hung both posters on one of the room dividers and covered the other with the old and faded blue and green quilt that had been hers since she was a toddler.

Now, home from her second hiking adventure with Jack, from her second experience with what kissing *should* do to a woman's body, she opened the front door, tossed the big canvas bag she used as purse and briefcase onto the kitchen table, glanced at the wall calendar—and gasped.

No! Not fair!

But there it was, in her writing, on today's date.

"P conf."

She had to see Peter, now, but Peter would be gone for a week. She had completely forgotten. He was so excited about a conference on effective advertising and promotion for small businesses, and she barely listened. That should tell her something.

What happened to her in that shed should tell her something too.

If she closed her eyes and let herself remember, she could still feel Jack's hard body against her, his warm hands at her waist. His mouth on her neck. She could still feel her breasts swelling, and the wetness and openness between her legs.

He tasted like *Mentha canadensis*. Maybe the herb had some quality she didn't know about. Maybe the smell or the taste, combined with whatever toothpaste he used, was a powerful aphrodisiac.

Maybe it was good that Peter was gone. It would give her a chance for some serious thinking. Was she ready to end a relationship of several years because of a few kisses? She didn't think Peter would be devastated but he would be baffled and hurt, and she had no desire to hurt him.

What should she be doing now? Should she call Jack?

Hi, Jack, it's Rose, and I'm calling to tell you we can't have sex this week.

Maybe a text. The fewest words possible.

Or she could not contact Jack at all. Not ever. Maybe what she felt up there in the woods was a fluke. Seeing him again, having him here, in the close quarters of her little home, might be a mistake.

Nope. She had to give herself a chance. Maybe nothing would be the same as up in that shed. But maybe it would. And she wanted very much to feel those feelings again.

——*Jack. P's out of town for a conference. Next week?*—

****

Rose slumped into one of the kitchen chairs. She wanted to smack her phone down on the table. She wanted to throw it to the floor and stomp on it.

——*In PA 4 or 5 more. Talk when I'm back.*—

Four or five more days! Why couldn't things ever be easy?

Because it'll put hair on your chest. That's what her father always said when one of his kids complained that something was too difficult or too complicated. It's good for you, he said. It'll toughen you up, put hair on your chest. She was eight or nine when she wailed back,

"Daddy! I don't WANT hair on my chest!"

Actually, she didn't say *Daddy*. She said *Deee-uh-dee*. She never realized she had a nasal upstate New York accent until she started taking language classes.

****

Jack could imagine what his college buddies would say now.

Sure thing, bro. She's gonna break up with the old boyfriend. Just not right now. Maybe next week. Oops. Maybe the week after that. Get real, bro. She's not dumping *him*. She's dumping *you*.

But he believed her. He stood in a field in Bennington County, shielding his phone with his cap so he could read her latest note, and he believed her. If Rose Gilhooly didn't want to follow up on what they started in that shed, she would just come out and tell him so.

****

For days now, for almost two weeks now, she'd been practicing what to say to Peter. *How* to say it to Peter. He'd been a friend for years now, and an on-and-off lover. She didn't want to hurt him. He was outside, pushing a hand mower back and forth on his tiny front lawn. He was the only person in Morrisville who used a hand mower. It wasn't a statement about the environment. Peter said he didn't worry about climate change, and he went on raking up and bagging his leaves and taking them to the dump even after Rose gave him an article about how environmentally friendly it was to leave them where they fell. Peter used a hand mower for one reason only: because there was an old one above the sign at his hardware store and it was good advertising if people drove by his house and saw him outside, using one just like it.

"Rose! You're early."

She had never thought of Peter as particularly intuitive, but he had such a strange expression on his face that she wondered if he guessed why she was there.

"No. I think it's just about nine." She got out of the car. "How was the conference?"

"Rose. We have to talk."

"I know. That's why I'm here, remember?"

"I mean I have to talk. I have to—"

"Me first." She squared her shoulders and met his eyes. "Peter, I've enjoyed these last few years. And I think we've developed a, a firm friendship. But—"

"Oh, lordy. Are you going to break up with me?"

"Well. I—"

Peter threw back his head and let out a long wavering howl. "Oooooooooooo!"

No! He could not possibly be that shattered! Rose refused to believe it. They had never once said they loved each other. He never showed any deep emotion at all, not even during sex.

The screen door opened and a dark-haired woman came out onto the porch, a cool and professional-looking woman dressed in ironed black slacks and a starched sleeveless blouse.

And, oh my gosh, high heels. The woman was wearing well-polished dark brown pumps with two-inch heels, pumps that matched the brown leather belt around her slim waist. Rose didn't know a single woman who wore pumps. Even the state legislators she saw when she visited Montpelier wore sandals in the summer and fleece-lined boots in the winter, with slip-on clogs or loafers the rest of the year.

"Lou! Lou, my lovely Lou!"

Oh. *Lou*. Not an agonized howl after all.

"Come on down here, babe."

Babe?

"Rose, this is Lou. Lou, Rose."

The woman's eyes held a mixture of polite warmth and wariness.

"Lou and I met at last year's convention and we've done some e-mailing back and forth. Then when we saw each other this year we—Something sparked." Peter pulled the woman close with one arm. "Let's just say we missed a lot of the convention." The sheepish and delighted smile on his face was something Rose had never seen. "We were finding better things to occupy our time. Weren't we, babe?"

"Pete!"

Pete. Not Peter. He always insisted that Rose use his full name. Even his poker buddies didn't call him Pete, as far as Rose knew.

"Well. That's outstanding. Excellent, Peter. Congratulations. To both of you."

"Lou's been managing her dad's hardware store in western PA. Ten years now."

"Almost eleven." The woman's mouth widened into a smile.

Wow. Lipstick. And blusher. And mascara.

"Lou's mother's been bugging him for years and he's finally selling out. The sale is next week and the two of them will be on the road to Arizona a few weeks after. Starting a whole new life. So will Lou. She's going to move up here and be co-manager. With me."

"And co-owner."

"And co-owner. And a few other titles. Isn't that right, hon?"

Peter, stolid boring always-in-control Peter, was blushing. His eyes were sparkling, his cheeks and ears were red, and Rose thought he was standing straighter than ever.

"Wife. Another title for lovely Lou. And, if we're lucky, Mom. We've been working on that for six days now."

"Pete!"

"Rose is an old friend. In fact—" He reached out and grabbed her elbow. "In fact, we just might hit you up to be godmother. How does that sound?"

"Well. I—That would be quite an honor."

"I'm telling you, Rose. I am so glad you broke up with me so I didn't have to break up with you!"

****

That was a surprise.

To put it mildly.

Peter was getting married. Peter wanted to be a father. Peter was happy, *glowing* happy, not placid and unemotional and mildly contented the way he'd always been with her.

Rose felt let down. Which was idiotic.

But she wasn't sure if what she felt in that shed was real. She wasn't sure she would feel that way again, ever. And if she didn't, now she didn't even have Peter to fall back on.

All right, Rose. Get your act together. What are you going to do next?

She pulled into the big garage, turned off the truck, and just sat.

I've done what I had to do. I've talked with Peter, she thought.

Pete. Now he's Pete.

But her thoughts continued. She didn't know if she wanted to sit across a table from Jack in a restaurant and make polite conversation. But she wasn't sure she wanted to ask him here either. That was like saying they'd go to bed, and they hadn't even seen each other for over two weeks.

What on earth happened to her that fateful day? She could still feel it. She could feel the ache in her breasts. Right now, sitting here in her truck, she could feel her breasts tighten and she could feel herself getting wet.

Why that particular man?

Maybe it wasn't him. Maybe it was just a ticking biological clock.

Jack was pleasing to look at, that was true. He smiled a lot and his eyes sparkled and he got enthusiastic about things. And he had great hair.

He wasn't very tall, and she almost always looked twice at tall guys rather than short ones. But he wasn't really short. He was taller than she was anyway.

He wasn't GQ-handsome, but then not many men were. And besides, those models looked as if they never laughed or sweated or got dirty. They were more like dolls than real people. She wouldn't know how to behave around a GQ model.

Whether or not Jack looked like a model was irrelevant. For some reason, from that first day when he smiled at her at Hunt's and stumbled all over his words asking her to get a milkshake with him, from that first moment she liked him. And she had to admit she liked his body. He felt so hard, in that shed. Hard thighs pressing against hers, hard back under her hands, hard shoulder blades. She had never given a second thought to shoulder blades before. Now her fingers and palms could feel Jack's shoulder blades flexing as he moved his hands along her arms. She wanted to fit her own hands around his shoulder blades. She wanted her palms and fingertips and the back of her hands and the insides of her wrists to memorize that man's shoulder blades. That one man's, out of all the men she'd ever seen.

She shook herself and got out of the truck.

****

Rose took her first lover in her last year of college. He was a sophomore, three years younger than she was because she'd taken time off to help get her parents' CSA up and running. She was inexperienced and so was he and they'd cheerfully gone their separate ways after three unsatisfactory encounters.

Then there was Theo, Rose's second lover. She was walking along State Street in Montpelier, admiring the statue of Ceres, goddess of agriculture, glowing in the sun from atop the golden dome on the capitol building. Ceres was the perfect symbol for her chosen state. There were fewer and fewer farms every year, but agriculture still played a huge part in the state's history. It wasn't dead yet, as proven by her brand-new job interpreting for migrant farm workers.

Her thoughts were interrupted by a loud laughing bellow.

"Rose! Is that little Rosie Gilhooly? All grown up and gorgeous?"

The big cheerful man looked only vaguely familiar.

"Do not tell me you don't remember! It's me. From good old Cranville-Easton Central School."

When her polite smile didn't immediately widen, the giant took two steps back, lifted his right arm, and pretended to throw a football.

"Teddy! Of course! My gracious!"

He was more than a head taller and almost twice as wide as she was, and he almost crushed her in a bear hug, but she came out of it laughing and delighted.

Teddy! Teddy Bear!

He was named Theodore Barrett, and his parents called him Ted, but starting at the end of middle school when he suddenly shot up six inches and became popular overnight, he was Teddy. He was two years ahead of her in their tiny high school, and he was a Big Man on Campus for more than just his size. He was quarterback and captain of the football team. He played basketball and baseball too, and was head of the student council for a couple of years. And he was always cheerful, always friendly to everyone, even the kids no one ever befriended. It was impossible not to like Teddy Bear.

"What are you doing here in Vermont? I know you got a football scholarship to Colgate and I heard you were playing in the pros and making gobs of money. Why aren't you living in some mansion in California by now?"

"Yes to the gobs of money and yes to the pros. And yes to the CA mansion. I'm here looking for a place to use when I want to ski." His big white grin made him look as young as he had in high school. "I blew out my shoulder after six years of pro ball, but by then I'd saved a shitload of money." He shook her arm gently. "All of us who learned Home Economics under Miss Deveny learned how to manage money, *or else*!"

Rose laughed. "She was something, wasn't she? She must have been in her sixties by the time we had her, but she still knew how to control a classroom of rowdy teenagers better than anyone in that whole building."

"She was the one who pushed through the idea that boys should take Home Ec, remember? Way back in the Dark Ages. It took a few more years before the reciprocal happened and girls were allowed in shop classes." He waggled his eyebrows. "You delicate little things."

"Oh, Teddy. It is so good to see you. Do you have time to join me for lunch?"

"With you, of course."

"Italian or Mexican?"

"Mexican. But one thing."

"What's that?"

"Try not to call me Teddy. I've got an image to maintain. I'm doing a lot of on-air sports announcing, and I am a serious and adult-sounding *Theo*."

Theo was in Vermont for several more weeks that year, searching for the perfect retreat for him and his wide circle of friends. After two lunches together, he invited Rose for an overnight in Stowe.

"Regular folks can't check in 'til three. But the guy knows my name so he's having our room cleaned first and we can check in at one. Let's go up early, have a spectacular lunch and then retire to our room. Does that sound good?"

The next three days were a sex marathon. But she began to get a bit sore and, worse, she began to get bored. What was wrong with her? There were countless women who would be delighted to walk into a fancy restaurant on the arm of a man who could only be defined as a hunk. To touch her wine glass to his and know they would soon be in his king-size bed in his king-size suite. Those other women would feel awash with sensual anticipation. They would be able to keep up with Theo's incandescent sensuality.

But by the end of the second day, Rose wanted a walk in the fresh air. By the next morning, she longed for a quiet corner and a good book. She liked seeing Teddy Bear again, liked sharing stories about high school friends, still liked his open friendly face and his boundless energy.

But she knew she just wasn't in his league.

And then there was Peter, and he'd found someone better.

Maybe she wasn't in anyone's league.

But she couldn't forget her response to Jack.

Chapter Seven

At Last

——*Jack. Come for supper Friday?*——
That's all she had to say. Plus her address.

He would know she'd seen Peter. He would think they were free to go to bed. Have sex. Make love. But she wasn't sure they would do that.

****

"Jack."

"Rose."

"It's good to see you again." She tried a little grin. "Finally."

"Yes. Me too."

She'd forgotten what a nice speaking voice he had. Baritone. Warm.

"Um. This might just be supper. Nothing else."

"Okay." He held out a bottle of wine. "I'm looking forward to spending time with you, Rose. Even if it is just supper."

She took the bottle with hands still wet from washing the salad makings, and when it started to slip Jack put both his warm hands around hers. Breathless, she looked up into his eyes.

"Good save." He took the bottle out of her hands and placed it on the counter. "Something smells wonderful."

"Oh. Yes." She turned away. "Fish. Cod. It's a new

recipe." Her laugh came out a titter and she was embarrassed. "You're not supposed to try a new recipe when you have guests but it's very like another recipe and I like that one so I figured—You're supposed to have white wine with fish but I think red will work because it's hearty. A hearty recipe." She looked around almost desperately and grabbed the corkscrew and thrust it at him. "Would you open it? Let it breathe?"

Jack wanted to tell her to do that too. Breathe. He knew he would be nervous. But he was surprised by her. Rose seemed so calm, so confident, every time before.

"Is there anything I can do to help with dinner?"

"I don't think so."

"May I wander around a little?"

"Of course!" She wanted him to move away from her. She wanted him looking anywhere but at her flushed face, thinking about anything but her breathless babbling.

"I like this place."

"I do too. Humongously. I've been here over seven years and I like it even more than when I found it."

He was looking at her bookshelf.

"Spanish dictionary. Chinese dictionary. Bosnian dictionary. Sci-fi. Romance novels. Lots of books about botany. You are a well-rounded woman, Rose."

He felt his neck and face get hot at the double entendre, but she was putting something on the table and didn't notice.

"If I hadn't gone the teaching route, I was going to be a botanist. Not the kinds of plants you find in nurseries, but the flora of wild America. That was going to be my specialty."

"Oh. Yes. The common water-whatsis."

"I'm astonished that you remembered."

"I am pretty sure whatsis isn't the correct name."

"But you were half right." She opened the oven and pulled out four large potatoes. "Common Water-Dropwort. I'd like to go back sometime and get photos, before the first frost."

"You've got many weeks still. Although one never knows in Vermont."

"Potatoes, cod casserole, peas, bread, salad. What else?"

"This is a feast, Rose. It looks as good as it smells. I had a home-cooked meal exactly five weeks ago, at my folks' house. Since then it's been blue plate specials at various diners, some good, some not so much. And two disgusting prewrapped sandwiches I picked up when I stopped for gas."

"Yuck." Rose gave the little spurt of laughter he remembered from their first date. "Two possible meanings. Stopping to get gas."

It took him a slow count of three or four before he followed what she was saying, and then he laughed out loud.

"So you've eaten those sandwiches too."

And suddenly they were normal again. They were the friends who laughed and talked through two diner meals and two hikes.

"I have and I never will again. Sit down, Jack. Will you pour while I dish out?"

The table was set the same as it always was when Peter came for supper. The same dishes, the same napkins, the same cutlery, the same mismatched wine glasses and water glasses. But for the first time ever, Rose felt a little surge of pride. The blue casserole dish she'd found at Goodwill matched one of the napkins, and Max's mother's twin white bowls were perfect for the peas and potatoes. She was pleased in a way she'd never been with Peter.

"I should have brought flowers. For the table."

"There's no room. Unless I go into the back of the closet and get out the extra leaf." She took the wine glass and held it up. "Cheers, Jack."

"Cheers, Rose."

The little clink felt like a punctuation mark, the end of the first part of the evening and the beginning of the next.

"Rose, I hope you forgive me. I had breakfast way early and I ate one of those little boxes of raisins for lunch. I'm not going to be much of a conversationalist until I eat some of this wonderful-looking food."

"Dig in then. Enjoy."

They were quiet until Jack's plate was empty.

"Seconds?"

"I would love some. Thank you." He leaned back. "I should say that again, Rose. *Thank* you. The food is beyond good. I'm happy to be here. And now I can relax and talk and be a better guest."

"I am too, Jack. Happy you're here." She heaped his plate again. "There's cake too, but this stuff is healthier."

He placed a pat of butter in the middle of a potato and watched it melt. "Tell me what your interesting and diverse career had in store for you these past few weeks."

"Hmmm. Well, apple-picking season's just starting, and most of the migrant pickers are from Jamaica. They speak English." Her grin was wide and easy for the first time. "Well, they speak something that bears a resemblance to English. It's going to take me a few more years before I stop struggling with the accent and the slang and the many words that aren't standard here in the states."

"So you're not doing as much translation, but still some?"

"A bit, yes. And I'm still giving the mandatory safety classes, and I've got two classes for adults who want to get Vermont drivers' licenses."

"I didn't know non-residents could get licenses."

"In general, that's true. But if you have proof that you're a visiting citizen of some other country, and you've got a specified length of stay, and you'll be in the state at least thirty more days, then you can. At some farms, workers get paid more if they can drive the trucks and deliver crates to stores."

"Makes sense." His words were almost lost in a huge yawn. "Sorry. Not boredom, believe me. Fatigue."

For the first time, Rose noticed that he looked exhausted. There were circles under his eyes and even his thick red-brown hair looked flatter than usual.

"Coffee? Decaf so you'll be able to sleep, which you look like you need. And cake?"

"Both. Yes." He half rose from his chair.

"Stay put." She took their plates. "I'll bring stuff over while you tell me how it's been going with Papa Bear, Mama Bear, and Goldilocks."

"Oh dear god."

"That bad, huh?"

Jack sighed. "I'm exaggerating because I'm bushed. Papa Bear has signed off on the number of collectors he wanted, every one anchored to solid bedrock and good until the end of time. Cost more than he hoped but he's getting financial help from Efficiency Vermont."

"And Mama?" Rose put a steaming mug in front of him. "I can't remember if you take anything in yours."

"I would be amazed if you did remember. One breakfast, one lunch, weeks and weeks ago. Half-and-half, if you've got it."

"Here you go." She handed him a carton and then lifted a metal cover off a plate on the counter. "Light chocolate cake with cherries in the middle and dark chocolate on top. Yes for you?"

"Chocolate, more chocolate, and cherries? Definitely."

Rose cut two pieces of cake, filled another mug for herself, and sat back down.

"And what about Mama Bear?"

"I can't remember how much I told you before. Mama Bear wants a bunch of collectors and she doesn't want them near the house. But everything that's not near the house is a swamp. She finally got over her utter disbelief that the state Department of Environmental Conservation won't let her dig around in wetlands, and she is now willing to consider something on the roof of either her house or her barn. *Maybe.* The woman is a stickler for historical accuracy, and both buildings are from around 1850."

"No rooftop solar panels back then."

"Not a one." He licked the fork he'd used for dinner and then took a bite of cake. "Incredible. Very, very incredible."

"I should have given you a clean fork."

"No reason at all."

She wiped her fork on her napkin. "And what about Goldilocks?"

"Goldilocks is going to be the death of me. The

death of all of us. Every single option is too something. If we put the collectors in one possible site, it'll be too distracting when she's sitting in her study." He gave Rose a look from under his brows. "Where she does her morning meditation."

"So distractions are a no-no."

"Precisely. But if we put them in another possible site, they'll draw the eye away from the inherent natural beauty of her ancient and gnarled apple trees. Direct quote. And if we put them in back of the barn, a big old maple will shade them and it's a *Druid* tree, according to her, so it can't be cut down. If we put the collectors farther from the house and garage, the temporary road for bringing them in will make a scar that will be just *too, too* obvious. We're all beginning to think she doesn't really want solar collectors. She just wanted to be known around town as environmentally friendly. Solar popped into her mind one day and so, without any research, she decided that was the way to go."

Rose leaned back and watched him talk. Yes. What she'd felt in that shed was real. For the first time in her life, she knew what it was like to want a man. To want one specific man. She wanted to feel him heavy on top of her and to tighten her fingers on his buttocks as she felt him driving in and out of her. She wanted to be above him, slowly lowering herself onto his cock. She knew, absolutely knew, that sex with Jack would not be like sex with Peter.

"So that's the saga. Weeks and weeks in that part of Vermont. Countless trips from Montpelier to Bennington. Countless nights in beds that aren't my own. All for one contract, one possible contract, and one increasingly improbable contract."

"I'm sorry for you. It's frustrating when you put effort into a job and the effort doesn't bear fruit."

"Precisely."

"Jack." She liked saying his name. "Jack. All those countless trips—You probably want to head home and, and fall into bed for about twelve hours."

He slowly placed his fork on his empty plate. "That is, no doubt, very sensible. But it's not what I'm wanting."

"Really?"

"Is that all right with you?"

"Oh yes."

She stood and held out a hand, and he took it. She led him across the living area to the bed hidden behind the screen and then let go of his hand.

They undressed slowly, watching each other, tossing clothing in the direction of her rocking chair without looking to see where it landed. When she took off her bra, he reached out and ran the edge of one finger along one breast, and she closed her eyes and tilted her head back and didn't breathe. And when he straightened up after pulling down his BVDs, she reached out and ran the edge of one finger along the side of his cock and he bucked and groaned.

They tumbled onto her bed in a tangled needy mass of arms and legs and mouths and skin and heat. He was almost inside her when he gasped "Shit shit" and fell sideways off the bed in his haste to get to his jeans. She wanted to tell him she was on the pill but then she thought of Peter and the woman in Peter's life and maybe some woman or women in Jack's life. Yes. It was safer this way.

When he came back, she had just enough time to

think that this was like a first for her, because he was thicker than the other men. Then there was no thinking at all. There was only feeling. Rose wanted it to last a hundred hours or more. She wanted it never to end. But Jack was panting, gasping, grunting, and much too soon he stiffened all over and she felt him pulsing and throbbing and jerking inside her.

For a second or two, there was no noise, no movement.

And Jack was a boneless weight.

She shook his shoulder.

"Huh? Oh!" He lifted up on his arms, reached down and pulled out of her, his fingers carefully removing the condom.

She rolled to one side so she could pick up the wastebasket.

He muttered something that might have been "Thanks" and then he was asleep again.

Those few minutes with Jack were better than anything with Peter. But now was much too familiar. He was asleep, and her whole body was tingling, throbbing, wanting.

With Peter, she usually went into the living area until he woke up and went home, and then she went back to bed and sometimes gave herself the orgasm he hadn't. But tonight, she didn't feel like leaving the bed. She didn't feel like making love to herself. She lay back down and Jack grunted in his sleep and put his arm around her.

That was something at least. He knew she was there.

****

Rose stirred and stretched, and her foot touched something hairy. A leg. Jack's leg. She opened her eyes.

Jack's sleeping face was inches away.

A glance out the window showed a faint glow in the east. The only man she'd ever spent the night with was Teddy—or Theo as he called himself—and the few nights with him were marked by frequent interruptions. She had never in her life slept with a man for hours and hours, sharing the same sheets and covers, their bodies touching whenever one of them moved, their breath mingling.

It was only a few steps from the bed to the bathroom, and she closed the door before she realized that she hadn't stopped to put anything on. That wasn't like her at all. She always pulled on one of her nightshirts before getting out of bed, every one of the not many times she had left a bed that had a man in it. She wasn't going to walk back out there naked, though. After a quick shower, she wrapped herself in a big towel and opened the bathroom door.

Jack was standing beside the bed, stretching and yawning.

"Rose. Do you have to go anywhere? Work? Anything?"

"No."

"May I take a shower too?"

"Of course. I was fast so there'll be plenty of hot water."

"Will you wait for me in bed?"

Oh. Maybe things weren't over.

Rose draped her towel over the back of the rocker. His and her clothing was on the seat, on the arms, all around the chair on the floor.

She slid under the sheet and waited.

She watched the bathroom door open, watched as

Jack walked across the living area, looked up at him as he stood next to the bed rubbing a towel over his wet hair, watched as he draped his towel over the back of the rocker, watched as he bent down, picked up his jeans, and then carefully placed a condom on the bedside table.

He took a step closer, reached out a hand, and began pulling the sheet down. Very slowly. The cool fabric slid along the slope of her breasts and stopped there, until he twitched one side and then the other and exposed her hardened nipples. She watched his face, watched him watching the sheet sliding over her rib cage, the curve of her waist, the dimple of her navel.

He met her eyes.

"We didn't say good morning yet. Good morning, Rose."

"Good morning, Jack."

Now she watched what he was watching, the sheet at the top of her pubic hair and then below, and then sliding slowly down her thighs and over her knees. She never thought of her shins as erogenous but as she watched the white fabric ease down, *felt* it ease down, knowing that naked Jack was watching naked her, her shins tingled.

When the sheet reached her ankles, he abruptly yanked it off, grasped her legs, and pulled her down and sideways until her legs dangled over the edge of the high bed. Then he spread her knees and knelt on the floor between them.

She felt his thick hair on the inside of her thighs and she whimpered, moving closer. When his tongue separated her, the heat and need from the night before were instantly there, magnified, multiplied. Rose arched, her head tilted back, her hands grabbing the sheet and

107

pulling and tugging. A huge need was in her belly, between her legs, heavy and dark and growing.

"Jack. Oh god Jack oh god."

And then it burst, exploded, shot down her legs and up her torso and down her arms and making tears fill her eyes and her throat.

Jack stood up and she watched, unfocused, as he opened the little package and rolled the condom over his swollen cock. Then he wrapped her numb legs around his waist and came into her.

This time lasted. This time went on and on and on. Rose tightened her legs around him and met his eyes. And he kept pumping, kept filling her, and she kept sliding back and forth to meet him and the need was growing again and he kept pumping and she was gasping now, she was the one grunting and moaning and then she heard herself make a noise like a howl and she couldn't believe it was her and she came again and he was chanting, saying her name over and over, saying *Rose* with every thrust he made, and then he came too.

And then they were both in the bed, limp, laughing, holding on.

And then they were both asleep.

****

Rose woke to sun painting a wide stripe of gold across the bed.

Jack was watching her face. "Good morning again." He looked tousled and a bit uncertain.

"Good morning, Jack. Again."

"I have to ask. Because I'm not sure. Was that, earlier, was that as incredible for you as it was for me? I hope?"

"Jack." She reached up and touched his face. "That

was… It was extraordinary. I can't…"

His smile spread from his eyes to his mouth to his cheeks. "I can't either."

"For some unknown reason, I'm ravenous."

"Me too. For that same unknown reason."

"There's a bagel place a few blocks away."

"Want to walk?"

"Let's." Rose was giddy, almost laughing aloud. "Oh, yes! Oh let's!"

****

"These are better than any bagel sandwiches I've had in Montpelier or Waterbury. And those two cities are, respectively, the state capital and the seat of a whole lot of the state's government." Jack stood up. "I'm going to have another. You?"

"No. Well, yes. If you're willing to eat half if I can't finish it."

"Deal."

Rose sat at a little round patio table, the sun bright in her eyes and warm on her face, and her whole body was happy, down to the tips of her toes and out to the ends of her hair. Too bad you're not here now, sister Lily, she thought. She would tell her that she finally understood what her sister felt when she touched Geoff, why she glowed when she thought about going to bed with him. Rose had always thought she was exaggerating.

"Here you go. And a coffee refill."

"Oh, great. Thank you."

Jack stared down as he carefully unwrapped his sandwich. "Rose. You don't have to answer. But I gotta ask. You talked with Peter, right?"

"I did. Yes."

"And?"

"And what?"

"And how did he take it? If he suddenly appears in front of us, is he likely to haul off and deck me?"

She gave a little snort of laughter. "I can't imagine Peter decking anybody. Ever."

"But would seeing you with me—Would we be rubbing salt in his wounds?"

"No wounds. Not even a scratch." Rose could feel herself flushing but she made herself look directly at Jack and finish the story. "I went to tell Peter I wouldn't be seeing him anymore. And he—He laughed out loud with relief. It turns out that Peter is in love. Peter is planning to get married. Peter is talking about babies. As soon as possible."

"Hold on. How did that happen so fast? Love and babies and everything?"

"It turns out it wasn't so fast. He met a woman at last year's small business conference and they've been e-mailing and talking on the phone for a whole year now. They met up again this time around. And, um, they gave me the understanding that they spent most of the conference in bed."

"Oh. That's good, isn't it?"

"It is, of course it is. Lou, her name is Lou, is in the same business as Peter. She ran her father's hardware store and now she's going to be partner in Peter's store here in Morrisville. And his wife. And mother of his probably multitudinous children."

"How do you feel about that?" Jack took a bite of his bagel sandwich and watched her face.

"This is idiotic, but at first I felt let down. Put down. Discarded. Betrayed, or something. But a few minutes later I felt a relief as big as Peter's. Maybe bigger."

"That's good."

"It is." Rose grinned. "Anyway, she's a way better match for him. She wears heels."

"Huh?"

"High heels. Like women do in cities. She was standing on Peter's little lawn, in Morrisville Vermont, and she had on a neat business outfit and shoes with two-inch heels." Rose shook her head. "And me with my hiking shoes, jeans, and tee shirt. She will be a much more appropriate date at the next Kiwanis Club dinner. Or when Peter gets some sort of award from the Better Business Bureau." She stood up. "Want to walk a bit more?"

"Sure. Show me your town, Rose."

"Not a whole lot of tourist attractions in Morrisville. But we do have a school named People's Academy, probably the only school with that name in the whole country. And a museum. And a hospital."

"Copley."

"Yes. And a country club. And a batch of distilleries and breweries. And it's a gorgeous day for a walk."

"Lead on."

****

"Wow. Just look at that bird."

Jack's whole focus was on Rose's hand in his, her arm brushing against him, the smell of her shampoo. "Bird?"

Rose nodded toward a tree just ahead of them. "How could you, a dedicated birder, not notice a pileated woodpecker?"

The big bird was working at eye level, excavating a long deep hole and tossing wedge-shaped chips onto the growing pile on the grass.

"There must be some mighty tasty carpenter ants in that tree. And that bird is going to get every single one. He doesn't even care that we're only a few yards away."

"He?"

"Males have that red stripe going back from the bill. Females have black stripes."

They stood, quiet, watching.

"That is an extraordinary animal, Jack."

"He'll probably stay here for another twenty minutes, until he gets every bit of nourishment from— Or not."

White patches gleamed on black wings as the big bird swooped across the street.

Jack grinned at Rose. "Every day is a good day when you get to see a pileated woodpecker up close." He tucked her hand under his arm and started to move forward, but Rose pulled him back.

"I never asked. You don't have to start back today, do you?"

"Oh. No. I don't. Was that an invitation? May I stay again tonight?"

"I'd like you to. Yes."

Jack inhaled so deeply that Rose wondered if he'd been holding his breath. "I accept your invitation. With delight and considerable anticipation."

"Will we have all day tomorrow too?"

He looked over at her, at the soft waves of her hair in the breeze, at her pink cheeks and bright blue eyes, at her beautiful, beautiful mouth. "Sadly, no. Very sadly no. I should start back south by two or so. I'm meeting Derek, one of my partners, for an early supper in Bennington." He waggled his eyebrows at her. "Derek says that Bennington is the culinary capital of the state. No. He said it's the *gustatory* capital of the state."

"I hadn't heard that about Bennington."

"Me neither. He might have been talking through his hat. But anyway, we two will meet, we'll eat, I'll catch up on what's been going on in the office and he'll catch up on the saga of the Three Bears and Goldilocks."

They walked a few blocks in silence. Then Rose slid her hand under his arm.

"Me too."

"You too what?"

"Delight and anticipation."

****

"How about finishing the cake for supper?" Rose turned from the fridge. "We took a walk. Then we, um, got a lot more exercise here. We've used up a gidzillion calories today."

"At least." He took the cake from her. "All that chocolate might keep us awake, though. We might have to find something to do."

Rose leaned forward to kiss him. "Oh yes."

She got out two plates and handed a big knife to Jack.

"Cut some humongous slabs. I'm starving."

"Will do."

"Here. We can finish up last night's salad too."

"A balanced meal."

"We've got decaf. Tea. A little wine." She poked around in the fridge. "Very flat ginger ale. And always peanut butter, strawberry jam, and graham crackers."

"A veritable feast."

"Do you mind if we both eat salad out of the same bowl?"

"Worried about sharing germs?"

"Just asking. Being a good hostess and all."

****

"Ahhhh." Jack leaned back and patted his flat belly. "A wonderful and healthy meal yesterday and lots of healthy exercise today."

"And a filling and, what's that word? Sybaritic? Yes—a sybaritic meal this evening. I'm stuffed and happy, and I second your ahhhh."

"Don't think I know that word."

"Sybaritic. It means sensuously luxurious. Self-indulgent."

"Perfect." He stood and gathered their plates. "And now, Rose. It is evening. People go out to the movies in the evenings. Or they watch TV. Or they take a post-dinner stroll. Or they play cards. Or Scrabble. Or they have friends over. What's your preference?"

"Let me think here. We've already walked quite a lot today. I don't know what's playing at the Cineplex but I'm not in the mood for a movie. Cards or board games are fine, I guess. But I'm thinking more along the line of—" She looked up at him. "Of more self-indulgent and sensuous pleasure."

"I'm beginning to wonder if I'll be able to keep up with you, Rose Gilhooly."

"I have faith that you are capable of doing just that."

"Your faith will keep me hard." He wrapped his arms around her. "And your kisses. And your lovely face. And beautiful breasts. And your belly. And your legs, which I'm becoming addicted to. And your whole entire body, which fits my whole entire body so entirely perfectly."

"We do fit well, don't we, Jack?"

"You're sure you're not getting sore? Tired out? Bored with the whole thing?"

She laughed and he had an immediate flashback to the first time he heard her laugh, in the little diner down the road from Hunt's farm. Of his desire, right then, to keep hearing her laugh, to keep her in his life, to look into her eyes and watch her smile and hear her voice for at least the next fifty years.

"I'm not sore. I am wanting you, though."

"Do you think we can shower together?"

"The stall's too small." She reached out and started unbuttoning his shirt. "Quick. You first."

"Rose. I think I've died and gone to heaven."

Chapter Eight

The Holidays

Shaking with the need to touch and taste, Jack pulled
Rose behind a large maple tree where they could say
hello without entertaining the truckers going in and out
of the rural diner. After several minutes, Rose pushed
back a little, breathless.

"My gracious. Hello. Very hello. We have... My
gracious, Jack. We have got to stop meeting like this."

"How would you like us to be meeting?"

She just looked at him, her eyes wide and glowing.

"Me too. Me too. Two more weeks." He kissed the
tip of her chin. "Hey. Here's an idea. Let's forget about
breakfast. Let's get a room at that motel. For an hour."

"Ohhhh." She pulled back his sleeve and glanced at
his watch. "You've got exactly fifty minutes before you
have to leave. We should probably grab some breakfast
and then—" She grinned. "Then we can duck behind this
tree again to say goodbye."

"Oh. Okay. You go ahead in and get us a booth. I'll
join you in a minute."

"All right."

She turned and headed across the parking lot, doing
a happy little skipping skip when she heard a soft mutter
behind her.

"Down, boy."

Her body, like his, would have announced what they'd been doing, what they'd been feeling, if it weren't for the very loose sweatshirt she was wearing.

Only two more weeks. Then Jack would be finished with what he now called his southern tour of duty. And harvest season would be over so Rose's job would be limited to occasional on-call interpreting and the Bosnian language class she was taking online, plus the immersion week on the Middlebury campus. Then he would be in her home for a week. One evening they'd get out the leaf for the kitchen table and cook a feast for Max and Xavier. A whole week, with all those days and all those endless nighttime hours. And after that week, they were going to spend a few days together at his apartment and then go celebrate Thanksgiving with his folks. Not Thanksgiving exactly, but Jack assured her it would look a lot like Thanksgiving. The Carmichaels celebrated HarvestFest, he said, instead of the destruction of whole cultures.

A broken arm and 200 pies scuttled all their plans.

****

"I like him, Rose. He's in a whole different category from that incompletely-stuffed scarecrow who used to hang around here."

Rose snickered. "Great description, Max. Peter's skin always did feel a bit loose."

"What I said. Incompletely stuffed."

The two women stood on Rose's front step, looking toward the sidewalk where Jack was talking with Max's tall quiet husband. Patches of early snow were melting fast in the unexpectedly warm December sun.

"How long have you two known each other?"

"Five months? Almost six. But we saw each other

only a few times those first two months, and then for only an hour or two at a time."

"Dates. I remember the concept."

"And then Jack got sent to southern California for a symposium. And I left for my parents' house three weeks before Thanksgiving." Rose laughed, the startled little laugh-snort that Jack fell in love with months earlier. "I remember telling my mother, years ago, that I wanted an *easy* love affair, one with no snags and no glitches." She shook her head. "It hasn't happened. Jack and I met almost six months ago and we've had a few diner meals, two short hikes, and two short weekends."

Max held up one finger, assumed a faraway look, and made her voice thin and halting. "Not the total of the life are to be measure by passage of time." She grinned. "How was that? Didn't I sound exactly like that wise little green guy in those space movies?"

"I could hardly tell the difference."

"Glorioskee. Your Jack just got my Xavier to laugh out loud. I would love to know what's so funny." She sighed. "But it's probably wiser to let the magic be."

Rose gazed thoughtfully at the two men. "Jack is a whole lot better than Peter. He genuinely likes people. He's funny and kind and energetic. He cares about the environment. And he's wicked smart, even though he sometimes acts the clown."

"Looks like a wrestler, with those shoulders. Long torso. Sorta short legs." Max turned her head and scanned Rose from feet to neck. "Yup. An ideal fit. But I already guessed that from the noises coming from your place that day I was planting bulbs."

"No way! You didn't—"

"I did. I heard every sigh, every whimper, every

moan, every—"

"Wait a minute. You knocked on the door while I was packing to go to my parents, and you said you were going to be planting bulbs outside my windows that very day. Jack wasn't even here!"

Max's gamin face relaxed into a big grin. "It was so fun to see that lovely color on your neck and face. A color, by the by, that tells me the noises I just made up have occurred. Often."

"Well. Maybe."

"Good for you. For you both. So. Thanksgiving. Ten dozen pies? I never quite got that."

Rose snickered. "My folks run a huge and growing CSA. That's Community—"

"Supported Agriculture. I know. I'm a Vermonter."

"Of course. Anyway, they've got an orchard as well as the veggies and livestock, and my mom makes a gidzillion apple pies for Thanksgiving and people order them along with that week's share. But she broke her arm."

Max shook her head sympathetically. "That's so common with older people. Their balance isn't what it used to be, so they fall. And their bones are brittle, so they break."

"You must expand your expectations of aging, Max. My mother broke her arm doing a cannonball into a swimming hole. While skinny-dipping."

"Really? Truly?"

"Really and truly. She and my dad took a picnic lunch to a deep pool in the stream that runs through their property. It's one of their private get-away spots and they figured it would be their last chance 'til June. They got there, stripped down and ran at the stream, just like always. But Mom slipped on wet moss. Dad said she did a mid-air flip that would have earned her at least 8.5 at the Olympics. She landed on her arm and broke both bones in her wrist."

"Ouch, ouch, ouch."

"Serious ouch. Pie-making, which Mom usually does effortlessly, turned into a major challenge. My brother Finn was straight out with the CSA and my dad has all the animals to tend to and my sister has a full-time job. It was sheer desperation that made Mom call me. I have always been, without any question, *the* worst pie crust maker, not only in our family but in the whole eastern half of the U.S. But I learned, and we made just over 200 pies in six days."

"Good god."

"I am now much better at making pie crust."

"Did you get to eat any of your efforts?"

"Of course! All but a dozen went to the CSA members, two were eaten at Thanksgiving, two went home with my brother, Mom put some in their humongous freezer, and three came home with me."

"Hmmm. Are your three gone already?"

"Jack and I polished one off last night. The others are still frozen."

"Great. You can bring one to Christmas dinner." Max turned to her, her face hopeful and a bit sheepish. "We were talking last night, Xavier and I. We know that Christmas Day is for families. But if you're going to be around, we would love to have you join us for dinner. And Jack too if he's here." Her brows lowered and her mouth turned down. "Our son is still gallivanting around the globe saving lives or some foolish thing like that, but our Christmas is going to include other family members.

Through no decision of our own."

"You're not happy about it."

"I am nauseated. I am pissed. I am irritated. I want to grab my hubby and run away to a distant island until mid-January." Max put both hands on her hips and scowled. "We weren't even given a choice. She left a message. Xavier's sister and her hubby *will* be here Christmas morning and they *will* stay overnight. Oh frabjous day calooh callay."

"You chortle in your joy."

"I long for the jaws that bite, the claws that snatch. Or whatever that line in the poem says. Or the vorpal sword! Yes! I would grasp the vorpal sword and go snicker-snack, once for the egregious Eneritz and once for her not-quite-as-egregious-but-definitely-not-enjoyable husband." Max held up an imaginary sword and made two vicious swipes in mid-air. "Swish! Swish! Ah-HAH!"

"Eneritz. Sounds like a posh hotel."

"It's a Basque name. The grandparents came from the Pyrenees." She gazed toward her husband, who was using both hands to emphasize whatever he was saying. "Xavier used to hate being Basque. No one even knew what the word Basque meant! And he particularly hated when people pronounced his name ex-AY-vee-ur. Now he just fixes them with his best professorial glare and asks them what's a short word for pizza. And when they say Za, he tells them that's what they should say when they say his name. Zaaa-vier."

"So is Zaaaa-vier fond of his sister?"

"Not hardly. She's almost twenty years older and she treats him like the baby brother she helped raise. The very young baby brother who needs her advice on every frigging thing." She heaved a huge sigh. "And she's got this loud nasal voice that never, ever, *ever* stops."

"And her husband?"

"Almost mute. He has to be." Her sigh started somewhere near her feet. "Anyway, Rose, we're hoping you'll be around. If you and maybe Jack join us, you might dilute her."

"Sounds delightful."

"I know. It's not fair to you. But I love my hubby, Rose. And he loves Christmas. He's not religious, exactly, but Christmas is a spiritual experience for him. It's a celebration two thousand years old, a celebration shared with all the millions who have gone to midnight mass and decorated trees, and carved turkeys and geese, and opened presents and sung carols. The millions who believe, if only for that day, an implausible story about a babe in a manger and his virgin mom."

"Don't forget the millions who overspend, overeat, and feel obligated to sit down with family members they detest."

"That too." She sighed again. "I want to give Xavier the Christmas he wants. And that harridan sister of his is threatening to ruin it."

"I don't know what Jack's plans are. He might want to be at his folks' house. But my parents are taking a real vacation for the first time in their lives. A whole week in Montreal. My mom's cast comes off the day before they leave, and they're going to see the Botanical Gardens and go to a show and a concert and, in my mother's words, walk a thousand miles and eat themselves silly. My brother and his girlfriend will stay at the farm and take care of the animals. That's his big Christmas present to them. I upgraded their hotel room; that's mine." Rose hugged herself in delight. "They're going to have a fifth-floor suite with a jacuzzi and room service and a whole wall of windows overlooking the city, instead of the little economy room on the ground floor they originally reserved."

"A lovely vacation for them."

"I think so. So I'll be here, in Morrisville." She pointed toward the main house. "And in your house for Christmas dinner. With bells on."

"Maybe the bells will drown out the insistent nasal whine."

****

"Jack, now that I've told you what we're walking into down there, are you still sure?"

"Turkey dinner with all the fixings? Your apple pie? Max's pecan pie? All the stuffing and gravy I can eat? I can put up with Xavier's relatives for an hour or two." He widened his eyes. "And Christmas fruitcake too! You may not believe this, Rose, but I love fruitcake. I have never once wanted to use it for a doorstop. Or put it out for the birds."

"You are peculiar, Jack."

"I am indeed." He turned and took her chin in his hand. "What about you, Rose? Are you dreading this whole event?"

"I am very fond of Max, and I like Xavier more and more every time I talk with him. But I'm glad your folks are pagans so you could be here today, instead of in the Northeast Kingdom with them."

"Old-style hippies. *Solstice* is the important winter holiday, not Christmas. I've never missed a one. They have neighbors over. They have a potluck feast that starts about three in the afternoon and lasts until dawn.

Everyone reads poems or short stories to each other and a few people play ancient music on recorders or fiddles or bagpipes. Everyone reflects on the past year. A Morris dancing group performs part of a medieval miracle play around a bonfire just before the ultimate moment when everyone joins hands and welcomes the return of the sun to the dark north country."

"That sounds festive and meaningful, Jack."

"It is that, Rose. Now, grab your pie and let's go meet a dragon for Christmas."

****

"Well. That wasn't too bad."

"Not at all." Jack took her arm as they headed across the frozen ground. "The food was incredible, our host and hostess were delightful, and the good guys outnumbered the skeletons at the feast."

"I felt a moment of pure fury, though, when she tried to enlist the two of us in her relentless criticism of her brother."

"But you turned your fury into a very effective smackdown."

"I thought I did too." Rose made her voice nasal and raspy. "Don't you agree that it's *tragic* that Xavier is wasting an excellent education? A *fine* intellectual upbringing? Our family's *innate* mental abilities? My brother could have been a full professor of history at a prestigious university here or even on The *Continent*." She snorted. "You could hear the capital letters. The Continent. As if North America isn't one."

Jack took over, his voice a good replica of her Eneritz-imitation. "Instead of *wasting* it all at an *unknown* institution in the wilds of Vermont. A so-called college that's nothing more than a relict of the hippy

124

era—"

"An era that deserves to be dead and gone and long forgotten." Her spurt of laughter made a little puff of cold mist as she bent to unlock the door. "We're good, Jack. We sound exactly like her!"

"But you so sweetly informed her that every graduate of that rural relict can not only *teach* history but *make* history." He quoted her words back to her. "Save forests worldwide, to counteract global warming. Change the course of climate change. Rehabilitate agriculture around the globe so the earth can feed its burgeoning population."

"I am very impressed by your memory, Jack."

"I was very impressed by your daring." He pulled her close for a quick kiss. "I am very impressed by you, Rose Gilhooly."

Praise always made her uneasy. She backed away, her cheeks pink from more than their short stroll across the cold yard. "Anyway, Za *does* teach history. He teaches History of the Northern Woodlands every semester, and it always has a waiting list. So there, dragon lady."

Jack hung up their coats. "Xavier and Max. Two unusual names."

"Max said their two X-es smacked together like magnets, and that was it. They were hitched."

"And now, Rose." His eyes glowed. "Now it's time for our own Christmas."

She looked over at the tiny tree in the corner of the room, dwarfed by the brightly wrapped packages her parents put in the car before she left the farm the day after Thanksgiving, along with a few new packages.

"We could wait until tomorrow." She turned and

looked again at the man who was becoming so important to her. "We could go to bed right now."

"We could."

"Yes." She reached up and pressed her fingertips against his lips. "Let's save presents for tomorrow morning."

"I am feeling a great deal of appreciation for that idea."

"Merry Christmas, sweet man."

"Merry Christmas, Rose."

****

After breakfast the next morning, Jack sat on the stuffed chair with Rose at his feet and wrapping paper on the floor around them.

"Great gifts from your folks, Rose. They know you and love you, that's obvious."

"They do. And I in return."

"Now open this one." He held out a flat box in silver paper. "This is a selfish gift. I got it because I want to see you in it."

Rose kept her eyes on the bow she was untying, preparing herself to feel embarrassed and foolish when she pulled out a skimpy bustier or a black lace teddy or something minimal and bright red.

"Oh!" She lifted out a silk blouse of shimmery blue, with a high black collar, long black cuffs, and a tight black waistband. "It's lovely, Jack. It is absolutely lovely."

"The same color as your eyes. I thought it was, in the store, but I wasn't sure."

"Jack, this is—This is gorgeous. Astonishing."

"The saleslady said it was supposed to be worn bloused. I'm not a hundred percent sure what that means but I said I'd pass it along."

Rose held the blouse against her. "It means you put it on, pull it down, and then pull it up a bit so it's loose above the waist."

"Try it on now?"

"Just a minute." She picked up another thin box, this one longer and narrower.

"My gift to you isn't nearly as beautiful, but it should keep you comfy while you're working."

He held the box up to his ear and shook it. "Comfy, huh?"

Rose always unwrapped her presents slowly, and she always smoothed the paper so it could be reused. Jack looked at her, grinned, and ripped his present open with both hands.

"Oh wow."

Inside the box were two pairs of polypro glove liners, a fleece neck warmer, and four chemical hand warmers.

"Rose, you are a lifesaver and a wonder and a beauty, all in one. Did you just guess or have I ever whined about the cold?"

"You have whined once or twice. Maybe a half dozen times. I stole that glove you thought you lost, the one with holes in two of the fingers, so I could get the right size."

"Do you know what's going to happen next?"

"No, Jack. What is going to happen next?"

"I am going to put on one of these pairs of glove liners. You are going to put on that blouse. We are going back to bed. Immediately thereafter, the glove liners and the blouse are going to be tossed across the room."

Rose came out of the bathroom wearing the silk

blouse and nothing else. The blouse wasn't bloused, but rather pulled down to its full length so the black band compressed some of her lush red-brown pubic hair and let the rest spring free.

She walked slowly toward Jack, holding out her closed fist.

"Here."

She opened her hand and he took the condom off her palm.

"This angle might not work. But I want to try it."

She leaned over the chair and Jack sucked in his bellyful of Christmas dinner and French toast breakfast so she could undo the button at his waist. He was so hard they weren't sure she could get his zipper down.

"Lift up just a little."

She opened his pants wider and freed his penis. Jack opened the packet with his teeth and watched while she rolled the condom on him.

"You have a beautiful cock. I don't think I ever told you that before."

He couldn't answer.

She straddled him, wiggling her knees back and sliding forward along his thighs.

"Yessss. I think this is going to work. Oh, yessss."

Rose lowered herself onto him excruciatingly slowly, watching his half-closed eyes with her half-closed eyes.

Back up. Down again slowly. Again and again until they were lost in a haze of sex and sensation and need.

They both made a noise when she sank down hard and fast, sheathing him entirely, grinding against him with her hips and her pussy.

"Oh god, Rose. Do that again."

Again, slow up, slow down, slow up, then a sudden shove.

"Oh god, Rose. Oh god. I can't stand it. Hold tight."

He cupped her bottom with his hands, fell forward onto his knees, and then she was on her back on the floor and he was riding both of them to the end, to the end together, to a groaning moaning gasping screaming end.

Chapter Nine

The Ugly Little House

Rose didn't know Jack like this. He was always upbeat, of course. Energetic. Enthusiastic. But this morning he was like a man who hadn't had caffeine for months and then slugged down a dozen double espressos for breakfast.

He'd left a cryptic message on her answering machine.

Got something to show you. Taking half day off. Meet me park-and-ride at 9?

Rose could feel the difference as soon as she got into his car. Jack barely glanced in her direction, tossing her a quick smile and a distracted "hi" and starting the car before she even had her seatbelt fastened.

And then he started talking, his usually smooth voice faster than usual and interrupted by occasional hitches and little gasps. He told her that his colleague Derek made a unilateral decision that the office should be dog-friendly like that computer company but his brand-new puppy wasn't housebroken and one of the engineers was the fastidious type and he was thoroughly disgusted and threatened to leave for the rest of the day and Derek agreed to wait another month before bringing the pup back to the office but now there was a strained feeling between the two men and the office didn't feel like it used to. And Jack had just heard about a local club for birders and he thought he might join up. It was called the BBC but not like the British one because this stood for Burlington Bird Club. Or maybe Burlington Birders Club, he wasn't sure. And he'd seen a Northern Mockingbird and reported it to e-bird and it got on the rare bird list and so other birders knew his name by now. And Jack's mother called and she was thrilled because Jane and Bernie Sanders stopped by the store on their way to some political event in New Hampshire, and his mother was more excited about Jane than she was about Bernie because Jane had done things with her life while Bernie was just a politician. But, Jack added, that wasn't true because Bernie used to make educational videos with some other guy from Burlington but he hadn't said that to his mother because she was so excited.

Rose opened her mouth to mention a nearby example of an excited person, but Jack went right on talking. About the weather. About the uncommonly warm and rainy January thaw and how it took away all those mountains of snow and now it was wicked cold with blizzard warnings for the weekend. About the garbage truck on his street that hit a power pole yesterday. About his neighbors who took down their holiday lights two days ago in that howling wind and Jack stood by the window with his cell phone the whole time so he could call 911 if they fell off the roof.

Rose felt herself withdrawing. Pulling into herself. She always pulled into herself in times of stress, like when her dad's leg got caught under a huge rock he was trying to lift. She was only six or seven and she ran all over the farm looking for their only hired hand, and the man said she was cool as cucumbers on a dewy morning and she didn't start crying until her father was safely sitting on his butt in the driveway, rubbing his bruised leg and praising his level-headed little daughter.

This wasn't the same kind of stress, this morning in the car with Jack. Of course not. But he wasn't normal. Rose was accustomed to feeling deliciously open with him, eager for his words and his thoughts and his laughter and his touch. She always felt alive and happy, with the constant simmering of lust underneath. But this morning she felt her whole body contracting, closing.

"Five more minutes, Rose! Just five more!"

He turned in at a dirt road.

"Last house on a dead-end! Perfectly perfect!"

Jack pulled up in front of a small house set back in a large lot. He threw himself out of the car and stood with his arms spread wide, looking back toward Rose with a wide grin.

"Wow." She left the car more slowly. "Congratulations, Jack." She wrapped her arms around herself against the blasts of icy wind. "You have found the ugliest house-painting job in the entire state."

"Butt-ugly, I agree. I think the paint was sold under the name Infant Diarrhea."

"Ewwww."

"But it can be painted over." He grabbed her hand and pulled her around so they could see the far side. "And it's only the front and one side."

"Oh."

"And there's only one window frame painted neon green, or lime green, or whatever."

"Oh."

Rose thought it was what her mother called a bungalow or a craftsman or handyman house. There was a wide porch across the front and a partial second story tucked under the eaves. It might be a pleasing place to live, with a great deal of work, but right now the square little building didn't look much better than some of the temporary housing for migrant farm workers that Rose saw in her job.

"The neighbor told me the original plan was for two houses on this lot but then the reservoir boundaries changed and there wasn't enough room. So this is the biggest lot on the street and no one can ever build any closer because of the reservoir."

"That's what the hurricane fence is?"

"Reservoir. Yup. Two sides of the lot. Great place for bird feeders because of the woods and the water nearby." He was still holding her hand and now tugged her across the yard. "I thought the listing said two-car garage, but it's two *garages*, one on each side of the house." He gestured toward a trim little outbuilding with old-fashioned barn doors and a rooster weather vane. "My dad is into brewing and I'm catching the bug. I could use this one for a home brewery. I considered a rooster-related name, because of the vane, but I wanted something wilder. Northern Lynx Lager. Fisher Cat Ale. Leaping Trout Beer." His eyes were sparkling now, and his grin was even wider than before. "But one day I was doodling at work and one of the engineers looked down and said my trout looked like a chubby sturgeon, and there it was. Chubby Sturgeon Beers and Ales."

"That would make a good logo," Rose murmured.

"Exactly!"

"Can you market brews from here? Zoning and all?"

"Nope. But my cousin has a restaurant in Swanton. He said if my brews are as good as my father's, then he can use pretty much all I manufacture."

"That's good then."

Jack reached out and ran his hand along a peeling windowsill. "This old gray stuff is probably lead-based. We'll have to use drop cloths and gather up all the chips and take them to the hazmat section of the dump."

We?

"Come on! I want you to see the inside."

"Jack. Stop." She tugged her hand free. "Why am I here?"

"I thought it would be obvious!" He turned to face her, his eyes glowing and the corners of his mouth twitching as if he could barely keep from grinning. "I am consider—I am thinking about—" He took in a gulping breath and made himself talk slowly and clearly. "Rose, I'm thinking of buying this house but first I need to know if you like it."

"That's…" Words tumbled through her head. That's what? Surprising? Startling? Unexpected? Crazy? In the end, she just shook her head. "What?"

"I need to know you're okay with this house before I make an offer."

"But that's—" She took a deep breath. "Jack. You're an adult. You don't need to check in with anyone else before deciding where to live."

"I'm not checking in with anyone else. I'm checking in with you."

"Jack." Rose frowned. "Jack, we are two separate people. We have two separate lives. We're not—" She gave a little laugh. "I bought a new sweater last week. It didn't occur to me, even fleetingly, to check with you before whipping out my credit card."

"This is not the same thing, Rose."

She stood stock still, on the frozen lawn in front of a derelict khaki-colored house with one neon lime windowsill, looking at a man she always enjoyed but right now a man who was catapulting her into panicky numbness.

"Jack." She tried to get a deep breath. "If it makes sense for you to buy rather than continue renting, if you want to accrue, or accumulate, equity or whatever—If this house pleases you, then you should buy it. Because *you* want to. Because it makes sense to you. You shouldn't be asking me."

"I believed that I should be asking you."

"But that's illogical. It doesn't make sense. We're two—"

"Two separate people. You said that. I thought, I still think, we are more than that."

"Jack. We…" How could she tell this wonderful and sunny person that she cherished the fact that they were friends, and lovers, but the very idea of "more than that" made her want to run away. "We haven't known each other very long, Jack. I shouldn't have any say in something as big as buying a house."

"Again. I believed you should. I jumped the gun." All the light and bounce and almost-smiling were gone from his eyes and his voice. "I should probably get you back to your truck."

****

Dumb. Dumb. Dumb.

He should have waited.

He knew he wanted to live with Rose. He knew that since their first date. He had managed to wait for months and months before sharing that conviction with her, but when the realtor showed him the house and he imagined the two of them there together, maybe with their kids, he believed it was time to tell her.

And now she was sitting like a statue beside him, staring straight ahead, mute.

He was so sure she'd catch on as soon as they arrived at the house. He was sure she would act coy and pretend not to understand. He imagined her stringing him along, behaving as if she had no idea why he wanted her to approve of the place, while her bright blue eyes twinkled with humor and excitement and delight.

But she had shown confusion first and then withdrawal.

He was so sure she was beginning to love him. She laughed with him. She shared her thoughts and listened to his. She made love with him so beautifully and so generously and so often.

But they never said the word *love*. Neither of them. He should have thought about that before showing her the house. He should have said it.

If he told her right now that he loved her, would she say it back?

Her hands were clenched together in her lap, her eyes huge and tragic. She wasn't ready. He had to face it. She might never be ready.

****

Rose stared straight ahead. She felt physically bruised. What happened back there? She never asked for the right to tell him what to do with his life. She didn't want to be that important in his life. She didn't want to be the person who determined whether or not he bought a house that he clearly liked.

She wanted Jack the way he had been for months now. The happy and optimistic and laughing Jack. She *hated* this anxious and hopeful face. She hated, hated, hated that she hurt him. She was angry at herself for hurting him and furious at him for putting her in a position to hurt him.

She wished she'd been quicker witted, back there at that ugly little house. She wished she could have made a joke of it, and she wished he had caught on and played along with her.

Jumped the gun? Did that mean Jack was sure they would live together someday, would buy a house together? Did he think it was a foregone conclusion? She didn't want him planning her life. *She* was the only person who was going to plan her life. Just her. No one else.

What could she do now? What was he thinking? He hadn't said a word since they left the house. Her wonderful time with Jack couldn't be over. He was too important to her. She loved the way she felt with him, the way she laughed and was herself and shared what she was thinking. That could not end over one misunderstanding. It was impossible.

"We're here." Jack pulled in next to her truck and stopped. "Your language class is next week, right?" He was still stiff, staring out through the windshield.

"The Bosnian week. Yes. I have to check in tomorrow."

He winced. "Rose, it's supposed to be snowing like a son-of-a-gun tomorrow afternoon."

"The college e-mailed everyone and recommended that we arrive by noon and beat the storm. We can get lunch and, um, chill out. Until the rooms are ready." She tried a little smile. "Our last chance to speak English. Once we check in, it's supposed to be nothing but

Bosnian until next Saturday morning."

"Immersion."

"All Bosnian, all the time. We're not even supposed to think in English. I…" What else could she tell him? What could she say to get them back to normal? "I reserved a single room because I never sleep well with anyone else. Well, except you. Of course. I sleep like a rock with you. Anyway, I counted and there's an even number of men but an uneven number of women so there had to be one single anyway. Unless they were going to make three women triple up and that's widely considered a fate worse than death." Rose knew she was babbling. She gulped and made herself wind down. "As your Samantha found out."

"Yes. Well. It'll be a good week, I think. For you."

"Jack. I am so sorry I rained on your parade."

"What?"

"You were excited about that house and I made fun of the color and I didn't want to see the inside and I— You stopped being excited right before my eyes. I feel sad and upset and sorry about it."

"It's okay."

"It's not. Not really."

He reached out and touched her cheek. "I got ahead of myself. Ahead of us. I'm the one who should be upset and sorry."

"Oh." She looked into his warm brown eyes and was completely without anything more to say. "Oh! Are you going to get an inspection? Before you sign anything?"

"Derek's brother does house inspections for a living. He'll go out sometime this week."

"Oh. That's good then."

Another long moment of silence.

"Rose. Will you kiss me goodbye?"

His mouth was gentle, familiar, welcome. But the kiss was very brief.

"I have to get back to work." He didn't have to. His next appointment was a few miles down the road and not for two hours.

"Oh. Yes." She bent and picked up her bag and then opened the door and got out.

****

Kiss me goodbye.

Goodbye?

Rose turned the defroster to high and sat watching Jack's car as he pulled out of the parking lot and merged into traffic. Goodbye until next week, when she was back from the Bosnian immersion week?

Or did he really mean *goodbye*?

That simply was not possible. A person didn't give up on a friendship, a relationship, after one wrinkle. One single time when they weren't perfectly in sync. That just didn't happen.

She had a sudden vivid recollection of sitting in the student center when she was a sophomore in college, listening to her roommate explain that she wouldn't date some boy because all the girls knew he was an *Allernone*.

"You know, Rose. You meet some guy and you start talking and you're still talking hours and hours later and it's, like, total magic. You and the guy laugh at the same things and you get pissed at the same things and you've read a lot of the same books and you even agree about movies, which I'm telling you, Rose, guys and us women usually do not do. Every single thing just, like, clicks. So you start seeing each other all the time, meeting for supper, walking to class, and everything is like hunky-dory one-hundred percent of the time. And of course the sex is, well, you know…" Her roommate fanned herself with her hand.

Rose didn't know, but she nodded anyway.

"And then one particular Saturday comes along and he wants you to go to some rock concert or hoops game or some such thing but you promised your best friend you'd be there to watch her debut as soloist with the college orchestra, and SNIP. He cuts you out of his life. Just like that! For him, it's total perfection every single second. Or nada. All or nothing."

"All or none."

"You got it, girl."

Maybe Jack was an Allernone. But she didn't think so. For one thing, they weren't college kids. He was a mature man. A whole man.

And, equally important, she was a full-grown woman, and she was not going to let him go *snip*. This was her relationship too, her friendship too. And he was important to her.

She wouldn't be able to text him or e-mail or phone for the week she was gone.

Unless she e-mailed him in Bosnian.

No. Probably not.

This afternoon she would gas up, pack, check in with Max and Xavier, chat with her parents and maybe her sister Lily, and contact Jack. In English. And tell him something. She had the whole ride home to think about what that something would be.

****

——Jack, are you available for brunch the Sunday after my class? Or supper that night or any night that week?—

****

He looked almost like the old Jack, standing in her doorway with his wide smile and his hair mussed up by the wind and his cheeks rosy and tanned.

"Come in! That wind is brutal!"

"It is!" He shrugged out of his jacket. "This winter will be remembered for endless, painfully cold, driving wind."

"And power outages."

"That too. I may not have ears anymore." He pulled off his knit cap and looked around. "But everything feels warm and cozy in here." He met her eyes. "I am very happy to be here, Rose."

"Come. Sit. Supper's almost ready."

"First." He reached out and pulled her into his arms.

Oh yes. Oh yes yes yes. He was Jack again and she was Rose and she felt her body reach out to him, every part of her, from her nose touching his cold nose and her mouth tasting his, to her swelling breasts and melting middle, all the way from her fingers in his hair to her toes curling in her sneakers.

"Much better." He pushed a curl behind her ear and grinned. "Now we're us again."

"And you don't have to work tomorrow?"

"I do. But not until a 3:30 meeting in Keene."

"New Hampshire?"

"Only one I know of. Have to leave by one tomorrow afternoon." He waggled his eyebrows at her as he pulled out a kitchen chair. His chair. The one he always sat in. "We have a good number of hours to spend as we will."

Rose turned away and opened the oven, smiling down at the casserole dish. Yes indeed.

****

She couldn't sleep. She was deliciously tired, and deliciously warm with Jack so close beside her, but she wanted to look at him. Watch him. He slept like a toddler, his limbs relaxed and his face wiped clear of worries and laughter both.

When he took her to see that ugly little house, did he mean he wanted her to live there with him? Yes. That was what he meant. And at that moment, without realizing she was ready to make a decision, Rose knew she wanted him in her life. Forever. If Jack wanted her to move in with him, she would, but she knew at that moment that she wanted to be married to him, to be his legal partner. Share his life. Have his children. She hugged herself with the abrupt and complete understanding, and he half-woke and moved closer and she turned on her side so he could wrap his body around hers. She lay awake in the dark, smiling and weeping a little and then smiling again.

There was light coming in the back window from the security floodlamp in a yard the next street over. It cast a shadow of their bodies on one of the room dividers that made Rose's bedroom wall. The dark gray shadow looked like one person, not two. Jack's round head with the thick curls was distinctive even in shadow. His back blocked hers from the light but she could see a vague outline of her hip behind his. Their two-person body had three legs and three arms because her leg was lifted over his thighs and her arm was wrapped tight around his torso.

Rose watched the shadow of their two-person body until she fell asleep.

****

"Have you decided about the house?"

Jack turned a strip of bacon with a fork and nodded. He was making either a very late breakfast or an early lunch, a flowered apron tied around his waist and his hair standing on end from their morning love-making. "I did, Rose. I put a down payment on it three days ago. Derek's brother gave the place a clean bill of health." He turned two more strips. "Ugly as sin but basically sound, in his words. The colorblind couple who had the house last put on a new roof and did a good job upgrading the wiring and insulating. And we—*I* won't have to be super careful about that paint on the windowsills."

Even from the back, his little wince was obvious when he corrected *we*.

"The windows were replaced only ten years ago. Double-paned and top of the line for back then, and still pretty good. The paint, Derek says, was sub-bottom. Of the line. But not lead-based. It's okay for now. He says I might want to put in a more energy-efficient heating system in the next few years, but there's nothing but cosmetic things that have to be done soon."

"Jack..." Rose frowned, staring at his back. "What did you mean when you said you had jumped the gun?"

"Oh. I—I had been seeing us there. At that house. Maybe our children too. But that day you came out, I realized I jumped way ahead of you. Maybe I jumped to a place you'll, you'll never be, with me. I hope that's not the case, but it's possible." He laid the bacon strips on a paper towel. "Scrambled okay?"

"Yes. Fine."

Tell him, Rose. Tell him yes, to the house. To a life together. To the children. Tell him you've jumped there too.

But she didn't. She ate breakfast without tasting a single bite, and she asked him questions about what he'd be doing in New Hampshire, and she told him more about her Bosnian week. And she kept thinking about how beautiful he was, how much she loved looking at his face and listening to his voice.

****

You are a coward, Rose Gilhooly. You are a craven, idiotic coward. Tell him. Say it. Say something. Anything. Don't let him leave.

She watched him pull on his heavy jacket and wool hat and gloves. Watched him turn and smile. Watched the door close. And then she looked through the window and watched him hurry across the yard and she threw open the door and rushed headlong after him, her bare feet slipping in the snow and ice and wet mud.

"Jack! Wait!"

He half-turned toward her and she grabbed his hand between both of hers.

"Will you marry me?"

For an instant, he looked completely stupefied. Then he pulled his hand away and stuffed it into his jacket pocket.

"I was going to do that!"

She felt his hand again, this time wrapping her fingers around the little box he'd pulled from his pocket.

"Rose, will you marry me?"

"I asked first!"

"Yes. Yes, yes, yes. I will marry you. Now your turn."

Her "yes" came on a spurt of laughter, and their arms were pulling each other close, closer, tight, and they were both laughing and maybe a sob or two as well.

"Rose Gilhooly! Are you out of your ever-loving mind?" Rose looked over Jack's shoulder and there was Max, hands on her hips and a fierce scowl on her face. "Your feet are bleeding and you're soaking up toxic ice-melt chemicals through the cuts right into your bloodstream. Are you totally crazy?"

Jack pulled away. "God, Rose. You're barefoot." She gasped as he scooped her up in his arms. "Open the door, Max!"

He deposited her on the couch, dug a bandana out of his back pocket, wrapped it around both her feet, and headed for the bathroom.

"Huh." Rose stared at the blood seeping through the bandana. "I must have been sliced up a bit when I broke through the ice. I didn't even feel it."

Max muttered something about being crazy in love.

Ten minutes later, Jack had dried her feet and ankles with a towel, smeared on antibiotic cream and decorated her feet with five smiley-face band-aids given to her last summer by the migrant workers' kids. He took the little velvet box, opened it and slid the ring onto her finger, and all three of them got a bit weepy. Now she had a cup of hot tea in her hands, the quilt from the bed tucked around her shoulders, and Jack's warm body next to her on the couch. And a ring on her finger, a rosy gold ring with a tiny blue gem that he said was tourmaline.

And Max was grinning like a Cheshire cat from her perch on the arm of the stuffed chair. "So it was a mutual proposal."

"It was." Rose turned to look at Jack's dear face. "And mutual yes-es."

"Amen."

"Jack!" Rose sat bolt upright. "You're going to be

late. You've got to get going, now!"

"Jeezum. Frig. Shit." He was already at the door, buttoning his jacket. "It's gotta be bad form to propose, and say yes to a proposal, and turn and run away, all within the same half hour, but I do have to go. Max, thank you for coming out when you did and saving this woman from frostbite and gangrene and who knows what else. Rose, I'll call you as soon as I get to Keene. I love you!" And he slammed the door and ran.

No! She still hadn't told him! She had to tell him! But Max beat her to the door while Rose was still struggling to get out from under the quilt.

"Hey, Jack," Max bellowed. "Rose says she loves you too!"

They heard his deep laugh, and then the slam of his car door.

Chapter Ten

From House to Home

"Holy sh…!" Max caught herself with a chortle. "You weren't joking."

"Nope." Rose stopped the truck and gazed at the shabby-looking bungalow. "There it is. Our own little baby shit home."

"It's yours? Yours too, not just Jack's?"

"It's ours, Max. We closed on it together."

"Good." Max unfastened her seatbelt. "Here's Xavier. Let's get you moved in."

Moving Rose out of the tiny house in back of 112 Spring Street, and into the house on Reservoir Road, took less than three hours including travel time. Max helped pack her books, two posters and clothing. Xavier used a borrowed dolly to load the dresser and rocker into his van. The three of them weren't even breathing hard when it was all unloaded.

It was cold and empty in the new house. And dark, even after Rose switched on the overhead kitchen light. Almost no furniture, no lamps, no curtains on the windows, no plants, no bright colors to catch the eye and break the sense of dreariness. Rose stood in the empty kitchen and ached to have Jack beside her, enthusiastic, positive, sure they were doing the right thing.

"You're going to be happy here, Rose."

"I know it, Max." She blinked and gave a little head shake. "At least I'm fairly sure. But I've lived alone for many years, and I liked it. I'm already missing my private little nest in your backyard. And I'm already missing you."

"I am not going to get weepy." But Max's eyes were damp as she took a few steps closer so she could hug Rose. "I might sniffle a bit, though."

"Me too."

Xavier came through the door, took one look, and wrapped both women in his long arms, holding them tight and rocking from side to side the way he used to do whenever their son was scared or sad. Rose hated to end the hug. She felt warm and secure in their arms. But she drew a deep breath and untangled herself.

"I'm fine. Really. You two have to get back to your own lives, and I've got work to do."

Xavier looked around the empty house. "Interior decorating?"

Rose's laugh was wobbly. "Right. But no. I'm going to drive to Jack's apartment and join the rest of the moving crew. He wasn't able to pick up the rental van until noon, so it will be a rush if we want to get him out of there and into here before dark."

"The rest of the moving crew?"

"Jack's friend Derek, the two of us, and of course his parents."

"Will this be the first time you meet the Carmichaels?"

"It will. And you know, I think it'll be a good way to get to know them. Lifting and sweating and grunting. More natural than sitting around a table in some restaurant."

"Good thinking. Well—" Xavier and Max gave her one last hug and then they were gone.

****

Jack had described his colleague Derek well. The blond man was stout, somber, strong, and quiet. He said he considered bringing his new dog but decided the beast was still too puppyish. And then he said almost nothing else.

Jack had also described his father well. Tom Carmichael wasn't built like a wrestler like his son. He was more like a scarecrow, but he had Jack's open friendly face and mop of unruly red-brown hair.

But Jack had not mentioned that his mother looked like an actress or a dancer or a world-famous model, not like a Vermont storekeeper. Yes, Rose thought. An actress. Put a fur hat on Magda Carmichael and she would make a perfect Anna Karenina. Or whatsername from *War and Peace*. Dark braids wound around her head like a crown, and not even old jeans and a stained white turtleneck could diminish the overall effect of regal beauty.

"We are so happy to meet you, Rose." The voice was perfect too, warm, slow and a little husky. "We were looking forward to HarvestFest because Jack was going to bring you, but I understand that thousands of pies stole you away."

Rose laughed and returned the woman's quick hug. "Not quite thousands, Mrs. Carmichael. But definitely too many for my mother to tackle with only one hand."

"Well, you are here now and we are delighted. And I am Magda, not Mrs. Carmichael. And we have work to do!"

Moving Jack out of his apartment required five

people and four hours. There was a queen-sized bed with a headboard and baseboard and mattress and box springs. There were two dressers, a couch, a round oak table with a monstrously heavy base, four straight-back chairs, and Jack's beloved recliner. There were his college stereo and rack of CDs, two bookcases and two file cabinets, a work desk and swivel chair and desktop computer. There were boxes full of sheets and blankets and towels, and other boxes holding pots and pans and plates and mugs, and of course boxes and boxes of books and clothes. It was almost dark by the time they finished loading the rental van, and the intermittent drizzle had changed to steady sleet.

"Tomorrow then. First thing after breakfast. We'll leave the U-Haul here and stay with my folks tonight. You too, Derek. The roads are getting bad."

They were damp, cold and hungry when they trooped up the stairs to the Carmichaels' apartment above the store. Forty minutes later, they were warm and laughing, thawed by physical warmth, shared affection, a crockpot of split pea soup, homemade bread, and mugs of a spicy brew that Jack said was Magda's secret recipe for mulled Ukrainian wine.

"Not this time," his mother corrected. "This is a wine from Hungary. But it's still Slavic, so that is all right."

Now Rose could see Jack in his mother's wide cheekbones and beautiful brown eyes.

"You're Ukrainian?"

"No. I was born Magda Kollarova. A Czech and Russian name, from my Czech daddy and my white Russian mamma, from Belarus." She held up a ladle of soup to see if anyone wanted more. "I was the only

Magda in my Boston high school. After a week or so, I found four others who were neither recent arrivals from South America nor Italians from an earlier migration, and we five called ourselves CEOs." She paused, smiling at all the puzzled faces. "Central European Outcasts!"

"Magda was never an outcast," Jack put in. "She was elected homecoming queen! She was the most beautiful young woman in all of Boston."

"Enough," said his mother. "Now, Derek, we've got several all-weather sleeping bags and two heated camp pads for under you. Will you be all right downstairs, in the office?"

"Sure thing. Do you have an extra pillow?"

"You've got it. Jack, you and Rose will have your old room. All your posters will give your lovely sweetheart an insight into the boy you used to be." Magda looked from one to the other of them and dimpled. "The bed is quite narrow. You will have to snuggle."

****

"I like your parents very much, Jack."

"And they like you. But then, what's not to like? Both ways, them and you!"

"Oh!" Rose was staring down at her cell phone. "Lily and Geoff are in Montpelier! They want to meet you and see the new house, and they can help us move you in tomorrow morning!... Lily! How wonderful! How exciting! Where are you, not at the new house I hope!" She looked up and mouthed *motel*. "We put off hauling anything in until tomorrow, because of the weather. We're at Jack's parents' place. We'll meet you at the house tomorrow—Jack, when should we say?... He says we'll have breakfast here, and we'll be at the house by nine at the latest. I am so excited that you'll be there! Oh, before you go! Remember! If you love me as a sister, there is one thing you must do. You MUST overlook the color. Do not notice it. Do not even see it!" She laughed, what Jack called her delight snort. "That's good then! We'll see you tomorrow."

She put her phone back in her pocket. "This is wonderful! You and your parents will get to meet my very favorite sister and my very favorite brother-in-law. The fact that they're my only, of both, is irrelevant."

Jack was looking at his phone too. "It's going to be quite a crowd."

"Oh?"

"Tomorrow's a regular Sunday bird walk."

"But you won't be there."

"Nope. But they will!" He looked up with a broad smile. "Some of them anyway. They'll be at the new house after their walk, and they'll be carrying food. Our home, some of our relatives, some of our friends, and a catered lunch!" He pulled off his still-damp sweatshirt and then looked at her with an odd expression in his brown eyes. "Tonight will feel strange, Rose. My parents met Samantha, of course. And I introduced them to my dancer girlfriend. But I have never slept under their roof with a woman. Not once."

"Then it's about time." She moved closer and wound her arms around his neck. "I like being here, Jack. I'm not at all surprised by your Star Wars posters, or the view of Earth from outer space. However, I am a bit bemused by your choice of rock bands. Some of these were ancient when you were a teenager."

"Ancient but still rocking." He nodded at one of the posters. "I picked up one of their LPs at a church rummage sale and listened to it until the whole thing was pale gray. One song used to give me chills. I was sure it was about old people in nursing homes and, at the tender age of fifteen or so, I was sure that was going to happen to Tom and Magda. Not eventually. At any minute. And it was waiting for me too, inevitably. I was going to end up locked in some place with nothing but images of sorrow and long nights of gloom, or whatever the words are." He shuddered, and Rose hugged him tighter. "Enough of that! You want the first shower?"

"I need one. But I didn't bring anything with me."

Jack plucked a green canvas bag off a dresser. "In here. Soap, shampoo, toothpaste. You can use my toothbrush if you want. There are towels in the cabinet just outside the bathroom door. And here—Aha! I thought so." He pulled open the bottom drawer and tossed her a faded sweatshirt.

"You are always prepared, my love."

"I try."

****

While Jack was showering, Rose washed her underpants and hung them on the radiator and then slid under the covers. Waiting. She wanted him next to her in this narrow bed. She wanted to feel his tight hard body. She wanted to run her toes along his furry legs. She watched through half-closed eyes as he opened the door and smiled at her and took off his towel and walked over to the bed.

"We're going to have to be quiet."

"Yes."

"I don't know if I can."

"Let's try."

He climbed in next to her and she wiggled around to

make room.

"We could wait until tomorrow. When we're in our own house, where we could yell and moan and screech all we want."

"If that's what you'd prefer." She could feel him swelling against her. "But it would be hard, Jack."

"It *is* hard, Rose. Maybe…"

Then he was on top of her and she opened her legs and he slid in so wonderfully and they both gasped and breathed more quickly and gasped again, but they didn't moan.

****

"Jack's birding friends must have figured we had a moving crew of dozens. Look at all these leftovers!"

"I liked those people."

"Me too."

Lily moved her coffee mug out of the way and peered at the food Rose was wrapping. "Is there another hummus and veggie sandwich? I'm still hungry. I'm always hungry."

"Me too. I shudder to think what the Gilhooly sisters will be like when we're pregnant." Rose turned and looked closely at her sister. "You're not, are you?"

"I don't think so. But it wouldn't be a surprise. I'm sure you and Jack will discover this, that living as lovers goes in cycles. Phases. There will be times when you just don't feel like being intimate, when you want privacy and space and the freedom of your own thoughts and your own body." She grinned, looking as lively and mischievous as she used to when she was in her teens and enjoyed teasing her younger sister. "And there will be times when the two of you hump like bunnies all over the house, all day every day, and you simply can't get enough of each other's bodies. This last week has been one of those phases for Geoff and me."

"I thought, until I met Jack," Rose handed her a sandwich, "that I would never feel what you feel for Geoff. I used to envy you so much!"

"And now you feel the same way. I can see it when you and Jack look at each other. And—" She looked up as Magda came back into the kitchen. "And I see it when Magda and Tom look at each other."

"You see *it*, do you?" The older woman raised one eyebrow. "*It* is evident between us?"

"It is indeed. We are three very lucky women."

"So, Rose." Magda sat down and folded her hands in front of her. "You and Jack are still planning on a wedding only three months from yesterday? At your family farm?"

"We are indeed."

"Family only?"

"Absolutely," she said. "Just you and Tom, Lily and Geoff, Mom and Dad, and my brother Finn and his girlfriend. And a Justice of the Peace."

"That will be similar to my wedding. Six people, two dogs, and a Wicca priestess who had a license to perform marriages. You have no desire for a big show?"

Rose pulled out a chair. "Magda, I almost got married once before. Years ago. And I saw—Lily, you saw it, too—what a big wedding is like. It becomes all about *things*. The flowers for the church, the flowers for the reception, the bride's bouquet, the boutonniere for groom's lapel. The exact tone of ivory for the invitations. The right *font* for the invitations, because apparently the marriage is doomed if the wrong *font* gets used. And the dresses, oh god the dresses. And the tuxedos. And the hair and the nails. The perfect shade for the bridesmaids' *shoes*, for Pete's sake. The anxiety mounts and mounts and mounts. Every single THING has to be perfect. The poor groom is almost forgotten, and the poor bride feels harassed every single minute of every day, for months! No. Jack and I want our wedding, our vows, our commitment to each other, to be about us two and our families."

Lily reached out and took both of her sister's hands. "You will be surrounded with love and affection and shared memories, Rose. And not a dry eye among us."

"That is so. That is indubitably so." Magda's eyes looked suspiciously damp already, and she looked around for a change of subject. "We are all behaving in a disgustingly stereotypical manner. The women in the kitchen, taking about weddings, and the men outdoors."

Rose looked out the window. "They've been doing that man thing, where they stand around not looking at each other, all staring in the same direction, and occasionally holding their chins in their hands. Speaking about one word per hour."

"What have they been staring at? There isn't a car out there that won't start, or a half-built firepit, or—"

The door was pushed open and Jack came in on a blast of cold air.

"Rose, my sweet woman. We are fortunate beyond words to have an architect in the family and another architect in the birding group. I mentioned to Geoff that we're thinking about adding on to the house someday, and he and Hugh from the bird group got to work with tape measures and notepads, and now Geoff and my father are out there planning a one-story addition with two bedrooms and a back porch." He wrapped her in a quick frosty hug. "If you and I decide to continue with Hugh, he thinks he can schedule the whole thing late this summer or maybe in the fall. He's going to send an estimate. But, of course, we're free to consult other architects and builders."

"It would be good to work with someone we know. Or at least someone *you* know."

"It would. It would. If Hugh can fit us in that quickly, we won't bother to get the back painted at all." He turned to his mother. "The crew that Derek suggested will be here in five weeks, with drop cloths and ladders and scrapers and brushes, and they will erase every memory of baby diarrhea and acid green."

"All up and down the street there will be sighs of relief."

"Probably so." Jack reached across the table to take Rose's hand. "Tom suggested, while we've got men here doing the addition, we should also get the half bath downstairs enlarged and made into a full bath. And he thinks we should make the new downstairs bedroom ours, with a nursery next to it—"

"Oh!"

"No, Magda. Not yet."

"Fooey."

"And my dad also suggested that if the upstairs rooms are mostly offices for the two of us plus room for overnight guests, then we could close it off during the coldest parts of the winter and save on heat, if we want."

"That sounds good, my love. The Carmichael family is always thinking."

"We aim to please."

Chapter Eleven

Married

"This is only the third dress I've ever bought." Rose removed the long plastic bag covering an apricot-colored garment. "Can you believe that, Lily? And Mom helped me shop for the non-wedding dress, so I guess this is the *second* I ever bought, truly." She pulled the dress on and smoothed the soft fabric over her hips. "I wanted something I could wash, and I wanted long sleeves because it's still chilly in early May in upstate New York. I wasn't looking for ankle-length, but I can always shorten it."

"Or you could leave it long, and you and Jack can become famous throughout central Vermont for elegant black-tie soirees at Chez Carmichael."

Rose gave a little snort. "Picnic table and scruffy denims are more our style." She moved to look at herself in the full-length mirror behind the closet door. "I feel like one of those women in olden days, the ones with the keys to the manor on humongous metal rings hanging from their belts."

"Chatelaines."

"Right! Chatelaines! I am the chatelaine of the manor!" Rose gave a little twirl, laughing from sheer happiness. "I thought this might be too plain. Same color, top to bottom. No pattern or design. The saleswoman kept saying it 'cries out for accessorizing', and then Max came up with the perfect accessory! Hand me that corset thingy, will you?"

Lily picked a blue velvet garment off the bed. "It's not a corset, Rose, even though it does have laces in front. It's sort of a vest. And these embroidered flowers are the exact apricot color of your dress."

"It looks like a flower garden, doesn't it? Max made it ages ago for a costume party at Xavier's school. The two of them went as Herr and Frau von Trapp. This was attached to one of those short puffy skirts Alpine women wear, whilst their men are out cavorting about the Alps in lederhosen."

"And yodeling."

"But of course!"

Rose pulled the vest on and tugged it into place. "One of the students spilled something icky on the skirt and Max couldn't get the stain out so she cut off the top and put it away for some other occasion." She turned with a radiant smile. "And our wedding is that occasion! Will you tighten me up?"

"Hoist your boobs."

"What?"

"If I tighten this now, it'll just squish you. But if the vest goes under your breasts, it'll lift them up. Like a…" Lily pursed her lips to exaggerate the word. "A boo-stee-yay. Hasn't that always been a secret dream of yours? To wear a booos-teee-yay?"

"Not even for one moment."

"Try it anyway… Yes. That is just perfect!"

"Wow. I've never had this much cleavage." She turned from side to side in front of the mirror. "I think I like it."

****

"Is the bride almost ready?"

"She'll be down in a minute, Jack." Lily looked him up and down and nodded. "Old Vermont chic. Very nice."

The groom was wearing tight new black jeans, a white long-sleeved shirt open at the neck, and wide suspenders in navy blue embroidered with tiny flowers of coral and pale green.

"You like the old-fashioned braces? They're from Max. She said they match something she gave Rose."

"Her boo-stee-ay."

His eyebrows shot up. "Rose is wearing a bustier?"

"She is indeed. And she looks—"

They both turned as the bride came down the stairs. "Wow."

"You look wow too, my love. Where did you—Oh! That's why Max was acting so mysterious!"

"She made us match." He put his hands on her shoulders. "Wow again."

"You're making me self-conscious, Jack." Rose looked down the hall toward the living room. "Has the Justice of the Peace arrived?"

"A scary-looking stranger came in a few minutes ago."

She tightened her fingers around his. "Then let's go get married, my love."

Her parents sat side by side on the couch, holding hands as they had during the non-wedding so many years ago. Magda was in the big old rocking chair, with Tom cross-legged on the floor in front of her and leaning back against her knees. Lily and Geoff shared the only upholstered chair in the room, the chair where young

Rose spent so many hours reading and weeping over fat romantic novels, her head on one padded arm, her legs slung over the other. Finn was standing by the door, cell phone in hand. His long-time girlfriend, a veterinarian, had an emergency call so he was making a video to share with her later.

Rose and Jack walked a few steps into the room and stopped in front of a tall stern-faced woman with a mane of silvery hair.

"It's good to see you again, Mrs. Nutting."

"If memory serves, the last time was in church, with the whole Whittaker clan glaring from the front pews." The woman took one of Rose's hands between hers. "I am truly delighted to see you with the right fella this time." She gave Jack a quick and comprehensive up-and-down. "I like his looks, Rose. And I like what I've heard about him from your family." She briefly touched a finger to Rose's cheek. "And I like the way he makes you look. Let's get this show on the road."

Rose had promised herself that she would at least get through her vows before getting weepy, but she could feel her nose starting to tickle already.

"This is absolutely perfect," she started. "Being here in this room where I grew up, with Jack here with me. Seeing all of you sitting in a comfy living room instead of lined up on hard benches. Being in a home, not an impersonal public meeting space. We are going to—"

She looked helplessly at Jack, and he took over.

"Rose and I will say our vows, and then we will yield the floor to the distinguished justice of the peace. After that, we will chow down on the feast our families have prepared for us, the feast we've been smelling all afternoon. And after *that*, we'll go outdoors for a gigantoid bonfire with various entertainments."

Rose raised her eyebrows. "Entertainments?"

"Your sister and her husband have something planned."

Geoff leaned forward around his wife. "Lily and I, with help from both sets of parents, have put together a slide show, a montage of photos from Jack's childhood and Rose's childhood. We expect a constant stream of *ahhh* and *cute*."

Jack had an unwelcome recollection of a bathtub shot when he was four or so. The overly innocent expressions on his parents' faces guaranteed that the photo would be featured.

"And Tom and Magda have prepared one or two poems. And I think Finn and his sweetheart have practiced a couple of love songs for fiddle and voice."

"If Celia doesn't get back in time, it'll be *one* love song, very brief, for fiddle only."

"And your dad and mom have promised an even half dozen stories from when you were growing up, Rose. Stories they promise will range from adorable to downright startling."

Rose groaned, but she dimpled at her parents.

"Thank you all. Now." She lifted her chin, straightened her shoulders, and swallowed hard. "Jack. I know many examples of lasting love. Mom and Dad. Lily and Geoff. Now Tom and Magda. Our friends Max and Xavier. And many others. But I had begun to believe that lasting love might not be part of my own life, my personal life. I wasn't really unhappy about that. It was just a fact. And I had a full life anyway. I had dear friends. I loved where I lived. I have a job that's always fascinating and rewarding, and often just plain fun. I thought my life was full. Until…"

She took a deep breath.

"Until the day I met you, Jack. After that first meal, in that crowded little diner, I couldn't stop seeing your smile. Your warm brown eyes. I kept hearing your laughter at the oddest times, all day long. And after our second meal together, I knew how much you care about other people and about our environment and about birds and nature, and I wanted to gush about you to everyone I knew, like a teenager with a crush on a rock star. And then, after that muddy geocaching adventure—" She made her blue eyes very big. "After that, Jack, my thoughts were full of tight buns and strong thighs."

Even the somber-looking JP cracked a smile.

"My life, that had seemed so full before, was suddenly bursting with new thoughts and images. My full life kept growing, kept getting fuller, every time we saw each other. Every conversation. Every shared meal." She reached up and touched his mouth. "Every kiss. To be standing here beside you, Jack, and knowing that we are being married—Drat. I meant to tuck a tissue into my sleeve."

Jack let go of her hands, reached into his back pocket, and pulled out a bright turquoise bandana.

"Thank you, my love." She dabbed her eyes and gave him a glowing, teary smile. "So. My vows. I know, Jack, that marriages change over time. The constant shimmery excitement I have felt for the past year might diminish. But I truly believe it will mellow into something equally wonderful and even stronger. You and I are smart enough and love each other enough to make sure that happens." Her fingers tightened. "Jack, you are the best friend I've ever had. You are my partner in everyday life and my partner in adventures. You are my lover and my mate. I trust you. I like you. I delight in you. I will continue to be your helpmate and your cheerleader. I will hug you when you need a hug, and when I need a hug, and for no reason at all. I will laugh with you and cry with you. I will cherish you. That I promise."

Jack used the bandana to wipe her wet cheeks and then his own.

"My turn. Rose. You mentioned that first day, when we met at Hunt's farm. That day, our very first day, I looked at you sitting across from me in that diner booth, and I heard you laugh, and I wanted—Right then, Rose, I wanted to look at you and hear your voice and your laugh for the entire rest of forever. And right now—Right now I am stunned by the realization that I can do just that. Hear your voice, hear your laugh, look at your tousled red-brown curls, look into your smiling blue eyes, kiss your rosy mouth, listen to your thoughts and worries, and your humor and your caring, hear stories about your work and your childhood and your family, touch and caress and love you. Every day."

He looked briefly at the ceiling, needing a few seconds to pull himself together, and then back down at her wet and smiling face.

"Before we started living together, Rose, I would get home from work and immediately go to work again, getting everything from the day organized in my mind and entered into computer files. I often worked from sun-up 'til dark and then more hours after that. But these last few months, I have felt excited on the drive home. Work, and work worries, just slough off my back. Because you are in the house, or you will be soon. Because I know we'll talk about our days. We'll laugh, or see each other angry or upset and feel angry and upset too. And then we'll fix supper and eat and sit together out on the porch or in the living room, touching, listening, thinking about each other."

Jack's uninhibited nose-blowing made everyone smile.

"When I was growing up, Tom and Magda always kicked me out of the kitchen a half hour before supper, and they would sit down on opposite sides of the table, their hands around mugs of tea or sometimes glasses of ale or wine, and they would spend those thirty minutes by themselves. Just the two of them. It was a mini-date, and it happened every single day. I learned early on not to disturb them unless blood was gushing from an artery. Or an arm or leg was dangling at an impossible angle. That was *their* time." He looked from his parents to the couple on the couch, his brown eyes twinkling. "And your parents, Rose. They take off in the middle of the afternoon and head for their private skinny-dipping spot. Just the two of them."

More laughter.

"Habits like those keep marriages strong and growing. I agree with you, Rose. We are smart enough and we love each other enough to develop something for us, for us alone. So here is my vow, Rose. I will talk with you, and plan with you, and think with you, and we will have time each day that is ours. Just ours. Time to reconnect and be those two solitary people who met and saw in each other something unbelievably special, something we wanted in our lives. Forever."

"Amen." That was Rose's father.

"Verily." Jack's father.

"My turn." The Justice of the Peace.

****

Jack opened his eyes.

"Where are we?"

"We're in Vermont. The Champlain Bridge fishing access, with the handy port-o-let."

"Ahh." The sun on the wide lake was much too bright so he closed his eyes again. "You go and then I will."

When she emerged, rubbing alcohol gel into her hands, her husband was standing on the shore, his back to her, one hand up and shading his eyes. She stood still, savoring him, how he looked in the black jeans he bought for their wedding and his favorite cotton shirt that once was gold and had faded to tan.

She wanted a photo, but her cell phone was in the truck. A mental picture then. Black and tan against the blue lake and white clouds, against the dark evergreens and early green leaves of May. Jack's beautiful long torso. The tight butt and thighs that flexed hundreds of times last night, driving in and out, over and over until they were both shaking and sweaty and sated. And then starting all over.

Her husband. Rose had the sudden thought that she wouldn't have to walk over to him, that she could glide effortlessly over grass and gravel like a magnet being pulled toward its mate.

"What do you see?"

Jack turned, grinning. "There was a pair of Wood Ducks on this side of the water but they flew over to the New York side when I got close. I swear Wood Ducks are more skittish than any other species." He stroked the side of her face with his fingers. "I was wondering what it feels like for ducks, once they are paired off for the breeding season. Do they feel lost, or like something is wrong, when their mate isn't close by? And geese. They mate for life. That's got to be a powerful bond. When they're flying in a huge vee, do they always know where the other one is?"

"I can only judge by us, my love. As I was standing over by the port-o-let, I had an image of the two of us as magnets, quivering and needy—" She cleared her throat. "Until we were pressed tight and everything was where it's supposed to be."

He looked over her shoulder at the car coming down the hill.

"I would love to kiss you, Rose, and keep kissing you until we fall to our knees right here and roll around on the gravel and—" His brown eyes were filled with want and laughter. "And put everything where it's supposed to be. But I think we would distract the fisherfolk."

The trio getting out of the car were laden with poles, tackle boxes, nets, folding stools, and creels.

"Probably." She took his hand and they walked toward her truck. "Are you up to driving the rest of the way home?"

"Sure. I fell asleep before we were even out of your folks' driveway. It's your turn to get some rest. Are you exhausted today? Or sore?"

"Jack, my love, my husband. My extremely studly new husband." She paused getting into the truck, looking at him over the roof. "My entire body knows that I have experienced hours and hours of sensual rapture. Emotional rapture too. I am neither sore nor exhausted, just happy. But I have a serious question for you, Mr.

Carmichael." She lowered her voice. "Did you take something yesterday?"

"Take?"

"You were hard for an implausibly long time. And implausibly frequently."

"No pharmaceuticals needed, Mrs. Carmichael. I had you."

"And I had you. Repeatedly." She got into the passenger seat and looked over at him. "Last night was unique. I think it was partly because it's real now, we're really married. And partly because we don't have to avoid getting pregnant. You and I have morphed from lovers to potential parents. That knowledge is solemn."

"And thrilling."

"Thrillingly solemn." She twisted to fasten her seatbelt. "Realistically, though, it'll probably be a while before we start a little one. I went off the pill two weeks ago, and the estimate I read was between three and twelve *months* before possible pregnancy."

"We'll work on it every single day."

"Twice on Sundays."

Jack guided the truck up the steep driveway.

"We had a perfect wedding, Rose."

"We did. It was a feast for the emotions. Exactly what we hoped. A blend of your family and mine." She opened her window and let the wind tousle her curls.

"Not one of us Carmichaels expected a real witch to officiate."

"Ms. Nutting is a garden variety Justice of the Peace! And my parents' closest neighbor."

"Garden variety, my eye. Any garden tended by that woman would grow, I don't know, poison nightshade. Belladonna. Eye of newt and toe of frog." He glanced at her out of the corner of his eye. "I'm telling you, Rose. I took a walk around outdoors while you were getting dressed and I saw a hefty broomstick hiding behind that big lilac. I spent much of the afternoon expecting Tom, Magda, and the witch to start dancing around and chanting pagan incantations, alienating your family forever."

"Not possible. They all see how happy you make me. You and yours can do no wrong, not even if one of you suddenly threw in some Wicca reference. Which you didn't. Your dad's poem about the end of cold winter and the beginning of growing and warmth was perfect."

"It was. I was so proud of him I almost burst."

"Not one of us Gilhoolys knew that May first is the Feast of Beltane, Gaelic May Day. It's a lovely thing to remember every year on our anniversary."

"Was the yurt-slash-honeymoon-suite your brother's idea?"

"It was his doing, but he was joking when he said it was his wedding gift to us. The farm's been getting by for years with family plus high school and college kids during the summer. But with the orchard expansion and the CSA and the chickens and all, they need more help. Finn was deputized to look for one or two farmhands and come up with a place for them to stay."

"Hence the yurt."

"After three months looking for a used trailer, he saw an ad for a Mongolian yurt kit that some guy bought but never even set up." She did her little gasp-snort-laugh. "Finn said the guy loves toys. Three fast boats in the backyard along with kayaks, paddle boards, and a canoe. Road bikes and mountain bikes and motocross bikes. A whole wall of skis and snowshoes. Indoor exercise equipment up the wazoo. A gigantic plasma TV and every kitchen gadget ever invented. The yurt was one more fun toy. But the guy opened the box, read the set-up instructions, decided it didn't sound like fun anymore, and closed the box again. The kit cost less than the trailers Finn had been looking at, and he and some of his friends made it winter-worthy for a few thousand more." She caressed his jaw and the side of his neck. "The new farm hands, a married couple, can't move in for two more weeks so Finn decided the yurt would be a perfect honeymoon suite."

"It was. We would have relished our wedding night even if we'd been upstairs in your old room, but it wouldn't have been as, as—"

"Uninhibited?"

He didn't take his eyes off the road, but his slow remembering smile made her breasts tighten.

"Uninhibited. Yes. Wild. Extraordinary."

"Athletic."

"Olympic athletic."

"Sensational. Oh! That could have two meanings. Awesome and also sense-ational."

"All five of them." Jack's voice was deeper than usual, and raspier. "All five senses."

"I just had a flashback of you, standing there in that yurt, hooking your thumbs under those beautiful suspenders, and slowly pulling them down off your arms. And me stepping closer and unfastening your—"

"Whoa! Was that a hawk?" He glanced at her out of the corners of his eyes. "Rose, I need you not to be talking about my pants and your fingers while I am driving."

"Oh, all right. But that *is* a very good memory."

"Later. When we're home."

"Was there really a hawk?"

"I have no idea. I was focusing on your fingers. You know, my love, saying we didn't want any gifts resulted in some incredible gifts."

Rose giggled. "It did, didn't it? I can hardly wait to see the photo albums from Lily and Geoff and their brand-new camera."

"Albums? Plural?"

"One digital and one hard-cover."

"Oh."

"And our own mini-orchard from Finn."

"I think I was in the house peeing when he mentioned that. What's a mini-orchard?"

"He's planning to come visit us in two weeks when Celia has a few days off, and they're bringing five different kinds of apples."

"Shit, Rose. I don't think we have room for that many trees, not where there's sun."

"No worries, my love. My incredibly smart brother has been learning how to graft fruit trees. He's going to give us only one trunk, the rootstock, with different kinds of apples grafted on to it. Northern Spy, MacIntosh, Cortland, Wolf River, and one other. He promised to label them for us."

"Wolf River. That's a new one on me."

"It's an heirloom variety, and huge. An orchard in the St. Lawrence Valley used to advertise *one fruit, one pie*." She grinned. "And now I know how to make a pie crust that's better than cardboard."

She twisted around to look at the huge blue cooler in the back of the truck.

"But that's the most extraordinary gift. The

humongous ice chest packed to the top with food from your parents and my parents. There's enough frozen food to last us for months, plus oodles of leftovers from yesterday's feast that we can put out and share for tomorrow's feast. Everyone from your office is coming, right?"

"Every one, plus the brand-new secretary guy."

"And Connie, Eileen, and Curt from VMEP. And some of the birding group. And Max and Xavier, of course. Plus I think most of our neighbors will stop over."

"Should we say our vows again? Or just eat and celebrate?"

"I think it'll be too informal for vows, with people coming and going." She eyed him. "But we could do some public kissing. And we can flash our new rings."

****

"Look, Jack! Everything is budded! While we were getting ready to leave for New York, I wondered if spring would ever come. It came while we were gone!"

Rose leaned forward as far as the seat belt allowed, needing to get closer to the tiny new leaves on the lilacs, the coltsfoot blooming alongside the road, the dogwood all in white. "I was eager to get home, of course. But I was also reluctant to leave my folk's place because they already have tulips and crocuses, and Vermont had snow. Heavy snow the last day of April!"

"I do believe, Mrs. Carmichael, that spring waited until we returned."

"I do believe that is the case, Mr. Carmichael. Hmmm. It doesn't appear that any elves or pixies came while we were gone, and painted the house."

Rose thought the ugly little bungalow looked lonely,

sitting in its big lot, left alone for five long days while its owners were in another state getting married.

"Soon, my love. Then the crew Derek found will make all the diarrhea and neon green disappear."

"And you and I will paint the porch and railing and window boxes, and we will feel like true homeowners."

"We will."

"They're going to leave the back unpainted, right?"

"The builders think they can fit us in this summer. But if not, it'll be early fall for sure. A new bedroom for us, with our own private little porch. A bigger bathroom downstairs. And a new bedroom for little Carmichael, whenever he or she chooses to appear."

"But for now, our own honeymoon house."

"You're still okay with six days here instead of six days in Barbados, or Cancun, or Paris, or some other exotic destination?"

"Six days and six *nights*, Jack. Do not forget the nights. I believe we will make better use of those days and those nights here, in our own home, instead of wasting a big chunk of that precious time in crowded airports and stuffy planes."

"You, Mrs. Carmichael, are a gem."

Chapter Twelve

The Announcement

Rose sat shivering on the hard plastic chair, trying to pay attention as a doctor with a mop of gray hair and deep circles under her eyes explained early miscarriage.

"It happens during the first trimester, Rose, most often within nine or ten weeks after conception. Early miscarriages are common. An egg and a sperm connect but there's something so badly out of whack that development stops before a true fetus is formed."

She wanted Jack. He would be better able to concentrate. He'd ask all the questions she couldn't think of and he would even take notes.

"What happens next? Today, I mean."

"You stay here for another hour or so. At that time, based on how things are going, you might go home and wait for the bleeding to stop. Or you might decide to take some prescription medication that will speed things up. Or you could stay here for an additional hour and have what's called suction aspiration, during which any leftover material gets removed and your uterus gets washed out with a cleansing solution. You don't have to make a decision right now. Rest a bit more." The doctor looked closely at Rose's face. "You need some sugar and you need to hydrate. I'll have a nurse bring orange juice and ginger ale and you should drink both in the next half hour. I'll have her bring you another heated blanket too."

"Thank you."

It was very quiet in the emergency ward. Rose sat with two blankets wrapped around her bare legs, sipping ginger ale and trying to decide if she should call Jack now or wait. She wanted him here. She wanted him to hold her and share her sorrow. But she didn't want him to drive all the way to Brattleboro. She should wait until she got closer to home.

But she wanted so much to see his face.

An outburst of noise at the end of the corridor was an almost welcome distraction. She heard a woman's voice, loud, agitated, panicky, the words indistinguishable. At least two other female voices, soothing and professional. And a man's deep groans.

As the noise got nearer, Rose realized with a jolt that the crying woman was speaking in one of the Bosnian dialects. Not Shtokavian, which she knew. Maybe Croatian. Or Ekavian. Many words were the same, but not all, and the accent was quite different. The Bosnian woman was repeating the same few words over and over, trying desperately to get someone to understand her. Bad, and blood, and hitting. And another word that Rose thought she might have heard during the immersion week but couldn't remember.

The noise level increased, the man groaning more loudly and the woman now sobbing.

Rose put both hands on the chair arms and heaved herself into a standing position. She still was wearing her neat blouse and cardigan, professional garb for that morning's conference, but below the waist she had on nothing but socks, her new running shoes, and a pair of pull-ups like those advertised for incontinent seniors.

She hadn't dripped any blood on her shoes, and that was good, but she could not walk out there in a diaper. She wrapped one of the hospital blankets around her waist, pushed aside the curtain and slowly, slowly walked out into the corridor.

The last emergency bay was crowded, with two people in white coats, a uniformed state trooper, an orderly who was wringing his hands as if he wanted to help but had no idea how, the agitated Bosnian woman, and a man lying on a gurney, curled in a fetal position, his whole body shaking. No one looked up until Rose cleared her throat.

"She says her husband was punched. Hit. In his belly."

Both white coats looked toward Rose as if she'd materialized from thin air, and the woman grabbed her arm and repeated much of what Rose had heard minutes earlier.

"She says there were two, um, bad people. Bad men. Boys. Maybe teenagers. Two young men, she says. And her husband had, um, I think she said surgery or an operation." Rose looked into the woman's eyes and asked a question. "Yes. Surgery. Just a week ago." The woman stabbed at her right side, just below the waist, and there was another spate of the foreign language. "The surgery was there, on her husband's right side. She is afraid the bad boys, um, broke him, broke her husband, where he had the operation. She is afraid he is bleeding inside of him."

"Ask her if he has taken any medication today. Or drugs. Of any kind."

"No. She says no drugs."

"Did he have an allergic reaction to the medications

they gave him for surgery?"

"No. No problems. Everything was good."

The white coats were all business now. "Blood pressure low and dropping." The young nurse looked at Rose. "Tell her husband we can give him something for pain, now that we know he's not on illegal drugs and isn't allergic." She cleansed a place on his arm and competently slid in a needle. "Then we'll be taking him to an operating room. Maybe you can stay here with her and help her give information to the trooper."

It took only a few seconds for the injured man's face to begin relaxing, and the nurses were able to help him lie flat on the gurney.

"Tell her we'll send someone for her in a very little while and bring her to the waiting room closer to surgery."

"She says thank you, thank you. She says you must save him. He is her life. He is her love." The woman said something more, but Rose was trying to stifle a sob and didn't catch it. They both watched as the husband was wheeled out. Then Rose turned to the trooper.

"My friend. The woman who brought me in. She's out there waiting. We were on our way—" Rose took a deep breath. There was no reason to explain why she and Connie were in Brattleboro Hospital. The young trooper didn't need to know that they had been at a conference in Boston and were on their way home when Rose started having cramps and bleeding. "She speaks more of the Bosnian dialects than I do. She would be a big help here."

Rose could have left after Connie came bustling in, but she didn't feel like returning to the too chilly and too quiet area down the hall. She sat huddled, wrapping both arms around her, and listened to the three-way interview, impressed anew at her colleague's skill and patience, and by the professional questioning from the policewoman who had looked out of her depth just a few minutes before. The Bosnian woman, still agitated but now noticeably calmer, said she and her husband returned from grocery shopping to the small house they bought a few weeks ago. The trooper looked down at a notepad, asked her to repeat the address, and then said that the house had been derelict for many months and was suspected as a drug house.

Yes, yes, yes, the Bosnian woman said. The house was filthy, disgusting, a barn, a… The next word had Connie baffled until the woman gave a realistic oink. Oh, yes. The house was a pigsty. She and her friends cleaned and cleaned and cleaned. Her husband put new locks on the doors and he put bars on some of the windows but he promised he would take the bars off later, once they felt safe. He told her he saw the same two cars go by many times and he was afraid of the people in the cars. He told her she must never be alone in the house. Their friends set up a schedule so there would always be at least one person with her. And there *was* a person with her, her husband was with her, when they got back from the grocery store, but it wasn't any good because they were carrying heavy bags when the car stopped and the two bad men got out and they said they wanted the stuff and they knew the stuff was inside. Her husband told them to leave. He said there was nothing inside. He said everything in the house was theirs and it was all clean and there were no drugs. But one of the evil boys got close to her husband and said what's in the bag and shoved her husband against the house and her husband couldn't push back because his arms were full and he told her to call 911 and she was starting to do it but the other man grabbed her and her husband dropped the bags and that's when one of them punched him. Hard punch. In his belly. And she pushed and kicked at the other man and screamed and screamed and the two bad boys got in the car and she finished calling 911.

"Boys?" asked the trooper. "They were young? Can you describe them? Or the car?"

Just then there was a loud rattling noise. The doctor Rose had seen earlier pushed open the curtain and barked, "You! Get up! This very minute!"

Rose had to grin when the young trooper came to her rescue, explaining how vitally helpful it had been to the medical personnel to have Rose as an interpreter.

"That is all very well and good. But this woman is a patient also." She held out her arm to help Rose up. "*My* patient. And she is coming with me now!"

****

Rose was ready to leave two hours later. She and the doctor agreed on a suction aspiration, which took less than a half hour. Rose rested horizontally for a while and then was allowed to put on a ridiculously huge pair of purple fleece snow pants from the winter survival bag that Connie always kept in the back of her car.

"Good look for you," the doctor murmured.

"I think so too."

"You might want to give yourself tomorrow to rest up, Rose. Sit around or lie around. Read, watch TV, doze. You can get up to fix yourself some food, etc., but basically give your body a chance to recuperate. And talk with your husband. He'll be upset too. After tomorrow, you can do pretty much anything you'd normally do, but hold off on sex for a few more days."

"I'm supposed to teach two first aid classes the day after tomorrow. Will that be all right?"

The doctor smiled, her first smile since Rose met her. "First aid, huh? No wonder you were so together when you came in."

"I was NOT together. I was scared stiff."

"You covered well." The doctor stood up. "You were an ideal patient, Rose. Except for the unauthorized jaunt down the hall. My colleagues are very grateful, by the way."

"It was lucky the woman wasn't speaking some language other than Spanish or Bosnian. Even French would have had me stumped."

"Maybe we'll see each other again, Rose. In *your* professional capacity next time, rather than mine. We call for interpreters fairly often."

Rose smiled. "I would like to see you again, Dr. Belinson."

"And don't forget. Even if you have another miscarriage, that's no reason to despair. Having one or even a few early miscarriages is upsetting, no question about it, but it doesn't mean you can't carry a healthy child to term in the future."

"Thank you. Again."

"Well." Their handshake was warm and heartfelt.

****

Rose didn't see Dr. Belinson for the second miscarriage. She was at home, and she went to her own doctor. This time she had been pretty sure she was pregnant because her period was over a month late. She knew Jack was sure, too, but neither of them said anything about it. They both tiptoed around the possibility as if mentioning it might jinx them.

This time, Jack was with her, beside her, from the moment she woke up and saw blood on the sheets. It was Jack who called the doctor, who bundled her up in more clothes than she needed, who drove so carefully, who held her hands and talked to her in his beautiful warm voice. It was Jack who teared up when she did, who asked questions and listened carefully to the doctor's responses. And this time, when they got home, it was Jack who sat with her on the couch while they both cried.

After a long time, Jack cleared his throat and wiped his face.

"Maybe it's something specific, between our two chemistries. Maybe we should try a fertility clinic. We might find out specific things we should be doing. Derek's wife had a few miscarriages and then they found out they should be making love six to eight days after her period instead of waiting 'til later like they thought they should be doing. Something about an atypical menstrual pattern."

Rose's little noise was part laugh, part snort, part tear-filled gulp. "That's what you guys do at the office? You sit around and talk about atypical menstrual patterns?"

He didn't smile. "Our wives and families are important to us. We talk about them."

"Oh. Yes."

"My point is that now Derek and his wife are expecting their first baby any day."

"Oh."

Rose sat hunched over, occasionally shivering. Her voice was so soft that Jack leaned closer to hear her. "One of my sister's friends went to a fertility clinic. She told Lily and me about months and months of taking her basal temperature every day, sometimes twice a day, and calling her husband at work to tell him he should come home and, and fuck her, because she was ovulating. And having to tell him they couldn't make love when they wanted to. And every single month finding out it hadn't worked, not yet." She looked up, her eyes brimming with tears. "At the end of eleven months, she came home one day and he had moved out, everything, clothes and tools and high school sports trophies. Even two six-packs of his favorite beer."

"That's awful, Rose. But that must not have been a very strong marriage to start with. And it's not what always happens. I bet lots of couples have success with those clinics." He jostled her arm, trying for some lightness. "The clinics would be out of business if they didn't have some happy endings."

They sat in silence for a few more minutes.

"Do you like making love with me?"

"You know I do, Rose. Immensely."

"I do too. Immensely." She took a deep breath. "Making love is an important part of our marriage, Jack. Of our relationship. Our love." Her little tear-streaked grin made his heart hurt. "It's pair bonding, like you always say about birds." She turned and took both of his hands in hers. "Jack, I don't want our love-making to have a secondary purpose. To be... To be for procreation. I don't want to feel like one of my parents' farm animals."

There was a long silence.

"Well then, maybe I should get a vasectomy."

"What?!"

"I hate the thought of putting you through this a third

time. Maybe we should forget about having our own kids. We can look into adoption."

Another long silence. Then…

"No."

"No to what part? Adoption? Not having kids? What?"

"Just no, Jack. No to all of it." She took a deep breath and pushed her shoulders back against the couch. "Give me a few minutes to get my thoughts together."

He waited, staring into her face, watching her gather strength and determination.

"I want to have a child that's ours. I want to have *your* child, Jack. I believe, I don't know why, but I believe we will get pregnant again. And I believe the third time will be the charm. I believe you will be there in the delivery room and you will see our baby being born and we will both hold that baby and love it and watch it grow up. I don't want to give up, not yet."

He cleared his throat again. "Rose. You humble me. But I gotta tell you. I'm going to be scared every time we go to bed. Afraid I'll be putting you through today and the last time all over again."

She leaned forward and grabbed his face in her hands. "You had better get over being afraid, Jack! And pretty darn quick! I'm planning for us to do it like rabbits, every single day, for months and months and months, until we are sitting together at my doctor's office and hearing her congratulate us."

****

Jack felt like a kid on Christmas morning. He was almost bouncing all morning long, all the hours that the birding group walked the old railroad trail at the national wildlife refuge. He could barely keep from skipping, and he hadn't skipped since he was five or six years old. He wanted to dash ahead of everyone so he could run full out, as fast as he could. He wanted to hug himself and laugh aloud. He wanted to toss his hat into the sky and yell aloud from sheer exuberance.

But every one of the twenty-plus birders was hoping to hear the fluting song of thrushes and the startling cry of killdeer. Every person there wanted to watch the male bobolinks as they rose above the grassy fields and tossed their rollicking bobolink-bobolink-spinkspankspink songs into the air. This was the group's biggest outing of the year. He couldn't ruin it for them, even though he was almost bursting.

For a while, as they all got an unexpected look at a least bittern, Jack was able to take a deep breath and focus on birding. It was his first-ever sighting of the smaller and much rarer bittern. A very elusive bird. A life list bird for Jack and many others that morning. After it flew away, the knowledge that he had seen it on the very day he was going to make the most exciting announcement of his life left him almost convulsed with glee.

He could hardly wait until lunchtime. He could hardly wait until he talked with Rose and heard her voice. He could hardly wait to hear that she had talked that morning with her parents and her brother and sister. They had agreed: family first, then other people. He talked with his own parents after supper the evening before. Once Rose's family knew too, he could make the announcement to his friends and birding buddies, the biggest and most important announcement in his life since telling his parents he had found the perfect woman.

****

Jack's cousin Bobby ushered the birders through the main dining room and through a wide doorway at the back. "The traditional private room, at your service." He pulled out a chair at one end of the long table and turned to the leader with a little bow. "And your traditional place, Miss Ivy, at the head of the table."

Bobby and his head waitress started taking drink orders while another waitress plopped a pile of menus in the middle of the table. Most of the birders had been there before, and there was an immediate chorus of orders for fried potato skins and nachos.

Jack stood up, digging a cell phone out of his pocket. "No matter how good the nachos look when they come, save a few for me. I'm going to check in with my wife."

****

"Is it done? The deed? The announcement to your folks?"

"It is done, my love. They're all excited and happy. And they send congratulations. I thought my mother and sister would react the most enthusiastically but I'm telling you, Jack, I have *never* heard my dad so excited. He's already talking about making us a nursing rocker. And showing the farm to our baby. Mom had to wrest the phone out of his hand to get in a word or two."

****

Jack came back accompanied by Bobby and the waitress carrying huge trays of appetizers, and almost everyone seated at the long table burst into song, in several different keys but with impressive volume.

"Food! Gloooooorious food! OUR FAV-OR-ITE DI-ET!"

The second the song stuttered to a ragged end, Jack picked up his glass and rapped it with a fork.

"Announcement!"

He cleared his throat and looked up and down the table, his eyes sparkling.

"Rose and I can make it official. She is the wife plus one. We are expecting our first child in just five short months."

All along the table, the birders called out congratulations. Little Molly lifted her glass. "To the proud papa and the incubating mama and the soon-to-be chick."

"Cheers! Cheers!"

"Thank you, thank you all. Refills on the house. On me, actually. You all pick your designated drivers."

Chapter Thirteen

Accident

The wetlands were alive with glossy male red-winged blackbirds singing from the tops of cattails. A cardinal, hidden in a tangle of sumac and grapevines, filled the air with loud sweet whistles. Goldfinches flew over the birders, sounding their little "potato chip" noise at the bottom of every swoop. Along the hedge-rows, song sparrows and savannah sparrows tilted their heads back and sang, their little feathery bodies quivering with the effort and with the excitement of spring and breeding season.

And from the marshes came rattling, chirping, scolding noises.

"Wrens," Jack muttered. "I hear 'em. But I can't see 'em."

"They come to the top of the cattails pretty often," Ivy whispered, "but usually just for a second at a time. You've got to be looking in the right direction at the right moment."

"I… No… YES!" He winced and lowered his voice. "Yes! I see one!"

"And we're going to get a good long look! See what he's doing?"

"Is that a nest? I'm gonna get to see the bird *and* its nest??"

"The entrance must be around the back." Ivy slowly moved her scope into position.

"This is awesome. My life as a birder is complete." Jack bent over the scope, watching the tiny brown bird as it wove a long piece of grass into a tennis-ball-sized clump hanging between two cattails. "I was beginning to think the words on my gravestone would be *He Never Got a Marsh Wren*. And now there she is!"

"He."

"Huh?"

"It's the male wren that starts building the nest. Lots of nests. Then he leads the female around and she chooses the one she likes best, and she mates with the architect and gets busy bringing in grass and cattail fuzz and making a soft little cradle in the middle of all the sticks."

"Like house wrens. Makes sense. Thank you, daddy bird. I hope you and your mate have many little wren-lets."

****

Jack fell in beside Ivy as they headed back to the cars at the end of the morning.

"If I'd been yakking in my usual manner, Ivy, that little marsh wren might have stayed hidden until we left. And if it hadn't been for you, I never would have spent that long watching. It was great."

"Thank you, Jack. I don't tell you this often enough, but I deeply appreciate that you're quiet on my trips. I know it isn't always easy." She looked at him affectionately. "For you, birding is a social activity. And being social involves talking."

"And it's not a social activity for you."

"Not so much."

He nodded. "Well, now that we're past the quiet part of the walk, I want to crow about something. A people something." He was glad Ivy was with him, so he could share his news without boring the others.

"You're always in a good mood, Jack, but you seem even more upbeat than usual today."

"Yesterday Rose and I went to her doctor's. We heard the baby's heartbeat of course, which we've done before, but yesterday the ultrasound picture was awesome. Little tiny fingers and tiny lips and closed eyes and all. She looked just like a miniature person."

"That's great, Jack! How exciting!"

"It was. It is." His face was suddenly somber. "We've had two miscarriages. That's why we didn't tell anyone until Rose started showing. We were basically scared every single minute for the first four months."

"I can't imagine how that must have felt."

"Simply awful. But now! The baby is so real to both of us. Now it feels okay to go buy baby clothes, and talk about names, and stock up on diapers."

Ivy smiled at the man next to her. "You and Rose are going to be awesome parents, Jack. That is one lucky little girl."

Again, he was glad it was Ivy with him, Ivy who saw his eyes mist over with tears.

"Thanks. That means a lot." He dug in his pocket for a bandana and blew his nose. "We've both been having anxieties. Fears."

"I bet that's normal, Jack. And if not, it should be! Any couple who blithely brings a brand-new human being into the world without doing some serious worrying beforehand probably shouldn't even start the whole project."

Jack gave a little snorting laugh. "The project. That's what Rose calls it." He made an attempt to imitate his wife's soft voice. "We're more than halfway through Phase One of The Project, Jack." He glanced over at Ivy. "Phase Two is infancy. Then The Toddler Years. And so on. For decades."

"When are you going to introduce your little girl to birding?"

Jack looked at Ivy out of the corner of his eye. "My kind or your kind?"

When she grimaced, he put a hand on her arm.

"We'll introduce her to both kinds. Let her enjoy both. She'll have my hyperactive birding and list-making." He raised his eyebrows and grinned. "A life list in the hundreds before she starts first grade. And she'll also have your slow and educational birding. Meditative birding. And as an added bonus she'll have her mother's amazing knowledge of trees and flowers and ferns and the like."

"Again, Jack. She will be one lucky little girl."

****

Jack headed across the lot at the park-and-ride, waving to the other birders who were already in their cars and ready to head home. Two dark green dumpsters at the back of the lot dwarfed his little turquoise-colored car and made it look like a gaudy toy, with its brown scales and fishy eyeballs and the lettering advertising Chubby Sturgeon Ales.

He'd see Rose in under an hour, but he dug in his pocket for his cellphone anyway. He always checked in with her when a bird walk ended. Sometimes they just said hello and he told her what he'd seen, or he shared some funny or wise comment made by one of the group.

Today he wanted to crow about the marsh wren and the perfect little nest that was almost ready for eggs and then for chicks. Rose would get a kick out of knowing about the tiny avian parents.

Sometimes she asked him to stop on the way home and get take-out Thai food from one of their favorite restaurants, or sometimes a pizza, or the makings for his famous ten-layer hero sandwiches. Or, given Rose's pregnancy urges, she might be hankering for chocolate gelato and five pounds of red grapes.

Hankering. That was one of his father's words.

Jack leaned against the car, his legs crossed at the ankles. It had been a wonderful day, starting with a fast-moving thunderstorm that left the air brand-new, and now with warm breeze from the south and clouds racing across a sky that was the color of a robin's egg. And he was going home to Rose, to his wife, his love, the center of his life. And to their baby curled up inside her.

"Rose? I now have a marsh wren on my life list!" His grin widened at the sound of her burbling laugh, her warm loving voice. "And, even better, if it's possible to get even better, it was a little guy wren making a nest for his mate. I figured it was a female but Ivy told me—"

He jerked his head up when a car horn blared from the other side of the parking lot. He waved, but the horn sounded again, longer this time, and someone yelled his name. Out of the corner of his eye, Jack saw a dark shape slowly rising into the air behind him, above his car. He had just enough time to recognize the dumpster and take two steps forward before he was hit hard on the side of his head. There was a deafening roar of glass breaking, metal crushing and bending. The pavement around him sparkled and he realized it was rounded bits of windshield, just before he fell to one side and blacked out.

****

Hands. Two hands were touching him. His throat and his shoulders and all along his spine.

Not Rose's hands. He knew what Rose's hands felt like. He remembered how her hands felt that very first time, when he fell into that stream and she thought he was injured and she patted him all over and he sat there in the icy water and loved it. And every other time, every single time, whenever she touched him with her hands, he felt it to his core.

Somebody was patting him now but it wasn't Rose.

Three hands. Maybe four. Patting him and pushing down hard on his leg, and that hurt a lot and Jack wanted it to stop. He moaned and tried to get his arms under his chest to push himself up but hands were on his back and for some reason he wasn't strong enough to push up against them.

"You're all right, Jack."

Molly. The tiny birder with the bouncy white curls. Her voice was often fast and loud and even boisterous, but now she was saying his name so gently.

"Don't move. Give us a few minutes to see what's what."

Ah. She used to be an emergency room nurse. She'd know what to do. She gently cleared blood from his face with something soft and then pressed down above his left ear.

"Hugh, how's the leg?"

Hugh too. Jack almost smiled. Maybe he would get to hear the tall man say more than a few words at a time.

"Wide scrape. Long."

Or maybe not.

Molly's fingers again, gently probing the back of Jack's neck and down his spine. "Can you open your eyes for me?"

"Was that a *dumpster* that hit me?"

"It was indeed. Can you open your eyes?"

"Sure. But all I see is pavement."

"Sorry I can't get you a better view, but we don't want to move you until the ambulance gets here."

"And red. I see blood."

Jack couldn't get a deep breath, and he hated all that red in front of him. That crashing breaking noise must have been his car. His sweet little car. Shit. Damn. Shit fuck.

"You've got a cut on your scalp. Anything on the head bleeds like crazy. Is this just water in your bottle, Jack?"

Bottle? Oh. "Water. Yes. Just water."

Molly's gentle hands were on his forehead again, this time wiping blood up and away with something wet.

Jack blinked. "Better." He turned his head a little in one direction and then the other. "Head stings. Leg hurts. I'm sitting up. Don't stop me." He got to his hands and knees and awkwardly rolled to a sitting position with his legs straight out in front of him.

"Lucky the whole thing didn't hit me." He reached out and touched two metal handles jutting out from the shiny green dumpster that now rested atop his poor little car. "Just these doodads I think." He stared at his fingers. "Yup. Blood."

"Any pain in your belly?"

"Told you. Head and leg."

Hugh was pressing on Jack's calf with both hands.

It hurt like hell but Jack knew he was trying to stop any more blood from ending up on the pavement, and that sounded like a good plan. The pool of red around his leg was growing, amazingly shiny in the sun.

The other two looked startled when Jack laughed.

"You two. Molly. Hugh. Mismatched pair of angels."

Now he was aware of a siren moving across the park-and-ride, cutting off a few yards away and leaving roaring silence in its wake. And the truck driver who had dropped the dumpster was standing in front of him, his eyes huge, trying to explain over and over and over. And there was a policeman, or maybe two. And there were other hands, other voices, more questions.

Jack thought about dropping back off to sleep.

Rose! He had to talk to Rose!

His phone wasn't in his hand. He had it when he got hit. He was talking to her. She must have heard the noise, the crashing, breaking, crushing noises. He had to find his phone! The EMTs were all around him, it felt like ten or twelve of them, and they were blocking his view and he couldn't see his phone and he had to call Rose.

"Get away from me! I'm fine! Give me a minute! I have to talk with my wife!"

Then, through a gap between two white jackets, he saw tall Hugh bend over and pick something up off the ground. His cell phone.

****

"Jack! Jack! Jack, what's happening? Jack, please talk to me!"

"Rose?"

It wasn't Jack's voice.

"This is Hugh, one of the birders. Just a minute. Let

me turn the phone around. Better. Rose, Jack is all right but there's been an accident and he'll be heading for the hospital in a few minutes. He threw his phone when he fell. He—"

"Stop. Tell me again. Jack was in an accident. What's wrong with him?"

"Let me put Molly on. She's a nurse."

"Rose? Molly here. Jack's got a gash above his left eye and a longer cut on his shin. Both of them will need stitches. Do you want to talk to Jack?"

"Oh god yes."

"Rose?"

Finally. Jack. Her heart slowed the slightest at his familiar voice. "What happened?"

"Well, you're not going to believe it. Probably not, anyway. I can hardly believe it and I was—" He gasped. "I was right here. Am right here." He knew he was breathing too fast and talking too fast, and he made himself slow down so he wouldn't scare her. "A dumpster fell on my car."

"What?"

"A dumpster. Crushed the car completely. Didn't crush me, though. I wasn't in it. In the car." He gave a little snorting sound. "Dumpster didn't get me. Didn't get my new binocs either. Lucky. Charlie was thinking about upgrading. Gave them to him for a few days. Loaned them. He borrowed my binocs. So they didn't get flattened. My poor car did though. Looks like something in the wrecking yard."

"Jack. Stop. If you weren't in the car, how did you get hurt?"

"Oh. Right. It knocked me down. The dumpster. Not the whole thing or I'd be as flat—Not the whole thing.

Just two little handles. I'm fine, Rose. Gonna need stitches. And should get the cuts and scrapes cleaned out. But I'm fine."

"I'll meet you at the hospital."

"Yes. Good."

"Oh! What hospital?"

Jack looked up at one of the EMTs. "Where are you taking me?... Central Vermont, Rose."

****

"You look so good sitting there, Jack."

"I do not look good, Rose," he grumbled. "My leg is bandaged from ankle to knee, there's another bandage on my head, and half my face is puffy and beet red." He touched his cheek and grimaced. "I have now learned the important lesson that lying with one's face plastered against hot black pavement isn't a good idea." He looked up. "Ignore me, Rose. I'm just whining. I'm hurting and I'm grouchy and I want to be better *now*."

"Jack, I'm going to say it again. I can't believe how good you look." Rose crossed the room and sat on the arm of his chair. "It's so frigging good to have you whole and healing and here."

Jack raised his eyebrows. "Friggin'? I've never heard you use that word. Not ever."

"I have never been that frightened before. I'll probably never say that word again, unless you make me that worried again. No more dumpster wrestling, all right?"

His smile was weak but there. "Okay. And thank you. For loving me. I guess I expected to come home and feel better immediately, except for maybe a bit of soreness where I got stitches. I didn't expect to feel like a, a Clydesdale has been rolling around on my body."

"It wasn't just a few stitches, Jack. You have forty-two on your leg and sixteen on your head. And you lost a few pints of blood. And you might have had a slight concussion."

"I didn't. At least the doctor decided that I didn't. They kept me overnight for nothing."

"It was precautionary." She smoothed his hair away from his forehead. "You haven't been home twenty-four hours yet. Give it time."

Jack knew the dumpster hit his head and his shin, but his whole body felt bruised. It hurt to sit. It hurt to lie down. It hurt to get up and walk to the bathroom. It hurt to chew.

"Jack, you need to eat something. How about a smoothie, with a banana and chocolate milk and some yogurt?"

"And a few strawberries?"

"And strawberries, my love. As many as you want."

****

Rose bolted upright in bed. The room was much too hot. The smoke alarms weren't beeping but she had to get up and walk through the house and find out what was burning.

As she threw back the covers, her hand touched Jack's shoulder.

There was no fire. It was Jack who was so hot. Jack was burning up.

Five minutes later, she had a thermometer in one hand and her cellphone in the other.

"A little above a hundred three."

While she waited for the ambulance, Rose wiped his head and torso over and over with cold wet towels, talking to him, telling him how much she loved him, how much their baby needed him, urging the ambulance to get there faster, talking to him again, petting him, trying to push her own strength and health into him through her hands and her voice and her desperate pleading.

Chapter Fourteen

Max to the Rescue

Rose didn't get home again until late the following afternoon. Or maybe two afternoons later. She wasn't sure. And once she was home, she wasn't sure what she should be doing. What she wanted to do. The house was cold, and it felt so empty she expected her footsteps to echo when she walked from the side door through the kitchen and into the living room. She didn't want to eat. She didn't want to make coffee or tea. She didn't want to get out of the clothes she'd worn for days. She didn't want to go to bed.

She just stood in the living room, alone, listening to silence.

After many minutes, she moved like someone old and sick over to the wall and turned up the thermostat. And then, like someone old and sick, she went back into the kitchen. There was a note on the counter with her name at the top, and she picked it up and glanced at it before wandering back into the living room.

The doctors told her to go home. They promised to call if anything changed. They told her to get some supper and some rest. They said she needed to think of the baby.

Rose fumbled in her jacket pocket for her cellphone, suddenly panicked. She had turned the ringer off when she was in the ICU waiting room! They could have called and she wouldn't even know it! And she hadn't recharged the phone in two days and she talked with her parents and Jack's parents. Maybe the phone was dead. Maybe the hospital called but the phone was dead.

There were four missed calls.

Rose couldn't remember her password, the password she used every single day, several times a day. She started to beat on her forehead with her fist, but then she remembered.

There were no messages from the hospital. Calm down, Rose. Everything's the same. Jack is still in the ICU and he's still breathing and he still has the infection but nothing has changed.

Her sister Lily wanted her to call when she had time for a good long chalk. Back when Lily was ten, three-year-old Rose confused the words *talk* and *chat*. Ever since then, family conversations were chalks. She didn't have the energy for a long chalk right now. Maybe tomorrow.

The two calls from work could wait. The last message was from Max. She could call Max. She could talk with Max.

"Rose? Oh good! How about supper tomorrow? You two and us two and salmon steaks on the grill. And strawberry shortcake. Xavier and I are going picking tomorrow."

"Oh. Dear. Oh. Max…" Her shaky gasp sounded loud in the too-quiet house. "You don't know. Of course you don't. How could you know? Wait. I have to sit down."

"Rose. What's going on?"

"Jack is—Jack had an accident, three, no, four days

ago. Or three. I'm not sure. It was a, a dumpster accident. Dumpster. But that's irrelevant. The fact that it was a dumpster. That's not the point. The point is that Jack needed stitches and he had to stay overnight at the hospital because maybe he had a concussion. But he didn't, so he came home the next morning. But now he's in Intensive Care. It's a superbug, Max. Those ones that resist antibiotics. He's in the ICU. I can't touch him. I have to stand outside a glass barrier and his bed is turned the wrong way and he can't even see me. And the—The nurses and doctors wear face shields and paper clothing and special booties and it all has to be burned when they come out. No. Probably not the shields. The paper things. Those have to be burned. Like Jack is a biohazard. Jack IS a biohazard. They all treat him like hazmat. Jack. And—"

"Have you had anything to eat today?"

"I… What? I don't know. Maybe. I'm not hungry, so I probably did. At the hospital. But not in the hazmat zone." She looked down at the crumpled note in her hand. "I've got plenty of food, Max. The bird people filled the fridge and freezer."

"Bird people?"

"That group of birdwatchers Jack joined. The ones you met. I found a note. They said they filled the fridge and freezer. But I'm not hungry."

"I'll be there in a half hour."

Rose opened her mouth to say she didn't need anything, but Max had already hung up.

****

"All right, sweetie. You sit and drink your tea while I scramble up some eggs."

"I told you, Max. I'm not hungry."

"And I'm telling you, Rose. You need to drink and eat. Jack is depending on you to protect that baby. And that means lots of liquids and regular meals."

Wow. Max was looking scary fierce. Jack wouldn't believe it.

"Drink. Now."

The tea was too sweet but it felt good going down, and Rose held out her mug for a refill.

"Those bird people did things up big. Lots of single-size salads." She opened the freezer. "And casseroles. That's very thoughtful. But for now—" She plopped down two plates of eggs and added a donut to Rose's. "Eat. Now."

Rose stared down at the plate, at her hand picking up a fork. Her eyes were blurred and they hurt. She saw the fork moving. Her arms hurt too. She was supposed to notify the hospital if she started having body aches. If she had a fever. She didn't think this was what they meant, though. These aches. These aches were probably from spending hours almost asleep across two hard chairs. And from tension. And fear.

"Ready for more?"

"What?" Her plate was empty. Even the donut was gone, and she had a greasy sugary taste in her mouth; she never ate donuts because she didn't like that left-over greasy taste.

"Salad? You said there was salad?"

"What kind?" Max had her head back in the refrigerator. "It looks like a few green salads, one coleslaw, something that might be Waldorf salad, and this—Yes, this is broccoli and bacon."

"That one. The last. No. Regular mixed salad. Green stuff."

"Dressing?"

"There's some in the fridge door." For the first time, Rose looked up and met Max's eyes. "I hate donuts. I don't remember eating that one but I guess I did. The salad will get rid of the yucky taste in my mouth."

Now that she was aware of what she was eating, she realized she was hungry. Ravenous.

"What else is there? No. Not the birders' food. Ours. There's peanut butter in the cabinet right above your head. And bread in the bread box. Unless it's moldy."

"Yes bread. No mold. Jam?"

"Fridge, I think. Unless we finished it."

Max made her a sandwich, poured the rest of the tea from the pot into Rose's mug, then sat down and watched her eat.

"Feel better?"

"Yes. I do. Thank you, Max. I didn't even know I was hungry."

"Shock. Upset. Worry. Now, what happened? Something about a dumpster?"

"Sunday morning Jack went with the birders. He called me from the park-and-ride. Oh! I just remembered! He saw a marsh wren." Rose felt the first smile in days lift the corners of her mouth. "Jack has been trying to see a marsh wren for, well, forever. Ever since he started birding. And Sunday he got to watch one building a nest. A male. He told me male marsh wrens build the nests." She frowned, remembering. "And then, while he was telling me about the wren, there was a dreadful, a truly dreadful noise. I kept calling his name, over and over. I was heading out to the truck so I could drive to the park-and-ride when Hugh from the birding group picked up Jack's phone. He said it got tossed onto the pavement when Jack fell. The phone did. He said Jack was going to need stitches. Or maybe Molly said that."

"Who's Molly?"

"Another one of the birders. The little woman with the white hair."

"Oh. Right."

"Hugh gave Jack's phone to her and she, she used to be a nurse I think, and she said he would need stitches. And then she gave the phone to Jack." Rose wiped her face with a napkin and took a deep breath. "He sounded perfect, Max. He sounded strong and fine and perfect. I met him at the hospital, in the ER. He had stitches on his forehead and they were still working on a long gash on his leg. Cleaning it out. And then they stitched that too. Jack told me he'd been leaning against his car when a dumpster, one of those big industrial dumpsters, got lifted up by a truck next to the parking lot but something went wrong and it fell off the lift and onto his car. It didn't hit him, the dumpster, not directly, but some sticky-outy part knocked into his head and when he was falling it gashed his shin too. But he was fine, Max! Strong voice, joking around with the hospital staff. He was Jack and he was fine. But the doctor thought he might have a slight concussion so they kept him overnight. To keep an eye on him."

Her eyes filled with tears.

"I could have kept an eye on him, Max. He wanted to come home. He said he felt fine and he'd be happier at home. But the doctor thought they should keep him overnight and I was so afraid something might happen here, when we weren't close to the hospital. I was wrong. I was wrong! I should have listened to Jack. I should have brought him home. I would have made him wake up every two hours to make sure he didn't have a concussion. But I let him stay there and that's how he got it, the superbug. In the hospital. I asked if it could have come from the pavement, from the dirt in his cuts, and a nurse said probably not because those cuts got really well cleaned." Rose's whole body slumped. "Not cleaned. Cleansed. That's apparently even better than cleaned."

"Hospital jargon."

Rose wrapped her hands around her mug as if it was still hot. "I should have taken him home, Max. And I should have realized he was sick the very next day because he said he felt as if, as if a horse rolled around on him. You know how horses lie down and roll around on their backs with their legs in the air? Jack said he felt like a Clydesdale horse had fallen on him and rolled around. I should have taken him to his doctor right then. That very moment."

"We should probably ask a medical professional to be sure, but I don't believe that the Clydesdale reference is a well-documented symptom of infection."

Rose gave her a weak smile.

"Rose." Max reached across the table. "You couldn't have known. And I bet Jack kept smiling. Maybe even joking a little. You thought he was getting better, and you had no reason to think otherwise."

"Until I touched him in the middle of the night and he was burning up. Hotter than I thought a human could ever be."

"And then you got help for him. Immediately. And now you have another job to do. You've got to eat and drink lots of liquids and sleep and keep that little infant inside you healthy. For Jack to hold and coochy-coo at and love, in only a few months."

"I know. I forgot for a while."

"That's why I'm here. And why I'm going to stay here, at least for tonight and through tomorrow and tomorrow night. To keep you from forgetting again."

This time the tears overflowed. "You are such a good friend, Max. I was so incredibly lucky that day I met you and got to live in your little ADU."

"My little what?"

"Auxiliary Dwelling Unit." Rose gulped and blew her nose. "That's what they're called now. Don't you read the papers?"

"Good." Max sat back in her chair. "You're sounding a bit more normal. Now you need sleep. Do you have an extra bed?"

"Oh. Dear. Not really. The addition's all done, of course, so we've got extra rooms up the wazoo. But no beds yet. The guest room upstairs has nothing in it but my sewing table and computer desk and some baby stuff we're storing up there until we paint the nursery. The nursery is completely empty. And once it has furniture it'll have a crib, so that wouldn't work anyway."

"How's the couch?"

"It's all right. I'll sleep on it, Max. I don't think I can go in and sleep in our bed with Jack not there. That's why I didn't come home last night. Maybe two nights now. I'm not sure."

"Time isn't normal when you're with a loved one in the hospital."

"No. It isn't." Rose took a deep breath, her whole face twisted and pained. "I was afraid, Max. I was so afraid of seeing our bed without Jack in it. I'll take the couch and you can sleep in there."

"I think you will sleep better in your own bed."

"Maybe. Yes." Rose stood up and squared her shoulders. "You're right. I can do it. Jack will probably be in the hospital for several days. I might as well get used to it. I'll go get a pillow and some quilts for you." She turned toward the bedroom. "Pillows. Sheets. I'm blanking. Oh, yes. Linen closet. And then I need a shower. I can't remember when I put these clothes on."

****

Rose woke up, panicked, again. Her cellphone was ringing and she couldn't remember where it was. It kept ringing while she felt under the pillow and all around her on the sheet and all over the top of the bedside table. It usually went to voice mail after four rings but she'd changed the settings so she wouldn't miss a call. And now it was ringing, ringing, ringing, and she couldn't find it! Sun was streaming in the windows and she had no idea what time it was and the phone was ringing and she couldn't find it.

The drawer. Of course. She put it in the little drawer in the bedside table because she was afraid she might knock it to the floor if it rang in the night and woke her up.

"Yes? Yes? What is it? What happened?" Her whole body sagged. "That's good, isn't it?... Yes, I understand... Yes, of course. Thank you so much for calling. Thank you!"

She looked up to see Max in the doorway, wiping her hands on a dish towel and looking both concerned and hopeful.

"Max! Jack's temperature was down a little in the middle of the night, and it's down a little more this morning. He still has a high fever but it's not as high as it was!"

"So he might be fighting the infection."

"Maybe. Yes. Maybe the antibiotics are working." Her sudden grin was wobbly but wide. "Or maybe he's just strong, wonderful Jack. Strong enough to fight a superbug." Rose jumped out of bed as if her body suddenly had springs. "What time is it? Gosh almighty! I slept—How long did I sleep? Eleven hours? Twelve? Yipes!"

"You needed it. And now you need to sit down and have breakfast. Or lunch. Maybe both together."

Rose opened a dresser drawer and tossed underwear and socks onto the bed.

"I'll go teach the Friday first-aid class at Hunt's—" She threw off her nightshirt and wiggled into a sports bra and what Jack called preggy panties. "It's at 1:30. Connie covered for me for four days. Or three. Maybe it was Connie and someone else too. Anyway, I don't want to muck up their schedules any more than I have to. And I'm the only one who's first-aid certified." She opened another drawer and pulled out a pair of slacks in blue and white crinkly fabric. "Mom's. From her three pregnancies. These things are almost forty years old. And this." She held up a gauzy blue shirt. "I'll be cool and comfy even if it gets hotter than Hades today, which it just might. I'll teach the class and then I'll go to the hospital and then, if you'll still be here, I'll bring home Thai food. Does that sound good?"

"There's lots of food from the birders."

"Oh! Yes! I forgot entirely! All right! Hunt's, hospital, home. Three H's. I can do that. Oh!" Rose stopped her whirlwind movement to stare at Max. "You don't have to stay here, you know. You can go home to your hubby. I'm all right now, I really am."

"I talked with Xavier this morning and told him I was staying today and tomorrow and maybe Sunday. He suggested there might be things you and Jack meant to get done here at the house, to be ready for the baby. He can come anytime this weekend and help out."

Rose felt tears prickling the back of her nose. "You two are such good friends, Max. Yes. We—Jack and I were going to paint the nursery this weekend. We wanted to make sure we left weeks and weeks and weeks for any lingering smells to clear out."

"That is a perfect job for Xavier! He's an awesome painter. One of those anal types who tape up every single thing first and then take the tape off at exactly the right moment, when the paint is dry but not one second too dry, and he puts down drop cloths even though there's never, ever, a single drip on them when he's finished. It's positively uncanny."

Rose giggled and then stopped moving, astonished. "I think I'm happy. I know it's temporary but I'm happy. For the first time in days and days. It feels weird."

"It should feel normal, my friend. You are a happy person."

"I am a lucky person. Anyway, what made me laugh is thinking about Jack painting. He's the polar opposite of your Xavier. Jack attacks painting with his usual energy and enthusiasm, and also with his usual speed. When we did the porch ceiling, I bet a third of the paint ended up on the drop cloth." She plopped down on the bed to tie her sneakers. "But he's very good about mopping up any drips that land where they shouldn't, so the final product ends up looking great."

"Your whole house is looking great, Rose."

"It is. I agree. All it needs now is my husband."

"Soon. Now you come eat and then you can show me exactly what you want done in the nursery."

Rose leaned back on her arms and studied her friend. "Max, you are a gift. Right now, at this very moment, it feels like things are back on course. I'm going to go back to work, at least part-time, and Jack will get better and he'll be coming home and the nursery will be ready and we will have a baby and—" She gulped. "And now I've really got to eat. I'm way past ravenous!"

Chapter Fifteen

Coming Back

Another morning yanked out of deep sleep by the ringing of her phone. Another panicky scramble to open the bedside drawer and fumble around inside and turn the phone the right way around and press the right buttons.

"Yes? Yes? Hello? Yes, this is Rose. Yes, of course. Of course I will! Oh yes!"

She sat up against the headboard, hugging the phone to her head.

"Jack? Jack, is that really you? Oh, my love, you sound so good. It's you! It's your voice! Are you out of Intensive Care? You are, aren't you!"

Rose was sobbing and laughing at the same time. Jack's normally beautiful strong voice was thin and raspy and breathless. But he was Jack, her Jack, and he was talking to her.

"Fever broke. Overnight. Normal, normal temp. This is... This is one of the nurse's phones. She could get..." He was gasping, drawing in breaths that sounded shallow and labored. "Get in trouble... but she... she believes... me. Hearing you... Rose, hearing you... best medicine. Make me better... fast."

Rose could hear his smile. She knew that wasn't possible but she could. She could hear him begin to smile and she knew his eyes were twinkling up at the nurse and she knew the nurse was smiling back at him because who wouldn't smile at Jack when he twinkled?

"Will you... bring... bring mine? Phone? Then we... We can talk. Every day we can talk."

"Yes my love, yes, yes. I'll bring it this morning. Very soon."

"Gotta go. Gotta give this back."

"Wait! Wait, Jack! What room are you in?"

A soprano voice answered her question and repeated that Jack's fever was gone and he'd been moved to a regular room where he could use cellphones.

"Still a long haul, Mrs. Carmichael. But we're all delighted with your husband's progress."

"Me too! Oh, me too! Thank you so much for letting him call me!"

****

"It looks like that nurse nailed it, Mom. The nurse who said Jack's battle with the superbug is textbook on speed. He's going through all the expected stages but he's going through them faster than expected."

"That's so good, sweetie. Your husband is a strong person. And he's got a lot to get well for. A lot to get home for."

"It'll be a while before he's actually home. Maybe another two days where he is, maybe more, and then a week of rehab. Maybe more there too. His whole body's worn out. He can get himself into a sitting position, which is progress, and today when I was there he was feeding himself. But it took both hands to hold the spoon." She grinned, remembering. "But he was determined! His appetite's coming back and he said even lukewarm hospital bouillon and slightly melted ice cream tasted like heaven."

"Did he say he was ravenous, like you always say?"

Rose's little spurt of laughter ended with something like a sob. "No. But it was so good to watch him chowing down. Well, maybe not chowing down, but at least putting food in his mouth. The doctor had said that Jack might not have any appetite for weeks, even months. As long as he's willing to eat, I want to keep him eating! I'm thinking of bringing him a mini-plate of Pad Thai tomorrow. I'll ask the doctor in the morning if that's all right."

"The man can barely manage a spoon and you're going to bring him noodles."

"Maybe I'll wait a few days."

"I would."

"Anyway, he's going to try a walker tomorrow. He has to rebuild all his muscles, Mom. Learn how to use them all over again. Walk and get dressed and get to the toilet alone and go up and down stairs and—Well, everything."

"I'll bet he's chomping at the bit."

"You know, he isn't. Or at least it's not obvious. Jack was so very sick and now he's not, and it feels like that's enough for now. He's happy just to be able to sit up, and eat, and use a phone. And he's so—" She was teary now. "So happy to be alive."

"What's on for today, sweetie? For you?"

"Oh gosh. I need to check my calendar every day now. There's so much to do and I want to spend time with Jack every day or at least talk on the phone, and this is just about the busiest time of year at work and—"

"Do you have to be working?"

"I want to, Mom. If I weren't working, I'd be spending too much time here, and home feels—It feels empty here, Mom. Too empty. And besides I don't like knowing that I'm not pulling my weight at work when there's no real reason why I can't."

"I guess that makes sense. I just hate the thought of your getting overtired."

"Me too. I was exhausted before Max came to rescue me, and I didn't even know it."

"So what else is filling your calendar? Besides work and hospital visits?"

"Well, the first birthing class is Tuesday. Jack was going to come with me, of course, and I don't know if I feel like driving all that way by myself and then driving home in the dark. I'm going to ask the instructor if I can get the information online. Or maybe even participate online, at least until Jack can start coming with me. And Thursday afternoon the people in my office are giving me a baby shower. It'll be fun, I'll enjoy it, but it'll cut into my time with Jack. Although—" She smiled, pleased with her idea. "I know! I'll take the gifts into the hospital for him to see. He'll get a kick out of how tiny, tiny, tiny the outfits are. And it will be good for him to focus on the baby instead of how many steps he managed to do with the walker and how long it'll be before he can put on his shirt and button it by himself."

"I have raised three very wise children."

"You are a very wise woman. You and dad both."

"Nope. He's all man."

They were both laughing as the call ended.

****

"Max! What a delightful surprise to find you standing right here in our driveway!" Rose jumped out of her truck.

"There's more of you to hug than just a week ago."

214

"True." She patted her belly. "Little Calloway Carmichael is big and active!"

"Calloway, huh?"

"We haven't decided on a name yet. But that's what we were calling her before we knew her sex. Jack found it in a list of gender-neutral names and it sounds nice and Irish." She stood back. "What are you doing here in the big city of Montpelier?"

"You've completely forgotten, haven't you?"

"Forgotten wh—Oh my gosh. I did! Totally! This is getting worrisome, Max. I could leave my own head behind if it weren't firmly attached."

"Are you still up for going out to dinner? And putting me up overnight so we can hit the car dealerships first thing in the morning? And shop till we drop while Xavier finishes up in the nursery?"

"I am, Max. Finding a car for Jack is at the top of my list. Come on in. I need to guzzle something cold and wet before I head out again." She unlocked the door and tossed her bag on the floor. "This week has been crazy. I've been spending time with Jack every day and I worked half days Monday through yesterday and I did two online birthing classes in the evenings, catching up for the first two in the series that Jack and I signed up for. And there was the baby shower yesterday. And today I ended up working more than I planned because one of the farm workers had some sort of seizure and I went with him to the ER so I could translate for him and the medical personnel."

"How is he? The farm worker?"

"It looks like he'll be fine, if he stays away from huge industrial agriculture. Ahhh." Rose plopped down in one kitchen chair and propped her feet in another while Max opened the refrigerator and pulled out a bottle of orange juice. "Eduardo worked at a huge vegetable operation in California before coming here, a place that uses both herbicides and pesticides. *Mucho, mucho* of both, according to him. Exposure to those kinds of toxins can hyper-stimulate parts of a person's neurological system. Thanks." She took the glass and downed half of it before continuing.

"The ER doctor went to a conference a few months back, specifically about farm chemicals, and he was almost giddy with delight when an actual case showed up while he was on duty. Eduardo and I both learned a lot today." She drained the glass and accepted a refill. "The first symptoms of that kind of chemical poisoning can be convulsions or seizures. Eduardo had a minor convulsion back in California, but he didn't want to leave the field to get medical attention. He was hoping it was a one-time thing. But this morning's seizure was a lot worse." She shook her head. "I'm telling you, Max, my translating skills were taxed to the limit. I was trying to understand medical terminology that was unfamiliar to me and then trying to change it into something a Spanish-speaking farm worker without much education might understand."

"And did he? Understand?"

"Well, he left the ER saying he wasn't going to work in California ever again. His brother works in orchards in Washington and Oregon, and Eduardo's going to try and go there next year. O-ray-GOON. And Wasss-ing-TOON. He was sweet. I hope he really does what he's said he's going to do."

"Me too. Have you had enough down time?"

Rose hauled herself to her feet. "Yes. And I'm

ravenous. Where are we going?"

"I've been hankering for Thai, and you said you and Jack found a good place."

"Oh yes!"

****

By the following afternoon, there was a five-year-old medium-sized SUV in the driveway, in front of Rose's truck. She and Max had looked at a half dozen cars and took three of them out for test drives, but she knew that her husband would have visited many more dealers and looked at many more possibilities and done a lot more bargaining. But Jack wasn't available, and he might not be for a month or more. And now she had one more thing checked off her list.

"Looks good there."

"It does, Max. I'm glad it's that metallic gray color instead of bright red or something, so Jack can get it painted like his dear departed Chubby Sturgeon car."

"It'll be a while before he's thinking about brewing and marketing."

"True." She sighed. "Well, let's go see what your talented hubby accomplished while we've been gone."

Both women stopped dead in the doorway to the nursery.

"Oh my goodness. Goodness me. This is astonishing. Outstanding." Rose turned to Max, her eyes glowing. "I had no idea he had this kind of talent."

"It is pretty remarkable, isn't it?"

The pale blue walls that Max and Xavier painted earlier were now decorated with occasional puffy blue-white clouds, turning the upper half of all four walls into spring-time sky, with a half dozen tiny birds silhouetted against the blue. Spiky foliage in many shades of green sprouted from the top of the baseboards, and a darker green shrub was painted from floor almost to the ceiling in one corner of the room.

"Oh my gosh again. That looks just like the old lilac outside. And—" Rose bent down. "I can*not* believe that husband of yours. This stuff around the bottom is—It's not grass! It's sedge! Buxbaum's! *Carex buxbaumii*! I cannot believe it! And red clover! And vetch! *Astragalus robbinsii*! What a hoot!"

"He probably got one of the profs at Sterling to give him some photos." Max looked as smug and pleased as the Cheshire cat. "I told you he was wonderful."

"You were so right. I can hardly wait for Jack to see this. I know! I'll take cell phone photos and show him tomorrow! Oh, little Calloway, you are going to love, love, love this room." She gave Max an impulsive kiss on the cheek. "When you get home, you have to pass that kiss on to Xavier. And give him a humongous hug from me too."

"A kiss and a hug from you. And then I might just grab his hand and pull him into our bedroom and give him something else, just from me."

"That is a great, and very proper, idea!"

****

Jack being back in the house didn't mean that he was home. Not the way he used to be. He sat in his old recliner all day, every day. Sometimes he was asleep, but sometimes she knew he had his eyes closed so she wouldn't talk to him, wouldn't make him focus on anything, wouldn't make him think.

Derek stopped by and tried to get Jack excited about a large project coming up in the next few months. Jack was polite, but he wasn't really listening. And when

Rose suggested bringing his computer downstairs and setting it up in the living room so he could do some work, he said he needed at least a few more weeks.

Rose sat on the arm of the recliner several times every day, and he always put his hand on her belly to feel their baby kick, and he talked with her about names. He was relentlessly cheerful and supportive. *That's a good one! I like that! I will like any name you choose, Rose.*

****

"Jack! Come see this! The house wrens have left the nest! There's a fledgling standing on the porch railing!"

He looked up and dropped the newspaper into his lap.

"That's cool, Rose. Very cool."

"Do come and take a look, Jack. The little guy doesn't even have a tail, just a few tiny thin feathers sticking up every which way. And he's more head than body. Oh! Here's one of the adults. Oh, Jack, you've got to see this. The second his parent appeared, that little one opened its mouth so wide it could easily swallow its own head. Yummy. Down the hatch. I think it was a fly."

"They had at least one healthy fledgling. That's good to know."

She turned from the window. Jack was looking down at the paper again. He hadn't moved from that darned recliner since he finished the rehab exercises before breakfast. He said he'd been doing the exercises three times a day, an hour and a half each time, and she knew he did them in the morning and evening because she was home then, but she wasn't sure about the afternoon time.

She used to think Jack never lied. But now he lied every time he smiled at her. He lied just a few seconds ago, when he tried to make his voice sound like he was excited about the wrens. Tried to make it sound as if he cared.

She stood staring at him. He was thinner. He was eating less than half what he used to eat. It was a struggle for him to get out of the recliner. He moved, when he had to, clutching the handles of a walker and taking small shuffling steps. He held the newspaper with hands that shook and sometimes he turned the pages but she didn't think he was reading. He didn't want to listen to music, although he always added that she should put something on if she wanted.

His skin had lost the goldy-brown of someone who spent a lot of time outdoors. His beautiful red-brown hair was flattened to his head and it didn't look clean but he said shampooing was too much trouble for her. When he took a shower, she had to place the little stool in the stall and turn on the water and adjust the temperature. She had to wait while he loosened his sweatpants and let them drop, keeping one white-knuckled hand on the edge of the sink. She had to help him get his shirt off and then hold both his hands as he let go of the sink and took two steps forward and lowered himself onto the stool. He could lather soap on his torso, but he couldn't hold his arms up long enough to shampoo his hair. She had to do that for him and then make sure the suds were rinsed out. And then they did it all in reverse: help him out of the shower, both of them afraid he might slip on the wet floor; bring the walker into the bathroom and make sure he had a good grip on it; dry him off; help him into clean shirt and sweatpants; watch him move so painfully slowly into the bedroom or back to the recliner. Watch him maneuver into a position that felt safe so he could let go of the walker and ease himself down.

She knew he was depressed. That was a classic sign of depression, not being interested in things he used to like. But she had no idea how to shake him out of it.

She turned away and went back into the kitchen. There was a canvas bag full of vegetables from the farmers' market for her to deal with. There was lunch to make. Saturday and Sunday should be their days. Together days. Maybe she could interest him in the birding magazine that came a few days ago. He could pick an article and she could sit on the arm of the recliner and read aloud to him and they could both look at the pictures.

She loved him. She should be able to think of something to do.

****

Jack watched her walk into the kitchen. He knew she wanted him to get out of his recliner and take hold of the walker and shuffle across the room. He knew she wanted him to join her at the window and watch the fledgling wren and maybe laugh with her. He knew she was upset, from the set of her head and shoulders. And from her quiet. Rose always made her own music when she was in the kitchen, singing or humming as she cut up vegetables or stirred soup or made bread or wiped down the countertops.

Of course she was upset. Unhappy. Tense. Tired. She was working five days a week and she had a second job here at home. *Him*. She was rushing home every day to make lunch and sit with him while he ate. She was doing all their shopping and cooking and laundry and cleaning. And she was getting bigger and bigger, with their child. And she was unendingly upbeat, except when she thought he wasn't watching. Then her shoulders slumped and her head sagged forward, or her shoulders went back and her whole body tightened as she readied herself to hold the weight of another few hours, another few days.

Both of their mothers offered to come and help out, but his parents were needed at the store and hers had to keep the farm humming along during the busy summer months. And he didn't want anyone else there, in their home with them. He didn't want anyone else to see him in sweatpants every day because sweatpants were the only thing he could put on by himself. He didn't want anyone to see him sitting like a lump in a recliner while his pregnant wife worked overtime. He didn't want to overhear whispered conversations, asking Rose how he had slept, how he was doing today, whispering about him as if he wasn't there.

He hated this life. They said he'd made rapid progress while he was in the hospital but now everything was stagnant. *He* was stagnant. He was exhausted all the time but he couldn't sleep more than a few hours at a time. He hated the walker. Hated seeing it in the room. Hated using it. Whether or not the doctor said he was ready, he was moving to a cane this week. He'd probably need two canes, but that would still be better than the walker.

He was bored and he was boring. He couldn't think of a single thing to talk about with Rose. He asked questions about her work but he couldn't concentrate on her answers. Reading gave him a headache. He couldn't even watch some dumb movie and maybe get a laugh or two because he'd have to get out of his recliner and set up his old DVD player and that would take forever and he wasn't sure he could make his fingers work. And nothing would strike him as funny anyway.

He was so *damn* tired of trying to sound cheerful every single minute Rose was home. He had to make his voice stronger than was easy right now, so she wouldn't get that worried little frown between her eyebrows. But, godalmighty, talking normally and smiling normally and being so frigging cheerful took so much effort, and he didn't want to do anything that took even a tiny bit of effort. He wanted to lie back in his recliner and doze and have no noise around him, none at all. He wanted to be left alone. Sometimes he even wanted to be back in the hospital, where he could press a button and get food without feeling guilty. Where he could close his eyes with another person right there in the room with him and not feel guilty because he wasn't up to smiling and making conversation. Where he could live through an entire day without knowing he was nothing but a burden.

An hour and a half to go before his next exercise session. An hour and a half of doing nothing. Just sitting. An inert lump in a beat-up recliner.

Shit.

Why hadn't he thought of that before?

If he could have, Jack would have jerked upright and leapt out of the damned recliner. He couldn't, but he still sat up so abruptly that Rose turned around in alarm.

"What's the matter? Leg cramp? Jack?"

"Nothing is the matter, Rose. I just had an epiphany."

She took a few steps toward him, wiping her wet hands on her denim-covered thighs.

"The doctor told me to do those exercises three times a day. But I don't think he said *only* three times. In

223

fact…" He bent forward, with difficulty, and felt around for the messy pile of printed instructions and information that began when he left the hospital and grew with every doctor's visit and every time Rose looked something up online and printed it out for him. "I think the at-home guide says *at least* three times. Not *only* three times."

"But you're not supposed to overdo it, Jack."

"I'm not overdoing it. Not now." He lifted the whole stack of papers onto his lap and started pawing through it, glancing at one sheet at a time and tossing one at a time onto the floor. "At first doing those exercises three times a day was all I could possibly do. I thought they were *more* than I could possibly do. I was more tired than I ever remember being in my whole life. But not anymore. Ah." He dumped all but one piece of paper onto the floor and leaned sideways to turn on the light. "Remember at the start? When I'd end up drenched in sweat and shaking like a leaf?"

She perched on the arm of his recliner. "I remember, yes. And yesterday evening you didn't look anywhere near worn out when you finished up."

"I wasn't. And not the other two times yesterday nor the two days before that. Yes! It says at least. *At least* three times a day." He forgot to pay attention to his voice so it was back to thin and shaky, but when he looked up his brown eyes were earnest, alert, more alive than she'd seen since before the accident. "Rose, I want to get my muscles back. I want to be able to do things I've done since I was a toddler. And a few minutes ago, I realized that there are only four things that will help me." He counted them off on his fingers. "The exercises, sleeping, constant hydrating, and eating lots and lots of your good food. That's all I can do. All the rest of every

224

single day is *wasted*. I have been doing diddlysquat for most of every single damned day. As of this very instant, Rose, I am done with that. Help me up."

"You're going to do an extra set?"

"One right now, one after lunch, and one this evening. That'll be four today. Four, maybe five tomorrow. And I want you to pick up two canes for me at that rental place, Monday on your way home from work. I'm done with the walker."

She took his hands in hers and they both got him up out of the recliner.

"Also, Rose, I don't want you coming home in the middle of the day. Do your work, finish what you have to do, then come home and stay home. There's nothing stopping me from making a pb-and-j sandwich."

She reached up and pushed a curl off his forehead. "I've been worried that you won't eat if I'm not here. That you won't want to… Um…"

"Get up off my butt? You were right. I didn't want to. I wanted to live and die right in that recliner. But that just changed."

He grabbed her hands again and he knew she could feel how weak he still was and he knew it scared her. So many things scared her. She had been as scared as he was and he hadn't given that fact as much attention as he should have. She was afraid to touch him, even in bed. She slept huddled over against the edge of the bed, afraid to bump against him in the night and make him hurt. It would have hurt a lot at the beginning. It might hurt a bit even now. But he needed her touches, and he didn't know how to make that clear to her.

****

When Rose opened the door Monday afternoon, she

smelled food. Hot food. A variety of smells that made her almost faint with hunger.

"My gosh, Jack! That smells fantastic! What did you do?"

He was back in the recliner, but he was grinning up at her. "I went rooting around in the freezer and found a container marked chicken cacciatore and I put it in the oven. It'll be ready in twenty minutes. Perfect timing, if I do say so myself."

Rose dumped her bag on the bench by the door. "From the smell I could easily believe you've been acting like a chef all afternoon. I am beyond ravenous. And I was feeling dismal because I couldn't think of anything I could throw together in a hurry." She peered at the foil wrapping on the counter. "I forgot all about this! It's from the birders, from your friends. There were two casseroles but Max and I polished off one of them. How extraordinarily yummy!"

"I found some frozen peas too, and what I think might be some sort of cookies, also from the birders. How does that sound for a meal?"

"Jack." She wanted to throw herself into his lap but she was afraid his joints and muscles still hurt so she settled for taking his head in her hands and touching her mouth to his. "That sounds outstanding. I've got to take a quick shower because one of the new alpacas at Hunt's drooled all over my front. Then I'll come and set the table and we can eat!"

Jack put both hands on the chair arms and hoisted himself upright. The two canes were leaning against his chair, ready. "I can hobble out to the kitchen, Rose, and I can manage to set the table."

"All right, my love."

He watched her leave the room. He would figure out how to balance on one cane while setting the table. He would pour the seltzer. He would start the peas. He would put the frozen cookies in the microwave. He'd let Rose get the casserole out. It took some fancy juggling to get it into the oven with only one hand. There was no point trying to get it out when it was hot, and ending up with their supper all over the floor. Then Rose would have to figure out something to eat, and she was tired and ravenous.

How often did she feel "dismal" as she climbed the porch stairs, as she opened the front door and thought ahead to the evening with him?

****

Okay, Jack my man. Today is the day. Out of the chair and out of the house.

There were four stairs down from the front porch, but only two stairs in the back. So Jack hobbled on two canes into their bedroom and out through the French doors and onto the little porch.

And stopped. The yard looked huge. The two stairs looked daunting.

One cane and a death grip on the railing. Down one step. Down two.

His feet were on the ground, on grass and dirt and pebbles and clover. He'd forgotten how much clover there was in the yard. It looked like every single plant had a white flower. He inhaled and the smell made him almost light-headed.

Come on, Jack. You're not out here to smell the pretty flowers. Turn around and go back up those two stairs. And then back down those two stairs. Keep doing it until you can't do it anymore. Then go indoors and drink a lot of water and rest for no more than half an hour and then do the rehab exercises, including all the stupid little gripping and stretching and pushing and pulling that's supposed to strengthen your hands and make your fingers do what you tell them to. And maybe someday you'll be able to pull on a pair of blue jeans and fasten them by yourself, like an adult.

****

The long scar on his leg was looking better, and the one on his forehead couldn't even be seen in some kinds of light. And Rose knew he was doing the rehab exercises four or five times a day now, because he did them on Saturday and Sunday when she was home. But he didn't tell her that on weekdays he exercised almost all day, every day. He didn't tell her the first time he went outdoors. He didn't tell her when he moved from the back porch to the front porch, or how many times he'd been up and down those four stairs. He didn't tell her when he walked to the end of their driveway and back, using two canes, or when he did it again the next morning and then three times that afternoon.

He didn't tell her when he started walking out onto Reservoir Road, or that he thought he might be able to get halfway to the corner and back by the end of the week.

Part of him wanted to share those triumphs with her. But a larger and more insistent part said *whoop-dee do*. So Rose had a husband who could go down four stairs all by himself. A husband who could hobble almost six hundred steps on two canes and didn't even need to lie down afterward and take a nap.

Whoop-dee do.

But at least she had a husband now who had meals

ready when she walked in. He found a place to order precooked frozen meals and he happily paid extra to have them delivered and then he balanced on one cane and put them in the freezer and there they were, good food that Rose didn't have to prepare. And not a bit like the old TV dinners. These were good food, with good local meat and organic veggies and Vermont cheese from up where she used to live.

And he sat beside her for two online birthing classes and he thought that next Tuesday he might surprise her by walking out to the car on his canes and telling her they could do the class in person, together, like any other couple who would be having a baby together in less than two months.

Chapter Sixteen

A Bright Pink Flamingo

"He's looking good, Rose. Infinitely better than when we saw him a few days out of the hospital."

The two women were sitting on the little back porch, watching Jack balance on one cane while he turned things on the grill and laughed at something Xavier said.

"He made the decision to get better, Max. And that's what he started doing."

"What are they talking about, do you think?"

"I bet it's that proposed roundabout. Jack's up in arms about how much wetland will be destroyed if the project goes through. He's probably enlisting your husband into some sort of citizen protest. Wetland warriors or something."

"Cattail hugging instead of tree hugging?"

"I wouldn't be surprised." Rose watched her husband for a few more seconds and then turned toward Max. "He does look great, doesn't he? Getting rid of the walker was a major confidence booster. Now he's generally all right with only one cane, and that helps too. He is so determined, Max. He's been exercising like a madman and it's given him back his appetite and makes him sleep at night." She snorted. "Jack is out cold right after supper every night and he doesn't move until morning. I thought I needed a lot of sleep, what with little

Calloway making demands on my body, but he's got me beat."

"Recuperation takes a lot of energy, Rose."

"We both have learned how true that is."

"You're looking better too, my friend."

"I hope so! It is *so* much healthier not being petrified all the time, afraid I'm going to lose my husband. And not be running around like the proverbial chicken with its head cut off, trying to keep up with work and grocery shopping and time with Jack and childbirth classes and— And on and on and on." She looked down at the two men on the lawn. "Right now feels pretty much like heaven."

"How much longer are you going to work?"

"I'm going to keep working almost full time for a while, between the farms and being on call for emergency translation. Like last week's auto accident involving two Bosnian speakers, which was tricky. And yesterday's wedding where half the attendees spoke no English and the other half spoke no Spanish. *That* one was fun!"

"What are you planning to do after the baby's born?"

Rose looked sideways at her friend. "Prepare yourself, Max. I am about to say something radical."

"Go for it."

"Jack and I are going to raise our own baby."

"You rebel you."

"At first, we thought we might use that daycare center near Jack's office. But the longer I carry this baby, Max, the more I hate, hate, *hate* the idea of handing Calloway over to other people. Letting other people see her first smiles. Maybe her first steps. Having other people know more than we do about what toys she likes, how she interacts with other little ones."

She leaned forward, her face flushed and earnest. "Back when I was a teenager and doing a lot of babysitting, there was this couple who had three boys, boom, boom, boom. The kids were two, three, and almost five when I started sitting for them, and I always wondered why the parents bothered to have children at all. They both had full-time jobs, and they were on a lot of committees and in a bunch of organizations. Their boys were in daycare starting at age six weeks or so, all day every day, plus there were babysitters three or four nights a week. I know I had a skewed view of reality, having parents who were around all the time. But even as a fourteen-year-old, I felt in my gut that those three little boys were getting short-changed."

Max was nodding. "We felt the same way. We were poor as church mice, but we agreed we'd both have part-time jobs until Josh left for college, so one of us was always home. We discovered, somewhat to our surprise—although I guess we shouldn't have been surprised—that Josh needed us as much when he was in middle and high school as when he was younger."

"That makes sense. The teenage years are a confusing time for so many kids." Rose frowned, staring again at the two men without really seeing them. "We keep reading about an epidemic of mental health problems in kids. Even kids as young as three or four! I am sure many daycare workers do an excellent job, but the children still get moved from adult to adult, house to house. Maybe our country's children need more security, more sense of home. Their own room. Their own favorite toys. Taking their naps in their own bed. Seeing their own parents most of every single day."

"I think many women feel guilty if they stay at home. Like they're not 'contributing'. Maybe stay-at-home dads feel that way too. And many couples feel they need two jobs just to get by."

"I know, Max. But I wonder if that second paycheck often gets spent for things that wouldn't be needed if one parent stayed home."

"Huh. Like proper clothes for work?"

"Transportation to and from work for two people instead of one," Rose continued, ticking it off on her hands.

"Childcare, which may be the biggest expense for many couples."

"Ordering in or picking up dinner on the way home from work, because both parents are exhausted from their busy days. It's gotta be less expensive having one parent at home doing meal planning and cooking."

"*And* it might avoid a lot of ultra-processed foods!" Max exclaimed.

"That stuff is pure poison!" Rose agreed.

"I read recently that a large percentage of store-bought baby food has too much sugar and not enough nutrition. I'm willing to bet the food you and your sister Lily got when you were little was way healthier."

"It was." Rose's sigh sounded as if it came all the way from her feet. "I wonder how many two-paycheck families need two checks not for the basics but for all the extra *stuff* most of us think we need. The very newest espresso machine. The next size up in plasma TVs. This year's clothing fashions, and take last year's to Goodwill. I sometimes think that simpler, less so-called advanced cultures had the right idea. Focus on family and on one's relationship to nature, and not on the acquisition of *stuff*."

"So you won't be going back to work after the baby's born?"

"I love my job, Max. Both of us love our jobs. And both of us feel that we're doing something important. But little Calloway here is more important." Rose rubbed her growing belly. "So we're going to juggle. Jack's company just hired a new employee to do what he does in the southern half of the state, leaving Jack free to focus on installations closer to home. He already does a lot of planning and mapping and consulting from his upstairs office, so he's going to set up a crib and later a playpen right next to his chair. He won't get the extra pay for working over forty-five hours a week anymore, but he'll still be full-time with full benefits.

"For me," Rose said with a smile, "September's usually the last busy month till spring, so that's good. I'll do safety lectures and English classes at four apple orchards and farms that have migrant workers. Two of them are dusty and chaotic, with unfriendly dogs racing around and cats that are pretty much feral, so I won't bring the baby with me." She grinned. "But my most favorite farmer, the usually somber Huntley Huntington runs a tight ship indeed, and he actually smiled when I asked about bringing the baby with me! He grabbed my arm and showed me a little screened-in porch with a rocking chair where I can nurse the baby without being disturbed. He said his wife nursed their daughter in that very place so it has good vibes. His phrase. I'm telling you, Max. Seeing Hunt grin and then hearing him talk about *good vibes* was a double delight!"

"Is there a Mrs. Huntley Huntington?"

"Oh yes, and she's a perfect mate for him. He's tall

and handsome, and she's tall and lovely. And serene. She and another woman run a yoga studio in back of the main house. They've got a separate driveway and parking area, so I don't always notice what goes on there, but it looks like there might be four or five classes a day. Plus some evening programs, I believe."

"If you're at work all day now, and Jack is asleep by—What? Seven-thirty or so? That doesn't leave much time for the two of you."

"We've got weekends, the same as we did before. And Jack managed to stay awake for two online birthing classes and one in person. But in general, Max—" She sighed. "In general, you're right. All that lovely golden evening time is gone. We used to talk and listen to music and watch movies and read together and laugh and cuddle—"

"And generally do what couples generally do."

"And now we don't." Rose gave a little shake and stood up. "But we will again. Hey, Jack! How's supper coming? We're ravenous up here!"

"Five minutes, my love."

Xavier turned and looked up toward the porch. "I think it's time to get the salads out of the fridge, Max."

"We'll do that very thing." She and Rose headed into the kitchen. "Your picnic table, by the way, is a thing of beauty."

"It was a housewarming gift from Magda and Tom. We didn't want anything for inside until we lived here for a while and got a feel for what we need. So she said, in her beautiful husky seeress voice, that outdoor people live outdoors as well as indoors so they were going to give us furniture for that part of our home."

****

"Ahhhh. That was a feast. A nourishing and belly-filling feast."

All four of them leaned back, full of baked potatoes, fat juicy sausages from a local farm, corn on the cob from the same place, strong cheddar cheese and smoked gouda and ripe tomatoes, and Xavier's sourdough rolls with six kinds of olives in them.

"Xavier, how about the Grand Unveiling?"

"Oh my lord. I almost forgot." He got up, took the porch steps in one leap, and came out seconds later holding a long cardboard box. "Max and I saw this at the craft fair. We looked at it, we looked at each other, and we both knew it was for our friend Jack. We're hoping you agree."

"Hmmm. Gonna need a knife to open it."

Xavier handed him a jackknife and Jack could feel Rose stiffen on the bench beside him, wanting to take the knife, wanting to open the box herself, afraid his fingers wouldn't work and he'd cut himself and there would be one more thing that hurt and one more reason to see a doctor and he would be embarrassed in front of their friends. But she didn't move, and it hit him again how very much he loved his wife.

He managed to open the jackknife with only a bit of difficulty, and hold it and slit the tape down the middle of the box and then close the knife and return it to Xavier. When he slowly pulled the flaps apart and started rustling around in the packing paper, Max couldn't wait another second.

"It's from that wood carver woman. You know, Rose, we looked at her chairs last summer?"

At first, the gift looked like a stick with a neon pink suction cup at the end. Then Jack pulled the whole thing out of the box.

"Oh my gosh! What a hoot!" Rose half-stood to look more closely at the cane's handle, a glaring pink flamingo's head with a huge orange and black bill.

"This was definitely made for me! Thank you, thank you!"

"Do real flamingos have bills in Hallowe'en colors, Jack? We were worried it might not be accurate enough for a birder."

"I have no idea, Max. I've never seen a real flamingo. But who would dare question this creature? Look at the expression in those little yellow eyes!"

"It's guaranteed, Jack." Xavier's precise voice was full of laughter and pleasure. "If it's the wrong length we can return it and the carver will either find one in her workshop that fits you, or she'll make you a custom-fitted one."

"It's even got wings!" Jack ran his finger down the little streaks that suggested tucked-in wings. "And feet! Scaly black feet with really scary toes." He threw back his head and laughed, his first real laugh since the morning he called and told her he'd just seen a marsh wren. Rose wanted to cry and laugh and jump up and hug him and hug both of their friends and then laugh and cry some more.

"That is too... Thank you, thank you, thank you." He glanced up at the sky. "It looks like it's gonna pour any minute so we should probably go inside. But tomorrow morning, my love, you and I are going to take a little stroll out on the road and we are going to dazzle the neighbors with this incredible neon pink flamingo cane."

"Maybe we can get the woodcarver lady to make a

second one for you."

"Not necessary. One will do." He met Rose's eyes. "I've been practicing. This glorious gigantoid pink flamingo will do very well."

"Jack Carmichael. I am getting the uncomfortable feeling that you haven't been completely forthcoming these past two weeks."

"I wanted to surprise you."

"You've been walking in the road?"

Two pink spots flared in his pale cheeks. "The yard, the driveway, and then the road. I've made it twice to the fire hydrant that's halfway to the corner."

"And back?"

"Of course back! You didn't find me waiting there, hugging the hydrant, when you got home from work."

He couldn't tell if she was angry or not. Her color was high, her eyes looked damp, and she wasn't smiling.

"Well." Xavier stood up. "It's starting to sprinkle. We'll help you get everything into the house and then we'll head for home."

Max looked from Rose to Jack and back again. "I would love to be a fly on the wall."

"I'm not angry. You don't have to leave. Honestly."

"It's time." Xavier was already stacking plates and picking up cutlery, and Max started gathering mugs and glasses.

Jack hoisted himself up on the flamingo cane. "The decision, my love, has been made for us."

****

It was very quiet in the kitchen. The dishes were washed and the leftovers were put away.

"You know what I'm thinking, Jack?"

"What are you thinking, my love?"

"I am thinking that if you're up to walking in the road, you might be up to other kinds of physical exertion as well."

"I might."

She took a step and put her lips close to his and she felt him kissing her back and then, for the first time in so very long, she felt him lift his hands and put them on her back and butt, felt him pull her closer.

"I've missed this, Jack. So much."

"I have too. But I've been scared."

"I know." She smoothed his hair back from his forehead, her fingers barely touching the v-shaped scar. "At first you were hurting too much."

"That's true. But even after I started feeling better, I was afraid I—I've been afraid I couldn't, Rose."

"If feels very much like you can."

Ahhh. That dimple. Jack realized with a jolt that he hadn't seen Rose's dimple in months.

"Now, yes. But not before."

He didn't mention his other fear, that Rose might not be attracted to him anymore, that she might see him as nothing but a worthless lump in sweatpants, spending all day every day in an old recliner, a lump who wasn't working and couldn't do anything at all around the house.

"I have an idea, Jack, and I believe it's an outstanding idea. We will go into our bedroom. We will get undressed. You will lie down on our nice firm mattress. Face up. I will straddle your thighs, with my knees on the bed so my weight and Calloway's weight won't be pressing down on you. And then, Jack—"

"Then what, Rose?"

"Then I will touch you and kiss you and maybe do

some licking and then, Jack—"

"Then what, Rose?"

"Then I will lower myself onto you. Very slowly."

"You're sure it'll be okay for the baby?"

"You heard the birth coach. Sex is safe all the way through a normal pregnancy unless your doctor tells you otherwise." The dimple again, as she carefully unbuttoned his shirt and bent to kiss his chest. "And sex is an excellent way of alleviating stress and anxiety. You heard her say that too."

"What you're saying, then, is that it's like a prescription."

"Absolutely."

"So we have to do it."

"We do."

"God, Rose. I might explode before we get out of the kitchen."

****

He's back. He's Jack again. Truly, completely, wonderfully Jack.

Rose stood in the doorway of his upstairs office, watching as her husband swiveled in his chair to look at the topographic map on the wall, moved the cursor over his computer screen, talked into his headset as fast and strong as ever, and lifted his other hand to beckon her in. His desk was covered with papers and felt markers and brochures and photographs. His thick hair was standing on end from his fingers pushing it off his forehead, and he was jiggling his knee in time to some music in his head.

"We can't fault their logic, Derek. Tracking collectors there will get them full benefit from the west and the south, even with those big conifers blocking the sun first thing every day. But if they would change the location just a few hundred feet north, they could go with stationary. I know they don't want to block the view, but it'd cost 'em less up front and probably less in maintenance going forward. You think you can convince them? Wait! Gotta word that differently! Derek, not one single one of us could do a better job of convincing them than you, with your earnest super-sweet honest face..." He threw back his head and laughed. "Coming on too strong, huh?"

He signaled to Rose again, and this time she stepped into the office and perched on the extra chair.

"I'll leave it to you then. And I'll get you the specs on the Hartford project later today. But now to the important stuff. How's life with eighteen-month-old Derek Junior treating you? Wait." He unhooked his headset, set it in the stand next to the phone, and switched to speaker. "Rose'll want to hear, too."

"You do remember he's not Derek Junior, right? Or has your near-death experience affected your memory?"

"I remember. But you gotta admit that your little Sebastian is a mini-you. Right down to the cowlick. Or right *up* to the cowlick. How is life with the little one?"

"It is a circus with three rings and clowns and wild animals and caramel corn. And now that we're past the sleep deprivation months, we can enjoy it."

"I can hardly wait. So. I think we're all set at work, at least for now. Text me if anything happens on either front."

Jack ended the call and swiveled in his chair. "You're home early today!"

"Everything left on my list can wait until Monday. I'm starving and I'd rather eat lunch at home with you than alone in a diner. Are you ready for a break?"

"I am, my sweet. My love, my wife, my gloriously huge woman, mother of my child."

"Gloriously huge, huh?"

Jack got up and stretched. "Yes. Gloriously. You are gloriously gorgeous and gloriously beautiful and gloriously vibrant."

She looked down and patted her belly. "I hope we never have twins."

"None in my family, as far as I know."

"Nor in mine." She took his hand and led him out into the hall. "We've got left-over roast beef and lettuce and onions and some of that horseradish sauce from your mother. And that good rye bread."

"That sounds better than perfect. And for dessert, I'm going to make us one of my world-famous two-person banana splits, featuring one or two kinds of the very best ice cream the state has to offer. Possibly three kinds, depending on what's in the freezer."

"You know, Jack. Some of my huge belly comes from what you've been feeding me this last month."

"It looks good on you. You got too skinny all those weeks taking care of an invalid husband." He winked. "Besides, you're eating for two."

"I am, that's true. And one of us made herself known in a big way today." She paused halfway down the stairs and turned to her husband. "My first Braxton-Hicks contractions!"

Jack stopped dead, his hand on her arm and his face both anxious and excited.

"It was so weird, Jack. I felt two hands grabbing my sides so I looked around, but of course no one was there. Then the hands pressed on my belly, and I felt fingers grasp my hips… And then it all went away." She started down the stairs again. "I had another one about five minutes later, and that was that. I spoke sternly to our baby and told her she was to stay right where she is for at least three more weeks."

"You think she'll be an obedient little girl, with the two of us for parents?"

"Well. Maybe not always. But I also tried logic. I told her that you and I want her to spend her first days here at home, with us, instead of in the neonatal unit at the hospital."

"That should do it."

She giggled. "A huge and odiferous manure spreader kept getting closer and closer while I was standing out there wondering if I was going into labor. Cramps plus the powerful stench of well-ripened cow manure." She patted her belly. "Lucky you, you couldn't smell it, could you?"

****

"Ahhhh. I can always think better when I'm not ravenous. And I think it's time for us to decide on a name."

"We can do that." He looked up from pouring maple syrup on the giant dish of ice cream in front of him. "But let's not allow that to distract us from this incredible dessert." He cocked his head. "More chocolate sauce? Or do you think what we've got here is enough?"

She laughed. "Yes, my darling. I truly believe it's enough. Give me a spoon and we can talk as we gorge."

"Wait! The crowning glory!" He jumped up, pulled open the refrigerator door, and pulled out a small jar. "The strawberry jam that didn't quite jam, from Max. This will be a perfect final layer."

"And truly beautiful." Rose watched him spoon out the glistening ruby-red sauce.

"I think this is my best effort yet."

"Oh yum yes." Rose concentrated on making sure her spoon had both flavors of ice cream, all three sauces, a few nuts, and a chunk of banana.

"So…" Jack said meaningfully without looking Rose in the eye. "We decided against sticking with Calloway because of the kuh-kuh thing? Calloway Carmichael. Although Callie Carmichael is sort of appealing."

"Maybe."

"Let's do the last name first. Do you want us to hyphenate?"

Rose raised her eyebrows. "That sounds indecent."

"Do you?"

"No and no again. Carmichael-Gilhooly would be unfair to our little babe. And I'm Carmichael now, so resurrecting Gilhooly doesn't even make sense."

"Just checking to see if you regret losing your family name."

"I love my dad deeply, and that's his name and his father's before him and so on forever. But Carmichael feels like *my* name because it represents a conscious choice of mine, not just an accident of birth. Besides, I think Carmichael is more mellifluous."

"Mellifluous, huh?"

"The Mellifluous Carmichaels. That's us." The dimple appeared in her left cheek. "Besides, we don't want our little one or her classmates looking up Gilhooly and finding out that one derivation means *gluttonous lad*. Carmichael, now, is noble. The Fort of Michael."

"I looked up Gilhooly too, Rose. You are descended

from some chief, something to do with the Four Tribes of Tara. And from a seventh-century king of Ireland. Can't get much more noble than chiefs and kings."

"Gluttons and kings then. Still not mellifluous."

"Maybe we can find something in your family tradition? What about a flower name, like you and your sister? That would be appropriate for the daughter of a botanist."

"I'm not a botanist."

"You've studied botany, you know about plants, you love plants. You're a botanist."

"Hmmm. Flowers. A lot of my favorites don't make great people names. Lilac. Clover."

"Clover's a name sometimes."

"But do you want it to be our little girl's name?"

"Definitely not. Wasn't there a porn film about being inside Daisy Clover?"

"No! That film starred Natalie Wood and it had nothing to do with porn."

"I am sure I watched a porn flick with that title. In college."

"Maybe the title got borrowed." Her little snort had her reaching for a napkin to catch the syrup dripping down her chin. "It is an obvious connection."

"Back to our task. What about naming her after some plant that's good for the environment and pollinators and birds and all?"

"Milkweed. Sneezewort. Tickseed! Turtlehead!" Rose's eyes sparkled. "Beardtongue!"

"Those last two sound like hobbits. What's that orange flower that throws its seeds if you touch it?"

"Spotted Touch-me-not. Also called Jewelweed."

"So what about Jewel?"

"I don't think so. Let's table flower names for now. They made sense for my parents because they were starting out as farmers. Growers." Another spurt of laughter. "But they started with nothing but cattle and apples. Lily and I are lucky we weren't named Holstein and MacIntosh!"

"What about names that were in your family, before the flowers?"

"I like that idea. We won't be carrying Gilhooly into the next generation, but maybe we can carry another historical family name."

"Grandparents? Greats?"

"Oh! My father's grandmother—No, his great-grandmother I think. Anyway, she marched as a suffragette with Amelia Bloomer, in Seneca Falls. Her name was M-A-R-E-N, but I don't know if she pronounced it like *mare*-in or *mar*-en. I like *mar*-en better." She reached across the table to grab Jack's hand. "Do you like that name?"

"I've never heard it before. But I think I like it. Maren. And it could hearken back to my dad's mother Marian. Do double duty." He nodded decisively. "Yes, I like it."

She leaned back and took a deep breath. "I do believe we have our baby's first and last names. You know what would be nice? If her middle name comes from *your* family history."

Jack's brown eyes sparkled. "Well, my dad's grandmother was named Idris, a name that was in the family a few times before her. It can be pronounced several different ways, but I think she said it with a both I's short. I don't like it much, though."

"What about names in your mother's family?"

"I'd have to ask her. No, wait. It's all coming back. Magda's favorite aunt was Branka. She died a few years back in an auto accident. And another aunt is Irina. And there's a Layla in there somewhere."

"I love that song."

"Me too." Jack was staring absently out the window, frowning, remembering. There was a smear of chocolate sauce on his cheek and Rose wanted to get up and lick it off.

"I've got it! Rah-EEE-sah."

"What?"

"R-A-I-S-A. That was my mother's great-aunt."

"Also Gorby's wife."

"That bendy green guy? Made of clay? He was married?"

"What?"

"You know. Decades ago. Toys, TV show, lunchboxes. Green clay animation. With a little red dog or pony or something."

Rose burst out laughing. "You mean Gumby?"

"Gumby! Yes! So who's Gorby?"

"Gorbachev. Russian leader back in the, um, eighties maybe. At the end of the USSR."

"Of course. How soon we forget."

"I did a paper on him in high school. He was the first Russian leader to have a wife who was a force in her own right. Her name was Raisa, like your mother's great-aunt." Rose was again sparkling and excited. "Raisa Gorbachev was a lovely woman. But you're supposed to call her Raisa Gorba*cheva* because she was Mr. Gorbachev's wife. Anyway, she was a teacher and an activist. Plus she was a major donor to some organization that had to do with blood banks, or training doctors, or something noble and useful like that." A frown wrinkled her brow. "But we would be saddling our little girl with two unusual names."

"She'll be strong enough, Rose, with you for a mother."

"And you for a daddy."

"But we have to realize that when our daughter graduates, the principal or dean or whoever will end up saying *Mary RAYza*. Or *Marian Reeeza*. Or some other bastardization." Jack frowned.

"And our feisty daughter, named for two upstanding and confident women, will stop dead right there on the stage, and correct him or her. Loudly."

"And we two will applaud from the audience. Loudly."

"We'll be so proud of our daughter that we'll just about burst."

Jack looked across the table at his wife, at the mother of Maren Raisa Carmichael. His eyes and nose were prickling with tears, but Rose was looking down at the remains of their dessert.

"If you don't act fast, Jack, I'm going to finish every last melting spoonful."

"They're yours." He pushed the bowl closer to her. "You know, Rose? I've been thinking about going on Ivy's F.A.T.S.O. walk on Sunday. There's a drawdown at Dead Creek, which means lots of shorebirds. It's less than a mile from the parking lot, so it won't even be as much walking as you and I have been doing every evening."

She plunked her spoon down with a clatter. "You are truly back!"

He grinned at her, his brown eyes twinkling and a

little mischievous. "We've had sex three times this week and I needed an afternoon nap after only two of those times. I have returned to the living." He reached across and covered her hand with his. "I'm not up for driving yet, but Molly can probably pick me up. And I don't have to carry anything heavy."

"And besides, you can't wait to show off your flashy flamingo cane."

"You know me well, Rose. You know me well."

Chapter Seventeen

Delphine

The wind started just after dawn, whining and moaning and strong enough to lift the folding chairs on the front porch. Rose and Jack took bagels and coffee outside and sat, anchoring the furniture and watching in relative safety as the tall evergreens across the road tossed and bent almost double, and leaves from maples and poplars made mini-tornados on lawns and driveways.

"Hurricanes are dangerous, of course. But right now this is sort of exciting."

"I agree." Jack reached over and took one of her hands. "We're gonna have to go inside soon, though. Leaves and twigs are already flying around. Bigger stuff is next."

"I know." She shook her head. "It doesn't make sense, but I feel safer out here watching. As if I might have some control if I'm keeping an eye on things." She made a little snorting sound. "Control over Hurricane Delphine, the strongest hurricane ever to hit Vermont. Sure thing! But hiding inside feels like... like... like poor Little Red Riding Hood huddling in a tiny hut while wolves circle and howl outside."

"We won't be huddling, Rose. We'll be living. Inside. Just like we do when it's pouring rain or snowing or wicked cold. I'll go up to my office and do some work until the power fails. You'll work more on the baby quilt, or maybe finish reading that mystery. We'll have lunch together. Later, we'll eat supper. And then we'll go to bed, together, either in our bedroom or down in the cellar depending on how things are going. We'll hold each other and cuddle and wake up in the morning to clear skies and sunshine."

"You are a sweet man, Jack." But her generous mouth was tight. She didn't like thinking about the two of them downstairs in the windowless cellar, unable to see what was happening outdoors, with the house collapsing above them. "At least Hurricane Delphine is coming today, instead of ten days from now."

"That would be an experience to remember. A gigantoid hurricane and a new baby simultaneously." He looked sharply at her. "You're absolutely sure Maren won't be early?"

"There's no such thing as absolutely sure. But you heard the statistics in class. First babies are late more often than early." This time her little snort sounded more like a laugh. "A whole 1.3 days late, on average. And my doctor said there's nothing to suggest Maren might be early. We should have at least a week left. Maybe ten days."

"You told her about the Braxton-Hicks episodes?"

"Of course." Rose felt the corners of her mouth turning up. Her husband knew all the terminology. He studied the sonograms, he memorized the stages of labor, he asked thoughtful questions in class, and he always took notes. She felt a surge of wonder that she had ended up with this man, instead of someone like the father-to-be in their classes who talked about "brixford whatsies" and announced he didn't want to be any closer than a football field away when his wife crowned. *Crowned. You'd think it was something royal or something. That video made me sick to my stomach.*

His poor wife.

The contents of a neighbor's recycling bin tumbled down the middle of the road, newspapers and junk mail and plastic yogurt containers and soda cans leaping and chasing until they were stopped by the reservoir fence.

"I'd be happier, Rose, if we were staying with Max and Xavier. Closer to the hospital, for one thing. But also, we're friends with a couple who has a bona fide Cold War bomb shelter in the basement, and we're up on the hill instead of down there with them!"

"That couple has a bona fide Eneritz sharing the bomb shelter with them, Jack."

"Point taken." He bent to get the coffee pot and topped up their mugs. "What's the story with the egregious sister-in-law?"

"I gathered from Max that Eneritz woke up two days ago and went about making coffee and having breakfast and reading the paper—"

"The *New York Times*, of course."

"Or the *Washington Post*."

"Also a good possibility."

"And she puttered around doing whatever it is she does of a morning and an afternoon. It wasn't until suppertime that she realized she was alone in the house. And she didn't figure out her husband was gone until she noticed some empty shelves in one of their bookcases."

"No note? No nothing?"

"I guess not. Yipes!" Rose sat up straighter. Now a metal lawn chair was sailing down the road, sometimes airborne and sometimes touching the ground and cartwheeling.

"Oh shit. It's gonna—" Jack stood up. "Oh shit. It did."

Even above the sound of the wind, they heard the crash of metal and breaking glass as the chair smacked into the side window of their neighbor's car.

Rose hoisted herself to her feet. "Time to go in."

"It is." Jack picked up the two folding chairs. "We'll be safe inside, Rose. We've given this a lot of thought. We're prepared."

****

Prepared. Yes. Two whole days of preparing. Jack's new-to-him car was safe in the garage. Rose's truck was parked on the lawn tight against the garage wall, with the heavy picnic table and benches upside down in the back and lashed down with rope. The grill and the chairs from both porches were in the house. They had food for several days, some of it in coolers so they wouldn't have to open the fridge while the power was out. Bottles of drinking water lined the kitchen counter. Five-gallon buckets of water waited beside the downstairs toilet, and every room had either a camping lantern or flashlights.

Rose had helped Jack make a corner of the cellar into an emergency refuge with sleeping pads and sleeping bags, flashlights, water, and food. She told herself, again and again, that their new bulkhead door would let them get out even if the house was in rubble over their heads. They would not be trapped. They could just wait until the noise stopped and then they would push open the bulkhead and step out into the air and take deep breaths and know they were alive.

"I'm going up to my office for a while. Yell for me

if—If anything." Jack reached for her chin and turned her face toward his and kissed her. "Anything."

"I will. You go and work."

****

For the next hour, Rose stood by the kitchen window watching the evergreen trees and the wind-driven debris. The rain started soon after Jack went upstairs, horizontal needles of rain that first turned the outside to gray and then completely obscured the houses across the street. As the wind grew still stronger, she began hearing cracks and crashes as trees around the reservoir lost large branches or toppled into each other.

"Mr. Cardinal," she murmured to the front yard. "I'm glad that your youngsters fledged weeks and weeks ago. I hope your whole family finds safe places to hide. Maybe against the trunk of a big sturdy oak. Oh!"

She stiffened and put both hands on her belly.

"A quick one. False labor, like at Hunt's."

Twenty-five minutes later there was another quick one.

"Walk it off, Rose," she muttered to herself. "False labor stops if you move around."

She wouldn't call Jack downstairs, not when the contractions were far apart and she didn't think they were real. But after another twenty-five minutes there was a stronger contraction, heavy hands pushing first against her back and then circling her waist and then pushing from the top of her belly down.

"Two more and I'll call Jack. Two more. Two more means it's real."

Rose waited through four more contractions, one after twenty-three minutes and the second after twenty. She turned when she heard Jack coming downstairs.

"Power's out," he said.

"Not surprising, with this kind of wind. That howling is beginning to sound animal, or maniacal, or something."

"It is indeed, my love. Is there any coffee left? Great!" He moved with his usual speed and energy toward the kitchen. "What have you been doing while I was finishing up a whole passel of odds and ends?"

"A passel, huh?"

"Maybe two passels. Want some coffee?"

"No. Thanks." She put her hands on her belly. "Jack. I don't think Maren's going to be 1.3 days late."

"What? Why?"

"I've been having contractions for over an hour."

Jack was at her side in two steps.

"How close?"

"First, twenty-five minutes apart. Now about twenty. I thought it was false labor but I walked around the house and they didn't stop and they're getting stronger."

His warm hands covered hers, both of them feeling the tautness and solidity of her belly.

"Well. That's… Okay. We'll be okay, Rose. You're healthy, the baby's healthy, and we know what to expect."

Rose thought, again, how fortunate she was to have found this man, this one man among all the thousands and millions of men out there. Jack's hands were shaking but his voice was calm, and he met her eyes, and he would be beside her no matter what.

"It's too dangerous to go outside right now. I'm hoping we can wait for Delphine's eye. Then either an ambulance will be able to get here or I can drive us to the hospital, and we'll both stay there until we head home tomorrow with baby Maren."

"That sounds like a plan."

"You should call your doctor now and let her know what's happening. Before we lose cell coverage."

"Oh. Yes. Oh!" She stiffened, her eyes wide, both hands against her belly. "You call, Jack. You call."

"How long since the last one?"

"Eighteen... No. Seventeen minutes. Between seventeen and eighteen."

While Jack talked with the nurse and then the doctor, Rose paced back and forth across the living room and kitchen and into the bedroom and back. She was still breathing deeply when Jack ended the call.

"Over?" he asked.

"Almost." Her grin was as welcome as it was unexpected. "You have *got* to feel the next one, Jack! It's totally amazing. I feel like—I feel like I dropped in at a friend's house and discovered he's a concert violinist and I never even knew he played. My body is showing me a skill I didn't know it had! I don't have to tell it what to do. It just does it!"

"You are amazing, my dearest love. And I definitely want to share the next contraction. And the one after that, and every single one."

"What did the doctor say?"

"Pretty much what we guessed." He glanced out the window, frowning. "It's too dangerous to be out on the streets right now. But the nurse looked at the radar map, and the hurricane's eye should be here in a half hour to forty minutes." He made a quick little head movement as if shaking off the worry. "And the doctor said we're her star pupils. If Maren gets here before we can leave, she's confident that we know what to do."

"Yes." Rose straightened her shoulders. "I'm confident too."

"Let's get the book." He looked up and gave her a real Jack grin, wide and open and so very dear to her. "I'm glad we bought the book instead of relying on the internet!"

"Why? Oh. Yes. The power."

"My backup source will last several minutes but that might not be enough. We do *not* want to feel confused or panicked."

"No panic. No worry. It may seem peculiar, but I don't feel at all panicky now."

Jack took her face in his hands. "Rose, my love. We will get through this. With flying colors. And at the end, we will have little Maren to look at and hold and love."

"I know." She didn't have to make herself smile at him. She felt the smile, the love for this man, start somewhere in her belly, right next to their tiny daughter, and then travel up until it filled her chest and flooded her neck and had to come out all over her face. "Let's get busy. I'll walk around and time contractions and you get everything we might need. In case."

Jack turned and headed for the stairs.

"Wait! Let's have something to eat first."

"Do not tell me you're ravenous."

"I am a very honest woman, Jack. I have to tell you I am ravenous. Because I truly am. And the doctor said it's fine to eat and drink a bit during the early phase of labor." She opened the bread box. "We've got really good rye bread, and sharp cheddar, and one last tomato, and one last cuke. And mayo, and maybe a bit of honey mustard. And pickles!"

"Rose."

She turned, laughing. "I know, my sweet man. I know there's a rare possibility that I might aspirate something into my lungs. I will be sensible and have juice and a mushed-up banana and a bowl of ice cream. You, on the other hand, will have a humongous sandwich. I'll watch you eat it. And I'll drool."

He knew he would never forget her little spurt of laughter as she stood there with her bright excited eyes and her swollen belly and the storm raging outside. The first time he heard that laugh, he wanted to hear it for the rest of his life. Now he wanted more. He wanted to hear her laugh for centuries, for millennia, way beyond their lives and the lives of their children and their grandchildren and their grandchildren's grandchildren.

"But you have to promise to make me a sandwich identical to the one you're going to have, just as soon as I've finished my task for the day."

"Consider it promised."

****

"Ahh. I'm no longer ravenous. But I can't say that ice cream is the best choice for a meal that's interrupted by a birthing contraction. I'm going to be impolite, Jack, and slurp up what melted during those minutes when I wasn't paying attention to food."

They both jumped when a tremendous crashing noise made the house shudder.

"Shit. That was big. And close." Jack peered out the kitchen windows, then the window in the side door. "Visibility sucks, but I don't think I'm seeing anything but empty space at the end of the street, where there should be that giant white pine."

"You think it hit anyone's house?"

"Can't tell. It might have. The top third might have hit the yellow house. Or it could be in the yard this side of the house. Maybe I can see from upstairs."

He was back downstairs within minutes.

"It looks like the yellow house is fine. Their garage is flattened, and the swing set in their back yard. But the house looks okay." He walked closer and put his hands on her shoulders. "The tree is lying across the road."

Rose was concentrating on the slow but inexorable beginning of another contraction, and she didn't immediately grasp what that meant for them.

"Oh. We can't get out then."

"Delphine's eye should be almost here. I'll do some scouting around and see if there's a way to get the car through a few backyards and out to the main road. Or maybe get part of the way and have an ambulance crew walk in and meet us with a stretcher. Gurney. Whatever."

"Yes. That's a good idea. Under fifteen minutes this time."

****

"You look like a logo for a frozen seafood company." Rose patted the front of Jack's heavy yellow rain slicker. "But you need one of those hats with a big brim. A sou'wester. A bright yellow sou'wester." She patted him again, delaying the moment when he would leave her alone. "I've never seen this jacket. What's it lined with?"

"Navy blue canvas. Weighs a ton, but rain doesn't dare get inside."

"It's still coming down pretty heavily, Jack. Maybe we should give up on the idea of finding a way out of here. Maybe we should just hunker down."

"There's almost no wind right now, and I won't be

gone more than twenty minutes." He cupped his hand around her chin. "Rose, if there's a way to get to the hospital, I'd like to try."

"All right, my love. But don't take any—Don't do anything risky."

Rose missed him before he reached the end of their driveway. She wanted him with her, next to her, holding her hand, sharing the new contraction. Sharing every contraction. She didn't want him outside when they couldn't be sure how long the relative calm would last.

Husband Killed By Falling Tree As Wife Gives Birth To Their First Child.

She shuddered. The house was cold. She had been comfortable while they were walking and walking, with Jack's arm around her and his solid heat against her side. Now she was beginning another contraction and she couldn't relax into it because she was cold and shivering and tense.

Get a grip, Rose! You are a full-grown woman and you're very capable and you have an extraordinarily important job to do. Both Jack and little Maren are counting on you.

Besides, Jack will be back in just a few minutes.

A jacket. Two jackets. Get moving again. And breathe. Breathe.

And don't forget to check the time.

Rose rested her crossed arms on the kitchen counter and concentrated on taking mostly shallow breaths with long exhalations after every fifth one, just as they practiced in class.

One more contraction down, unknown number yet to come.

I can do this.

I want Jack here.

The house was too dark and gloomy. She walked into the living room and took one of Jack's camping lanterns out of its box.

"Can be used for up to five days without recharging. That should do it. Five days of the hurricane, five days of labor. Piece of cake." She pressed the switch. "Ahhhh, wonderful!"

The bright light was a blessing, a gift. Rose switched on another lantern and put it in the darkest corner of the kitchen.

"Much better."

Jack would be back before the next contraction.

Was the wind picking up again?

She opened the door to the front porch and stared across at the spruce trees behind their neighbor's house. The tops of the trees were bending, but it wasn't nearly as bad as it had been in the morning, when she and Jack sat on the porch and shared coffee and bagels.

The wind wasn't howling. She heard nothing but a sustained whoosh.

Oh please, Jack.

The next contraction came and grabbed and tightened and lasted, and then left.

Thirteen minutes this time.

Oh please, Jack.

****

Both wind and rain returned before Jack threw open the kitchen door, ducked inside, and shook like a wet dog.

"How far apart now?"

"Twelve minutes."

He plopped down on the bench to take off his

sopping shoes and socks. "I'm sorry. I knew you'd be worried but I kept wanting to check one more option and then one more."

"Here." Rose held out a bathroom towel. "What's the word?"

"The word—" He rubbed his thick hair until it stood up all around his head. "The word is: we're stuck. There's no way to get a vehicle out. So I thought we could walk across the street and into the woods and get to the main road that way, but there's no real trail, and bushwhacking through dense woods when you're pretty far advanced in labor doesn't sound like a great idea."

His brown eyes were gentle and worried. "And it wouldn't do us any good anyway, even if we could walk out. Fred Whatsisname in the yellow house was on his porch. He's been listening to an emergency scanner and he said all the roads are closed. All of them. Everything's covered with debris and fallen trees and downed wires." He gave her a little grin. "You should have heard him cussing out the idiots who didn't put away their patio grills and trash cans and lawn furniture. Now not even emergency vehicles can get through."

"Well then, my love. We're here. Safe at home. And it's just us."

"And our baby."

"And our baby," she agreed.

"And your strong, amazing concert violinist body."

"Well then, my love, let's do this thing."

****

Rose's labor seemed stuck at twelve minutes. For the next two hours, the contractions were like clockwork. And Jack was there with her for each one, breathing with her, his hands on her sides and her belly, watching her face, murmuring encouragement.

"I thought it would feel like, like metal bands or something. But it's more like giant elastics, Rose. Giant wide bands of elastic that start out tight and then get tighter and tighter. How is little Maren not getting squished? She must be as tough as you are!"

Between contractions, she and Jack walked around and around, through the kitchen, around the living room, along the little hall to the bathroom, back into the kitchen.

"Let's dance."

"What?!" he asked, stunned.

"Walking is getting boring." She held up her arms. "Let's do some dancing."

"You are a crazy woman, Rose my love." He took her hand and she put her other arm around his shoulder. "But you are *my* crazy woman, and if you want to dance, we'll dance."

"We should have music. Do you remember any songs from your childhood?"

"Hmmm. Magda used to sing a Czech lullaby. I think it was Czech. Something about horses in the cabbage patch."

"Sing it."

"I don't remember all the words."

She gave him a look from under her brows. "Do you think that matters right now?"

"Good point." He gently swung her in a sedate twirl as he started singing and humming and singing again.

"That's a lovely melody."

"It is. But I think the words are about how much damage the horses do and how the family will starve that winter without their cabbage crop."

"That doesn't sound very restful for a lullaby."

"Neither does the bough breaking and down will come baby, cradle and all."

"True. Pop Goes the Weasel? Three Blind Mice?"

"Chopping off tails? Definitely not!"

"Row, Row, Row Your Boat."

"Okay. That's one."

"Old MacDonald. I don't think anything bad happens to any of the animals."

He whirled her again. "Itsy Bitsy Spider. The spider gets knocked down but starts back up the waterspout the minute the rain ends. It's an anthem to determination and—"

"Oh!" Rose moved out of her husband's arms so she could see the kitchen clock. "Not even eleven minutes! Either dancing was the perfect thing to do, or my body just decided it's time to move things along."

They stood still, her hand clutching his arm and her eyes wide.

"This one's bigger, Jack. Or tighter or something."

"Do you want to lie down? Or sit down?"

"Not quite yet. Do you think we can stay up here? Or should we go down to the cellar?"

"Fred said the wind in the second part of Delphine won't be anywhere near as strong as it was this morning. I think we can stay upstairs, Rose." He pulled the futon off the living room couch and dragged it to the hall near the bathroom. "Between interior walls. Safest part of the house."

"Good." She was panting, holding her belly and leaning over the kitchen counter. She didn't notice when Jack galloped upstairs and galloped back down a minute later. She didn't notice when he spread a plastic shower curtain over the futon, covered it with a clean sheet, and dropped a pile of backup sheets and towels nearby. The contraction was just beginning to ebb as Jack ducked into the bathroom and came out with a roll of gauze and bottles of antibacterial soap, rubbing alcohol, and iodine.

Rose took a full deep breath and straightened up.

"That, Jack, was the real thing. I forgot to check the clock at the start but I think it lasted almost two minutes."

He turned the gas on under the tea kettle.

"Okay. We've got the birthing area. We've got disinfecting stuff. In a few minutes, we'll have boiling water so I can sterilize the kitchen scissors. We've got plastic bags for, uh, waste disposal. Wicked icky term in my opinion, but that's what it said in the video."

He looked at her from under his brows and she saw excitement, happy excitement in his eyes, even more than the nerves.

Oh, yes. Oh Jack.

****

Later, Rose remembered Jack beside her when she walked, beside her when she finally sat cross-legged on the futon. She remembered him rubbing her back, massaging her shoulders, wiping her face with a cool wet cloth, holding the cloth against the back of her neck. She remembered him getting her sips of water, walking around with her again, breathing with her through every contraction, feeling every contraction with his hands.

But at the time, she mostly noticed what her own body was doing. She felt herself becoming huge. She felt herself growing, spreading, expanding, until she and her body were bigger and harder and tougher than the entire universe. She remembered Jack later, remembered and loved and was grateful, but for a few hours Rose's laboring body was the only truly clear thing in her universe.

****

"She's beautiful, Jack."

"She is."

"She looks strong and healthy."

"She does."

"I think she likes being born. Being here."

"I think so too."

Outside, the wind still howled around the house. Another tall white pine fell, this one in the woods across the road, and there was the incessant shrill warning of a car alarm. But Jack and Rose were oblivious. They sat shoulder to shoulder, leaning against the wall, in a cocoon of quiet delight.

"She has more hair than the baby in that video we saw."

"She does."

"I think it's going to be red-brown, like yours."

"Hmmm."

"She caught on to nursing immediately."

"She did."

They looked down at the tiny face against Rose's breast, at the tiny fist suddenly thrust into the air and waving around.

"We made a person, Jack." Her eyes were wide and amazed.

"Yes, Rose. We certainly did."

"She is one hungry little one."

"It's hard work, being born." Jack stood up, digging his cell phone out of his pocket. "I want to take some photos to share with Maren in years to come. Showing her where she was born, in the hall on the floor, during a hurricane. I want her to know that her first bath was with my handkerchief and warm water from our best cooking pot. I want her to know that her mother sat up against the wall and held her and gave her some healthy chlorophyll—Cholesterol?" His laugh sounded a bit manic and Rose thought he looked even more tired than she felt. "I had that word memorized for our last birthing class but now it's gone."

"Colostrum."

"Right. That stuff." He knelt on the end of the futon and took several shots of the baby's head against Rose's breast. "Protecting little Maren from infection. Giving her a healthy digestive system. Good stuff."

She leaned her head back against the wall and closed her eyes. "Whew. I'm tired."

"No wonder."

"I'm also ravenous." She opened her eyes and looked up at him, one brow raised. "And you have a promise to fulfill."

"A… Oh yes. Rye bread, sharp cheddar, tomato, and cucumber."

"And mayo and honey mustard and pickles!"

"Coming right up."

Epilogue

Hurricane Delphine knocked over, broke, and uprooted thousands of trees in New England. The winds ripped millions of leaves from their branches and sent them whirling and tumbling and racing north into Canada. But once the wind stopped, nature was determined to celebrate survival. Trees seemed to stand taller and stretch their branches farther. Individual leaves vied to be the most brilliant, to have the deepest wine red, the clearest orange, the most glowing yellow. Even the somber brown oak leaves showed off with a glossy elegance that went unnoticed in normal autumns.

The golden time lasted all of October and through most of November. And then, overnight, it was winter. December and January brought Vermont the longest unbroken spell of frigid weather in the history of the state. And then came the snow. Six inches one day, twelve the next, four or five inches every single day. A popular weatherman lost his trademark toothy grin and bemoaned that there was not one single person left in Vermont who hadn't begun to hate winter.

The weatherman was wrong.

"Rose, my love, I do believe this is the most perfect winter ever."

She looked up as Jack threw open the door on a gust of cold air and energy, tugging off his wool hat. "It's like a painting out there! Heavy snow on dark evergreens, mountains of white everywhere." He hung up his snow-covered parka and plopped down on the bench to take off his boots. "The drifts at the end of our road are almost as high as the roof of the Hurleys' shed. I'm telling you, Rose, this is a winter to remember!"

"It is." She answered absently, concentrating on measuring vanilla extract for her mother's favorite apple cake recipe. "Even some of your birding friends fled the state."

"True. True. They usually find pleasure and excitement in winter diving ducks and snow buntings and hawks, but this year is just too much. But our little family is safe in our little house, and we two adults don't have to brave cold or snow every single morning to go to work." He padded across the room and met her kiss, his face reddened by cold and wind, his thick hair tousled. "How is the littlest Carmichael this morning?"

"She was solemnly contemplating one foot, Jack, but the moment she heard your voice she started kicking both legs and wiggling all over her happy little body. She truly loves her daddy!"

"Of course she does. And he truly—" He bent to pick up the cooing infant. "Oh gasp. Oh pee-YEW! How can such a sweet-looking morsel of humanity produce such a staggeringly foul smell!? Yuck, yuck, yuck."

"So that's why she was so quiet and thoughtful! She was a busy girl."

"We will be back soon, Rose, with Maren returned to her appropriate sweetness."

Rose stopped stirring to watch him carry the baby toward the bathroom. Every morning and every afternoon he shoveled the porch steps, the walkway, and the driveway, reveling in his newly-returned strength.

And every morning she thought how much better he looked than the day before. Today he looked like a sexy lumberjack in dark turtleneck, flannel shirt, and threadbare corduroys tucked into thick woolen socks. A sexy, happy, *healthy* lumberjack.

He was right. It was the most perfect winter ever. First it had been too cold for landowners to schedule extended site visits. Then there was too much snow, and Jack had to rely on photos and phone conversations as his team began planning three new solar installations. He had been gone only six days since the end of November, and she'd had only eight calls for translation work, and one of those was online.

She wouldn't say this to anyone but Jack, because every person she knew complained bitterly about the weather, but it almost felt that nature was compensating them for those frightening days back in the summer. Or maybe repaying them personally because they both celebrated nature in their jobs and their hobbies. Because they planted native trees and shrubs and flowers, and they didn't litter, and they were careful about using fossil fuels and… She knew life didn't work like that.

Still, she liked the thought.

****

"Okay! All clean and dry and smelling like a daisy!" He came back into the kitchen and carried the baby to the window. "You'd like to see the snow, wouldn't you, little Maren? You probably don't remember the holiday cards that crossed your path last December, but this looks like one of them, with all those snow-laded evergreen branches. No, that's wrong. It doesn't look like a boring old holiday card, with sentimental perfectly blue skies and sappy perfectly gold sunshine. Outside our window,

Maren, is a *noir* holiday card, more monochromatic and thoughtful." He looked down at the baby's face. "*Noir*. That's another new word for you. Be sure to remember it so you can wow your kindergarten teacher."

Now Rose's snort-laugh mixed with the baby's chortling as Jack held her up and rubbed his face on her belly.

"You've got a job tomorrow, right?"

"At the State House, yes. Under the golden dome. Something to do with establishing a sister city relationship with Visegrad in Bosnia, which has about the same population as Montpelier, and is right on a river, like Montpelier, and has had significant flooding the past two springs, also like Montpelier."

"How long do you think it'll take for the dignitaries to exchange compliments and all?"

"I have no idea." She nuzzled the side of his neck with her mouth. "But as soon as I am no longer needed, I'm heading for that store on Main Street and I'm going to buy a big fat photo album, the kind with plastic windows for each page. Plus a giant box of stick-em doohickeys and a batch of colored pens that are guaranteed not to fade for decades. And photo paper. If we print out some favorites when I get home, then I'll get started on the album for Maren."

The file on Jack's computer had almost two hundred photos already. Photos of the baby with Jack's parents, his dad cuddling the tiny infant in both arms while Magda unfolded a crib quilt they'd made together, using an old pattern called The Road to Grandma's House. Photos with Rose's parents, who took turns in the rocking chair and didn't want to stop holding the baby even for supper, and photos of them next to the bounty that traveled with them to Vermont: a gigantic pumpkin, a box of winter squashes, canned jams and pickles, two fat roasting chickens, and more.

Photos of the baby with Lily and Geoff, tears pouring down the new aunt's face as she smiled from ear to ear. Photos of the swinging cradle made by Rose's brother Finn, from an ancient apple tree that broke during a central New York snowstorm.

Photos of Maren with Max and Xavier, standing next to the kitchen table covered with all the sweet and filling treats they brought because Max said nursing moms are always hungry.

And many, many photos of little Maren so her parents wouldn't forget the day-to-day changes. The first time she held her head still. The day she really smiled for the first time. The first time she raised her head and chest off the blanket, resting on her elbows and looking around with an expression that was clearly infant pride. Photos of the baby chuckling, really chuckling, as her daddy made faces at her.

"What's this one, Jack? A way to show Maren where she was conceived?"

It was a picture of their bed, the sheets and covers askew and the pillows tossed onto the floor.

"That, Rose, is for us. Not Maren. That is to remind us of the two-day orgy that started about one hour after your doctor said we could—how did she word it?— resume marital relations."

"Oh!" She laughed and flushed. "Oh yes. That was, um, an outstanding event." She gently freed her nipple from the baby's slack mouth and lifted her to her shoulder for a burp. "An event that warrants repetition. I am going to put Maren in her crib. Then I am going to take a shower because I've got milky vomit all over my shoulder and down my back. And then. Then I am going into our bedroom, Jack. And I am going to place my naked self in the middle of our bed, with my arms to my sides and my legs slightly apart, and I am going to wait for you to join me."

"You will not wait long, my love."

"Oh goodie."

A word about the author...

Maeve Kim is a teacher, nature guide, gardener, musician and writer. She is known in her home state of Vermont for lively and often humorous articles, programs and classes about the beauty of birds and the benefits of the outdoors. In her books, she combines nature, love and eroticism into stories that are heart-warming and touching.